## ACCLAIM FOR E.K. BLAIR'S
## ECHO

"The plotting is genius. It's shock after shock after shock. I loved the writing—it's dark and incredibly suspenseful."

**— Vilma's Book Blog**

"*Echo* is a brilliant web of deceit, mystery, and darkness. This book is a solid punch to the gut and a blow to the mind! A must read."

**— Book Crush**

"As the story progressed and wo~~rk~~ ~~do~~ we were teetering on a knife e~~dge~~ ~~ity~~ abound in this second installm~~e~~ ~~stomachs~~ in knots!"

~~y~~ **Booked**

"*Echo* was everything I ~~wished it~~ would be and more! E.K. Blair does dark and twisted like no other."

**—A Literary Perusal**

"Echo is my new addiction. E.K. Blair writes the words like she was born to tell this story. Hold on tight, because you're about to be taken on one hell of a ride through the dark crevices of your tangled psyche!!"

**—The Book Avenue Review**

"E.K. Blair's beautiful, twisted mind kept me guessing until the very end."

**— Aleatha Romig,** *NYT best-selling author*

"There is nothing predictable or safe on these pages, and there is nothing common about the way E.K. Blair's words will make you feel."

**—— Jay Crownover,** *NYT best-selling author*

"It's dark, twisty, and absolutely unputdownable. Prepare accordingly for the inevitable book hangover."

**——-Chelsea M. Cameron,** *NYT best-selling author*

"Once again, E.K. crafts a spell wrapped in darkness. *Echo* is a fabulous continuation to Bang."

**— Pepper Winters,** *NYT best-selling author*

# THE BLACK LOTUS SERIES
## BOOK TWO

# e.k. blair

*Echo*

Copyright © 2015 E.K. Blair

Editor: Lisa Christman, Adept Edits

Photographer: Erik Schottstaedt

Cover Designer: E.K. Blair

Interior Designer: Champagne Formats

ISBN: 978-0-9963970-1-8

For My Fans

"You would have to be half mad to dream me up."

-Lewis Carroll

echo

# prologue

## (BENNETT)

I DIDN'T EVEN take another second after I found out about Nina. Elizabeth. My wife. Jesus, what the hell is going on? The only thoughts in my head since hearing the truth an hour ago are confusion and fear and getting my ass to my attorney's office. I don't know what Nina is up to. Shit, I don't know anything right now. I haven't even had a chance to look at the dossier because I had to make sure that the only other person I care about, aside from Nina, would be taken care of no matter what. My mind is spinning and thoughts are beginning to swarm now that I've made it back to The Legacy.

Pulling into the garage, I park in my spot, grab the file, and rush inside. It's like a thousand hammers beating inside of my chest as I push through the doors, raking my hand through my hair.

"Mr. Vanderwal!"

I stumble in my step when I hear Manuel call my name from

across the lobby.

"Mr. Vanderwal," he repeats as he stands up from behind the desk. "I have something for you."

Ice swims through my veins when he picks up a small manila envelope and begins walking over to me.

"Who delivered this?"

"Said her name was Mrs. Brooks and that it was urgent. She was extremely persistent that you open it right away," he says with an outstretched hand, and I take the envelope.

"Thanks." Giving a quick nod, I make my way to the elevators. I recognize Jacqueline's handwriting on the envelope and wonder why she didn't just call me. When the doors open and I step into the penthouse I've been sharing with my wife, the panic manifests into an insurgent need to understand what's going on.

Tossing my coat aside, I head straight to my office and close the door behind me. I take a seat and immediately open the dossier to find a few photos taken of Nina walking out of what looks to be a residential building, most likely McKinnon's. The thought turns my stomach to think about what she's been doing with him all this time I've been away on business in Dubai.

My suspicions started at the masquerade ball. Something was off with her. I could sense it. Her emotions were all over the place—it was evident in her eyes, yet she played it off well and I never really questioned. When travel picked up and I was away for longer spans of time, I grew lonely and thought she might be feeling the same. There was an instance I arranged to have her favorite meal from Cité delivered to her only to find out from the restaurant manager that it was undeliverable because she wasn't home. After I called Richard, I found out that Jacqueline had mentioned Nina not being around as often as she used to. The red flags were there, so I admit, I had her followed. It didn't feel right, but I couldn't bear the thought of losing her. I needed to know, and now that I do and that it was Declan, I want to kill that son of a bitch.

More pictures of Nina, now with *him*. His hand holding hers. Her smiling up at him. His hand in her red hair. Her arms around his waist. A hug. A kiss. Hand on her ass. Hand on his face. Her body pressed against his, all while standing among the busy city traffic.

*Fuck!*

That's my goddamn wife! The woman I love beyond my own life. What the fuck is she doing? And when I flip to the next piece of information in the file, I'm reminded that she's not Nina when I see a picture of her. She's young—really young. A scanned page from a yearbook with her school photo and name printed right beneath.

Elizabeth Archer.

In ink, there's a note that reads:

*Freshman year.*

*Bremen High School. Posen, Illinois.*

Jesus. How did she wind up in Posen?

My eyes are fixed on the grainy black and white photo. She isn't smiling, but she's beautiful. I see the woman I married, and when I close my eyes, I can see *her*—Elizabeth.

And now I feel it.

Guilt.

I set the file down and lean back in my chair while I attempt to grasp on to reality, but my emotions are too conflicting. I can't even think straight. My wife isn't who she's pretended to be since the day I met her. But why? What does she want? I should hate her, be furious, be in a state of rage. Instead, I feel like driving back to the hospital so I can touch her, see her, hold her, and ask her why, and tell her that whatever it is, I'll fix it for her because I love her.

God, I love her.

What the hell is wrong with me? I should be enraged. Right?

I take a moment and close my eyes when I feel the pulsing of a headache beginning to form. Loosening my tie, I open my eyes and they land on the manila envelope. With curiosity, I open it up to find a flash drive along with a note that reads:

*Bennett,*

*I don't want to say too much, but after overhearing a very strange phone call Richard was having the other night, I've been worried. I wanted to call you since I knew it had something to do with the company, but after finding this flash drive, I got scared. I don't exactly understand what's going on, but I fear it could be really bad. Please look at this ASAP.*

*Jacqueline*

Opening the lid to my laptop, I plug in the flash drive and click on the only file that pops up. It appears to be the company's financial spreadsheet, but the numbers are way off the normal spectrum. I scroll through the information, and when I hit the bottom, I see the account name and panic ignites.

"Oh my God."

My eyes widen as I lean in closer to the screen because I can't believe what I'm seeing. My stomach lurches when I notice faint noises on the other side of the door. Before I even have a second to think, the door flies opens, smashing into the wall.

The man's face is a blur behind the stainless steel barrel of a pistol that's aimed right at me. Chills spark throughout my body, causing my lungs to collapse as I desperately try to speak, but he speaks first.

"You won't ever fucking touch her again," he snarls as he moves towards me with his arm straight out in front of him, marking his target.

I quickly stand on weak legs, holding my hands up in surrender, and plead through my crashing panic, "Declan, don't do th—"

(bang)

one

(bang)

CRIMSON SOAKS THROUGH the white cotton, spreading its death through the fibers of his shirt as he stands there, wide-eyed. My body goes numb as I watch him slowly stumble backwards. The weight of the pistol becomes too much for my delicate fingers to hold, and the gun slips out of my hand, falling to the floor with a thump at the same time Pike does.

I'm frozen as I stand here, looking down at my brother. His body begins to spasm, his eyes never blinking, and the gurgling sounds in his throat turn violent as he starts choking on his own blood.

I don't move to help him; instead, as if I'm watching a horror movie, I become a voyeur.

*This isn't real. This is a dream; it isn't real.*

The terror in his eyes is chilling as they glaze over, dilate, and stare into negative space.

His body stills, paralyzed to the ground, and then silence takes over. It's in this moment that I begin to feel the warmth of blood flowing through my veins, and I move. Inching slowly towards Pike, my trembling body kneels next to him, but I'm too scared to touch him.

*Is this real?*

Simply observing, I note a tinge of blue blooming on his lips. I sit. The world unmoving. My mind drifts to a faraway place where nothing exists. It's pure and empty and free from emotion. I settle in this solitary space, breathing in white noise, when suddenly the body next to me convulses. A retching of coagulated blood splutters out of Pike's mouth as his stomach contracts in alarming pulses, and then instantly stops. My heart pounds in an unsteady rhythm as I watch Pike's body soften into the floor beneath him. And when there is no more life, I wake up, snapping out of my trance as reality barrels into me.

*Holy shit!*

Grabbing his arm, I panic, jerking him. "Pike?" Shaking his arm, I murmur in fear, "Pike, wake up. Pike, come on." I move to hover over his lifeless body, gripping his shoulders and shaking him profusely, begging louder, "Wake up. Wake up! This isn't funny." Tears burn my eyes, and I choke on my own words. "Wake up, Pike! I'm so sorry. Oh my God, I'm so sorry. Please, wake up!"

His eyes are still wide open, but there's no movement. They're frozen, locked in place, and utterly black.

*What have I done?*

Pain stabs my lungs as I throw my head up to the heavens and release the most God-awful severing cry, but there's no sound that comes out of me. The agony is too much, so I wail in a torturous breathlessness. My heart, splintering, ripping apart, takes on a new meaning of misery, creating an emotion that never existed before this very moment, but it's too much. I can't bear it, but I feel its birth inside of me.

Looking back down, I no longer see the man I hated only moments ago. Instead, I see the boy who desperately loved me his whole life, and I crumple over, shifting his arm so that I'm able to nestle in the crook against his chest. He's still warm, and like I've done my whole life, I selfishly take comfort from him. I'm nothing but rot, using Pike, even in his death, in an attempt to soothe myself. I wrap myself around him and cry, breathing him into my soul. His shirt is a soggy combination of blood and sweat, yet I can still smell the ever-familiar fumes of his clove cigarettes as I close my eyes.

*"You're gonna be okay."*

His whispered voice startles me, and I pop up to look down at him. He's alive, blinking, and I see his lips moving when he speaks again.

*"Don't cry, Elizabeth. I'm still here."*

"Oh my God, Pike!" I murmur in disbelief.

*"It's gonna be okay,"* he assures again, and I cry, "How?"

*"Because I love you, and I believe in you. You're a fighter. A warrior."*

"I'm so sorry. I didn't mean to shoot you. God, I'm losing control, but I can't lose you."

A hint of a smile appears on his lips. *"You'll never lose me. You're my sister. I've never loved anyone as much as you. All I ever wanted in this world is for you to be happy. You're a survivor."*

"What do I do?"

*"Run."*

"What?" I question with a slight shake of my head, and

when my eyes meet his again, cold, black orbs greet me. "Pike?" Pinching my eyes closed, I open them back up, but the vision remains. He's dead, and I'm losing it.

His words sink in. He's right. I'm a fighter; he taught me how. So with that, I feel my spine straighten, and I take in a couple slow, calculated breaths. I lean down and capture his lips, taking my second kiss of death today. When I pull away, I drop my fingertips to his brows and gently run them down his face, closing his eyelids so that he can sleep peacefully. Wrapping both Pike and Declan safely in the steel cage around my heart, I swallow hard as I shift to stand. Today I lost the two pieces of my black, black heart, but now I have no other choice than to save myself.

I move quickly around the trailer, stripping out of my bloody clothes and changing into a pair of Pike's sleep pants and an old t-shirt. I need the smell of him on me because I'm scared to be alone. Gathering my belongings, I make sure to grab the file Pike took from Declan's before I wipe my fingerprints from various surfaces. Looking back at Pike, who lies dead in a puddle of darkened blood, I release a silent goodbye and thank him for saving me by giving me every piece of him. My body fights hard against the boiling pain that's begging to erupt, and I shove the thoughts away that it should be me lying there—dead. At least then I would be with Declan.

Declan.

*Fuck, I'm not strong enough to do this.*

My chest heaves and the cage weakens as I shut the door on my past and walk into the unknown future with Bennett's gun tucked into my bag.

As I pull out of the trailer park and onto the main street, my cheeks are coated with tears.

I'm lost.

Alone.

All I can do is go back to my phony life because what other choice do I have? Three men—men that are all linked to me—have been murdered. Bennett, Declan, and Pike. I try to get focused so I can create a plan on what to do when my gut twists in fear as I see Matt's car pass me by, going in the direction I just came from.

*Shit!*

I could turn around, catch him, explain what happened, but then I hear Pike's voice urging, *"Don't stop driving."*

So I don't.

Shadows of the city pass by as I make it back home and pull into the parking garage.

Wiping down the gun and placing it back in Bennett's car—one bullet short—I rush into the quiet building and up to the penthouse, undetected.

I take a quiet step across the threshold, and when the door slams behind me, I collapse to the floor. And this time, when I wail, my voice erupts in a fiery sob that burns in my soul. Vulgar cries, ripping through the cords of my throat as they expel into the hopeless air, echo off the walls and evaporate into silence. Tears mix with the dried blood of Pike and Declan, dripping from my chin, and fall lifelessly to the tile beneath me. When I see the swirled, translucent red, I let go of my voice and choke on my breath. I'm lost in the splatterings of my pain merged with all that's left of my loves.

*Who do I ache for more?*

And like the animal I am, with hands braced on the chilling

floor, I lean forward on my knees, and I lick the blood.

My salt.

Their metal.

My heart's elixir.

Peeling off Pike's clothes while I make my way to the bathroom, I stare at the blood that's dried on my body, and with no control, I begin to lick that too.

Fingers, hands, arms, knees.

I take it all, loving Declan and Pike, making a home for them in the depths of my body, deep inside. Everything's a haze; my only goal is to consume every last piece of vitality.

And I cry.

Eyes burning.

Lungs aching.

Hope disintegrating.

I'm all powdered ash, so hold your breath before a drift of air picks me up and carries me away to nullity.

"NINA."

Tension aches in my muscles as I stir awake. When I roll over and open my tear-stung eyes, I notice Clara, the housekeeper and cook moving around the room.

"It's nearly noon. You've been sleeping all morning." She speaks in a gentle voice before pulling the drapes back.

Light flashes, burning my eyes, and I jerk my head away, squinting against the sun's rays that pierce the room.

Clara walks around the bed and takes a seat next to me, stroking her fingers through my tangled hair, and the touch awakens the swollen wound in my heart that only sleep can soothe. Tears leak out onto my pillow, and I close my tired eyes.

"You should eat, dear. It might help you feel better."

I shake my head. Food can't heal this. I'm not sure anything can. I've lost everything. My baby, Declan, Pike . . . everything that mattered to me. And for what? Everyone is dead and there's nothing gained. Nothing but misery. The constricting around my heart makes each breath unbearable, and I desperately want to drift away. More than drift, I just want Declan to hold me. To anchor me by wrapping his warm arms around me, cocooning me into his chest, and filling my lungs with his scent—his life.

The one man who showed me what it was to be loved . . . truly loved . . . in the purest form is gone. Gone at the hands of my brother . . . my other love, my protector.

"Maybe a shower?" Clara suggests, but I don't respond. I just keep my eyes closed.

It isn't but a moment until I hear her sniff. When I peek my eyes open, I watch as she brushes the tears away from her cheeks. I shift my body against the tender bruising that remains from Pike's brutal beating a few days ago, the beating that killed my baby and led to the deaths of my husband, my lover, my brother, and my own soul. Clara looks over to me when I sit up and wince.

"I'm sorry. I don't mean to cry."

I don't say anything as I watch her try to recompose her poise through the sorrow she feels. I feel it too but for entirely different reasons. So I pull on my mask and continue my role, saying, "It feels so lonely without him. I keep thinking he's just away on another trip and he'll be walking through the door any minute."

She nods while her tears continue to fall and then looks to

me. "I'm worried about you."

*I am too.*

"I'll be okay."

"Bennett wouldn't want you to be suffering like this."

What she doesn't know, what nobody knows, is that I'm not suffering for Bennett. I'm not the harrowed widow mourning over her husband. No. I'm mourning over the man I was cheating on my husband with and my brother that no one knew anything about. My hidden life. My clandestine existence.

"How could I possibly not suffer, Clara? He was my husband," I choke out. "How am I supposed to live without him when he was my reason for waking up every day?"

"Because the world doesn't wait on us. It keeps moving and expects us to move right along with it."

"I'm not sure how to move right now."

"Well," Clara begins, resting her hand on my knee. "You can start by taking a shower and trying to eat something." Her eyes are sad and filled with concern. When I nod my head, a small smile breaks upon her lips, and she gives my knee a gentle squeeze before getting up to leave the room. Turning back to me, she adds, "Oh, while you were sleeping, your attorney called. He'd like to schedule a time to meet with you to go over Bennett's will."

This was the moment I had been working years for. The moment Pike and I dreamed about. This was supposed to be the moment that brought me victory and happiness. The money. The power. Payback and retribution. And now it means nothing without Pike by my side. I married Bennett to destroy him, but it didn't make anything better—it's just worse.

"I'll give him a call after lunch," I respond before Clara

walks out and closes the door behind her.

Getting ready is a blur. I make the movements but then can't remember how I got from point A to point B. Clara is in the kitchen, cleaning up after lunch while I sift through the sheaf of messages from all the calls I've missed since Bennett's death. I'm sure it's all over the news, but I can't bring myself to turn on the TV for fear I'll hear something about Declan. I'd crumble for sure.

I have messages from everyone. I know I need to contact Bennett's parents, and also Jacqueline, since I can see she has been calling excessively. God, the last thing I want to do is deal with these people, and as I'm about to walk away, the phone rings. I let Clara answer it as I head back to bed.

"Nina, it's the funeral home," she calls. "They are needing approval on a few final details."

Drained of energy, I respond, "I'm sorry. I just can't," before dropping my head and walking out of the room.

What the hell do I care about Bennett's funeral? Toss him in the lake for all I care. The bastard continues to ruin everything, even in his death. The anguish wells up into my throat as I fall onto the bed and cry into my pillow.

I fucking hate that man. I hate him for everything he was. Misplaced aggression or not, that asshole took everything away from me.

I cry like mad, trying to expel some of this misery, but I can't sit still. I lurch off the bed, and in a haze, find myself in Bennett's closet, ransacking everything. Ripping clothes from the hangers, thrashing shoes across the room, grunting with each volatile purge until I'm against the wall, slamming my palm into the drywall over and over and over. I beg for the infliction of pain, but the only pain I feel is in my heart. So I clench my fist and pound harder and harder and harder and harder . . .

"Nina! Stop!"

Harder and harder and harder and harder and . . .

two

"MRS. VANDERWAL, THANK you for coming in. I'm so sorry for your loss. Your husband was a good friend."

"Thank you, Rick," I respond as I stand in front of our attorney's desk and shake his hand.

"Please," he says, gesturing to the chair, "Have a seat."

I look at the man I've known since my engagement to Bennett four years ago as he sits down and pulls out a file of paperwork.

"I wanted to visit with you personally so that we can go over the terms of your husband's will and estate. I know this is a difficult time for you right now, but the day of Bennett's death, he stopped by to visit me."

I nod my head, recalling the phone call that was made in my hospital room. It was the last time Bennett was with me, when he found out that I wasn't really Nina, but Elizabeth, and that I'd been sneaking around with Declan.

Declan.

My throat tightens at the thought of him, but I push it down to focus on Rick as he continues to speak.

"A few amendments were made to the will," he tells me, pulling out a sealed, white envelope from the file. "He instructed me to open and read this to you privately upon his death."

Forcing out a tear, I sit and stare—nervous—but I play it as calm as I can.

"He must have known," he states blankly.

"I don't understand how any of this is happening." My voice quivers around the words, and Rick hands me a tissue.

"Have the police said anything to you?"

"No. But they took almost everything from our home office. The last I heard is they think it's business related."

"Money will make people do sick things," he says, and the chill that streams under my skin causes a sinister reaction inside of me.

He has no clue how close to home his words are hitting right now as I sit and wait to hear my reward for this game of revenge I've played over the past few years.

I dab my eyes with the tissue, and he asks, "Do you need a moment?"

I shake my head, and he takes his letter opener, slicing it through the lip of the envelope. Unfolding the paper, he takes a moment, and I watch as his eyes skitter across whatever is written. Rick clears his throat and shifts in his seat before reading aloud Bennett's words.

*My beautiful Nina,*

*I'm so conflicted writing this letter. The moment I met you, I knew the man I wanted to be. The type of man worthy enough to stand by your side because you are beyond magnificent.*

17

*But the conflict there is that you were never the woman I thought you were. I'm pissed at you. I know the woman that lies beneath the fallacy. The fallacy I fell deeply in love with. I don't pretend to have the answers for what you've done, but don't worry, my dear. Don't be scared, because I never told a soul. I'll take my friend, that little girl with the red pigtails, to my grave. Whatever it is that you wanted from me, I hope you found it. I hope that you can forgive me for what happened to you. I don't know the details; all I do know is that I feel responsible.*

*You weren't the only one who was dishonest though. I lied to you too. There is no easy way to say this, so here it is:*

*I have a son.*

*His name is Alexander Brooks.*

The utter shock at those words knocks me back, and I'm disgusted at myself for not being able to see what was right under my nose. He was fucking Jacqueline behind my back. My loving husband and my so-called friend.

*She was the biggest mistake of my life. It only happened once. The details aren't important, because I've regretted that moment since before it happened. Because it was you I wanted. It's always been you. I laid my hand on her that one time but never again after. Never did I want to because all I wanted was to be covered in you. To be covered in your love that I felt was so real, but I learned today that it wasn't real. Nothing is real, and I don't know what to believe.*

*What I do know is that I cannot trust anything. I have instructed that this letter only be read in a private setting between legal counsel and you, Nina. It is with this letter that I claim my paternity to Alexander Brooks. A DNA test was conducted shortly after his birth and can be found in a safety deposit box, which I leave to the hereby mentioned custodian, Attorney Rick Parker of Buchanan & Parker. I further move to amend my will to ensure Alexander Brooks is the sole heir to all business assets of Linq Steel*

*Co. and that Nina Vanderwal be sole heir to all personal assets upon my death.*

*All monies gained from Linq Steel Co., including all materials of the business estate, will be deposited into a trust fund under Alexander's name, which the trustee, Rick Parker, will oversee until Alexander reaches the age of 21.*

*Rick Parker will notify Jacqueline Brooks in a private meeting to go over the terms of this amended will, and I please beg of you, for the sake of my son, that none of this information leave the parties involved.*

*Nina, I lied about one more thing. When I said in my vows that I would love you till death do us part, I wasn't being honest, because I doubt death would be enough to make me stop loving you.*

*Bennett Vanderwal*

That bastard. And here I thought I was a good actress, but it was *them*. They fooled me—played me. They were deceivers just as I was—just as I continue to be. I always knew Jacqueline wanted to fuck my husband, I just never knew she actually had. So now I sit here, stoic. I want to laugh at the circuitous nature of it all—the incessant game that continues to reveal hidden secrets, but ironically, they're now someone else's secrets.

Rick sets the letter down and leans forward, pinching the bridge of his nose. Releasing a heavy breath, his eyes finally meet mine. "Did you know?"

I shake my head.

He shifts in his seat, regaining his composure, but I can see his discomfort slicing through his weak façade. "Well, then . . . as you're probably aware, the majority of his assets are named under the business. That's not to say that you won't be left with a considerable inheritance though."

Feigning irritation, my words bite when I state, "It isn't the money I care about."

"Of course not. I apologize. I didn't mean to insinuate that—"

"It's fine. I'm a little overwhelmed with everything right now. So if we're through . . ."

"Yes," he responds, standing and walking around his desk. He holds his hand out for me and I take it as I stand up.

"Thank you."

Rick leads me out of his office, and when I step onto the elevator, he sticks his arm out, preventing the door from closing and offers, "I'm so sorry you had to find out about Bennett like this."

"Well, I guess nobody's perfect, are they?"

"No. I suppose not."

He drops his arm, allowing the doors to shut as he gives me a nod of sympathy, but I would only need it if I cared for the two people that I just found out have been betraying me. Only I don't. His son can have the business assets, because honestly, the money feels tainted now. I'll take it, find a way to start a new life, but that money will always be marked in Declan's blood—my heart's blood. Bennett's death was never worth the life of Declan. Nothing is worth the life of the man who owned every piece of me.

MINUTES TURN HOURS turn days.

A monotonous routine of depression follows me everywhere I go. The razor sharp agony of my bleeding heart aches painfully for Declan. I miss him. Sometimes I think if I cry hard enough, he'll come back. As if life would be that giving.

No.

Life is a piece of shit.

It gave me a taste—one taste of sweetness—before ripping it away from me. The moment I decided to believe in hope, to believe in goodness, it was taken, only to remind me that I'm all alone in this world. But for once, I wanted to believe. I wanted to dig deep to find the good in me so that I could give it to him, however small of a piece it was.

I don my ink, bathed in black, to mourn my loves, but it isn't their funerals I attend, it's *his*. I don't even have to pretend for family and friends because the depth of my heartache runs deep inside of me, only it runs for Declan and Pike, not Bennett, whose funeral I am preparing to leave for.

I've stayed far away from any news on Declan and Pike; their funerals have come and gone, I'm sure. But to show my face would be foolish. I can't link myself to them if I expect suspicion to remain off of me. After all, I'm the spider's silk that webs this whole game together.

Smoothing the wax of deep red lipstick along my lips, I remember how warm they felt pressed against Declan. His sweetness burned into them. Sometimes I couldn't control my love for him, needing more, I'd bruise myself. Driven by pure desire.

I stand back, observing what's left behind. Soft waves of red hair fall over my thinned shoulders, eyes sunken in from the sorrow that eats away at me, but with a few eye drops, my blues beam bright and I'm reminded of my daddy's eyes that shone the brightest of them all. Loss is all around me; it's all my life has ever been. I run my hands down the smooth black fabric of my shift dress and right myself for my husband's funeral because this is a loss that I welcome with a full heart. Bennett is one of my few victories, albeit bittersweet.

The day is frigid and covered in grey. A light mist falls down on the cold earth as I drive across town to the cemetery where Bennett's parents own family plots. I go alone—the black widow. Everything is black, including the limos and town cars that line the winding street, skirting its way through the immaculate grounds of Bennett's final resting place.

As I park the car, I take a moment to breathe before I notice Baldwin walking my way, carrying a large umbrella over his head. I haven't seen him since I let him go last week. Bennett is gone, and it's time to start eliminating the remnants of him entirely, including his staff. I always liked Baldwin—I liked Clara as well—but after I let go of Baldwin, I said goodbye to her too. They both understood as I explained my reasoning. Clara was the hardest because a small part of me always felt connected to her as a mother figure to me, even though she was never mine to claim.

"Mrs. Vanderwal," Baldwin acknowledges when he opens my door and takes my hand to help me out of the car.

"Thank you," I murmur, eyes guarded behind my dark sunglasses.

His eyes are soft, full of concern, and I can tell he wants to say something, so I give him a smile filled with sorrow and he nods in shared pain, only mine is deceitful.

I loop my arm through his as he leads me over to the burial plot where Bennett's casket is perched above ground, flanked by numerous sprays of fragrant flowers and weeping loved ones. I join them as tears roll freely down my face and drip slowly from my jaw. This asshole they mourn is the pure hate that festers in me. And these tears aren't for him—they're *because* of him.

As I'm led to the last empty chair, next to Bennett's mother, my eyes meet Jacqueline's over his casket. I want to smile at that pathetic woman, but I don't, and she quickly looks away from me, shifting in awkwardness. She knows I know. The attorney called me the other day to tell me that he met with her to discuss Bennett's will and trust for their bastard child.

I sit.

Time passes.

Words of hope and the glory and abundance of God wane on.

*Life is a gift,* the priest praises.

Bullshit.

The sounds of rain trickling down and people crying dissipate the longer I sit. Many stop and offer me their condolences as I cry and pretend the words that were just spoken here were really meant for Declan and Pike. I sit and reflect on them, honoring their lives today, not *his.* So I nod and quietly thank each person as they one-by-one turn their backs and walk away, emptying the cemetery.

Richard and Jacqueline stop, and in a very out of character move on Richard's part, he gives me a hug, albeit short and tense. Looking over to the betrayer, she tilts her head in unspoken sorrow before opening her arms to me. I take her offering for appearance's sake.

"I'm terribly sorry," she whispers her multi-layered sympathies.

I pull back, keeping the interaction short.

"Thank you for being here."

"Call if you need anything," she says, which I'm sure is more for keeping her husband aloof than it is sincerity for me.

I nod and then Jacqueline walks off with Richard without

saying another word.

Only a few people linger when my heart catches at the sight of Callum, Declan's father. I've been purposefully hiding from everything Declan because my heart just can't take the pain, but when Cal's eyes meet mine, I stand and walk toward him.

The endearment he always held for me is no longer there, only the stone face of a man who has just lost his son.

"Cal," I whisper, approaching him as he stands under a large tree. He doesn't speak. "I didn't expect to see you here."

"Your husband was a man I always admired. You know that."

I nod and nearly choke on my own fractured heart when I respond on broken breath, "Your son . . . I am so sorry."

I attempt to keep myself as poised as possible, as one would expect of a business associate. Because to Cal, that's all I was to Declan. He's oblivious to the fact that we were so in love, wanting a life to call our own, and sharing the dream of having a baby together—a baby that once lived in my now rotting womb.

"Life isn't fair, darling," he tells me in his thick Scottish accent, and within it, I can hear Declan's brogue. I drop my head and hold on as tightly as I can to his voice, never wanting to lose it, when Cal's hand cups my cheek. Looking up into his eyes, his face is blurred from the welling of agony in my eyes. He slowly drags his thumb over my skin and collects my tears as he tilts his head and says, "Funny isn't it?"

I blink a few times at his curious words before he continues, "Both men . . . murdered in their own homes within days of each other, and police are coming up blank as to who's responsible."

His words release a violent chill up my spine, and before I can form a cohesive thought, he kisses my forehead and walks away. I watch his back as the rain falls over him and drop to my knees in the mud. He's the last one to leave and I'm alone, hands bracing and sinking into the soggy ground, screaming silently, but it's so loud inside my head.

# three

IT'S BEEN TWO weeks since Bennett's funeral, since I looked into the eyes of my love's father. I'm alone and I'm drowning. There's no one left in the world for me, and the only place I find any semblance of peace is in my dreams—so I sleep. I used to always dream of Carnegie, the prince-turned-caterpillar my father once told me about when I was a little girl, but lately, when I close my eyes, it's Declan I see. I dream about what our life could have been: living in Scotland in the estate he used to tell me about, having a baby together, loving each other. The vision covers me in warmth, but the moment my eyes open, I am greeted with the dank coldness of my reality, reminded once again that fairytales are shit-filled lies.

Pulling out another suitcase from the closet, I continue to pack up my clothes. I can't stay in Chicago. This isn't my life—not the one I want because what I want doesn't exist anymore. It's simply another fallen star that I was wishing upon. What I want is the dream, so I decided yesterday that I would go get a glimpse of that dream, of the what-could-have-been, of the what-*should*-have-been. Because the dream is all I have left of him, and I want to see it. I *need* to see it, to know it was real. So I'm leaving for Scotland. I don't know what I'm doing, but I can't stay here any longer.

I continue to move about the penthouse until the phone rings.

"Mrs. Vanderwal?" Manuel says when I answer. "Mrs. Jacqueline Brooks is here to see you. Shall I send her up?"

"Oh," I murmur, not expecting any visitors today. "Um, yes. Please."

I hang up, wondering what it is she's wanting. We haven't really spoken since the paternity of her son was revealed, but what is there to even say? It's not like she was ever truly my friend, just someone I pretended to like for the satisfaction of Bennett.

I open the door when I hear the knock and am greeted by Jacqueline holding Alexander in her arms.

"Jacqueline, please, come in."

Her eyes barely meet mine as she steps inside and slowly walks to the center of the room before stopping and turning around to face me. We both stand here for a moment while I watch her tears well up.

"I'm so sorry," she says on a shaky breath, and I shift my eyes to look at her baby. When he becomes restless in her arms, she sets him down on the floor and he focuses on the stuffed frog he's holding.

Walking closer, I kneel down in front of him and our eyes lock. I take this moment to observe his features, and beneath the pudge, I see Bennett. I never cared enough to ever look at this child in the past, but I should've because it's glaringly obvious.

27

He's right there within this little boy, and my stomach knots. My teeth grind when I feel the heat in my blood surging with a need to slam my fist into this baby's face. My palms are actually tingling with desire, begging my fingers to ball so that I can hammer my knuckles into Bennett's legacy. I hate this child because he is the one thing that carries the life of the man that destroyed mine.

Alexander reaches up with a smile and touches my cheek, and I have to swallow back the sour bile of loathing. It takes great strength to pull back and not knock this little shit across the room.

When I stand, Jacqueline breathes in shame, "Nina . . . I'm sorry."

"Why?" I ask with no influx of emotion.

"For hurting you."

But I'm not hurt, so I simply respond, "Everybody has secrets, everybody lies, and everybody cheats their way through life for self-fulfillment. We wouldn't do it if we felt sorry; we do it because it's our human right to seek happiness."

My words take her by surprise, and when I ask, "Did fucking my husband make you happy?" she takes a deep breath as more tears fall and answers, "Yes."

I nod my head when she adds, "But it didn't make me happy to know I was hurting you."

"People are bound to get hurt in our journey for happiness. If fucking my husband made you happy, don't ever be sorry for that."

She tilts her head with a look of pity.

"Don't worry about me," I continue. "You didn't break me. You can't break something that was already broken."

"He never loved me," she confesses abruptly. "He never

wanted me. I took advantage of him when he had too much to drink. I knew it made him sick to look at me after what happened, but he kept up his pleasantries for the sake of Alex. He merely put up with me because he refused to turn his back on his son."

Jacqueline grows more upset with each word while I stand and listen. Her voice cracks in heartbreak when she adds, "But it was always you he loved."

Releasing a heavy sigh, I give her a weak smile, shaking my head, and saying, "I guess in the end, it doesn't really matter. All we are left with is ourselves."

She wipes her cheeks and takes a couple deep breaths in an attempt to compose herself before reaching down to pick up Alexander, and then asks, "So what now?"

"That's a good question, one that I need to find the answer to, but I won't find it here."

"You're leaving?"

"Yes," I say with a nod.

"Where to? For how long?"

"I don't know," I tell her, not wanting her to know, and when I give her son one last look-over, I turn my attention back to her. "You aren't the only one with secrets. We all have them."

She gives me a slight nod and starts moving towards the door. I follow and say goodbye to the woman who blindly found herself tangled in my game of lies. But she'll go back to her husband, Richard, who believes that baby is his, and continue to live her life while I get myself ready to go see what could have been mine. If only . . .

*"I'm sorry, Elizabeth."*

My heart catches at the sound of his voice as I close the door, and when I turn to look over my shoulder, I see his face, and suddenly I'm soothed. He stands right by me, dark hair, sad eyes.

"Why?"

Pike hangs his head, shoving his hands into his pants pockets, and I can see the tension in his muscles under his ink-covered arms.

*"I took that away from you,"* he says as he raises his eyes to me.

"Took what?"

*"What she has. What you deserved."*

"Maybe you did me a favor," I respond. "I would've been a shitty mom anyway."

Shaking his head, he counters, *"No. You would have been a great mom."* Pike takes in an uneven breath, and I can feel his regret with each word, *"I'm sorry I took that away from you."*

Truth is, I don't know what kind of mom I would've been, but I was willing to take the role with Declan by my side. I trusted him to keep me together. Trusted that his love would be enough to make me better. But I'm not better, and without him, I'm nothing.

Empty.

"It's life, right?" I say with a defeated shrug of my shoulders.

*"Not the life I wanted for you,"* he says, stepping closer to me. *"All I ever wanted was to give you a better life. All I wanted was to rip that lock off that door when you were little and cut you free from that fucking closet. I wanted to take away all the times I was forced to rape you. I wanted to take away all your beatings, all your hurt. But I fucked up."*

With no need for my steel cage with him, I let my tears fall, and I cry because that's all I ever wanted . . . for my life to disappear. I want to forget all the horror.

*"I never meant to destroy you like this."*

"I know."

*"I panicked. I got scared, and I lost it,"* he tries to explain through his strained voice that threatens to break.

"I miss you, so much, Pike. I don't even know how to live any more. I have no one. Not one person on this Earth," I cry and then crumple to my knees. But he's right there with me on the floor, hand on my back, as I heave and sob, "What do I do?"

*"You live."*

"How?"

*"You breathe. You fight. You take everything that was meant to be yours in this life because you deserve all of it."*

"I'm just so tired of fighting for nothing," I tell him.

Taking my face in his hands, he wipes my tears, saying, *"You're not alone. I'm here. Do you feel me?"*

"Yes."

*"It's not for nothing. Never stop fighting."*

I close my eyes and relax my cheek into his hand, taking in his touch and truly feeling him. With a deep breath, I inhale his words and search for comfort in them, search for any shred of strength. Strength to breathe, to move, to open my eyes, and when I do, he's gone.

Looking around the room, there's no trace of Pike, no movement, no smell, no sound. Sitting back on my heels, I observe the penthouse, the illusory world I've created, and I hear his faint whisper, *"This was your creation, and you were strong enough to master it."*

And he's right.

I was strong.

But that's when I had something to fight for. That fire in me is gone. Only ash and embers remain. Echoes and shadows.

Darkness and death.

Pike is right though; I need to move. If I'm going to live, I need to remind myself that there is good in this life. Even if the good comes in miniscule drips, I have to believe the pain is worth those moments, because I've experienced it. It was real and alive and I would go through this agony all over again just to feel the love of Declan for one more second. I never thought the world could be that good, but it was.

For that moment . . .

It was so good.

Picking myself up off the floor, I steady on my feet before grabbing my coat and keys. As much as I've been avoiding the reality of Declan's absence, I need to face it. To remember that it was real and it's worth this pain.

I pull my car out onto Michigan Avenue and start heading north. The city is alive and moving all around me. I ignore the excitement and smiles and keep straight to River North. Turning onto Superior, I slow down. Suddenly, I feel cold and my clammy hands grip the steering wheel more tightly. There's a sick churning in the pit of my gut as I roll the car along the curb in front of Declan's building.

Shutting the car off, I sit for a moment in the stillness. The only sound is the pounding of my heart as it beats through my chest. This used to be my solace. My little piece of heaven located at the top of this building. When I get out of the car, I look up and see the greenery on his rooftop courtyard, but I know that's the only life up there. His name is no longer on the intercom system in the lobby, only the number for the realtor that is listed to sell his penthouse.

The coolness of the steel on my fingertip hollows me even

more, and the masochist in me begs to push the button.

So I do.

I buzz his floor, knowing that this time, his sweet voice won't be greeting me. Instead, it's my phone.

Pulling my cell out, I look at the screen but don't recognize the number. As I take a few steps back toward my car, I answer, "Hello?"

"Miss me?"

It takes a moment to snap out of my thoughts of Declan to recognize the voice on the other end of the call, and a surge of panic flashes through my system. Quickly composing myself, I answer steadily, "What do you want, Matt?"

"We need to talk."

"About?"

"Do I really need to say it?" he taunts, and I don't need a reminder to know that when I passed him in my car the day I shot and killed Pike, he was heading straight to his trailer. Words aren't needed; we both know what I did.

"When?"

"Tomorrow."

"I can't," I tell him as I get back into my car and shut the door.

"You have something better to do?"

"As if my doings are any of your business, but yes. I'm leaving town, so if you'd like to talk, it would need to be done today," I bite in irritation. Matt has always been a source of friction for me. I've put up with him because of his friendship with Pike, but he's always given me the creeps. Still, there's a part of me that's grateful for him, because it was him that gave me one of the greatest gifts, and he gave it from a pure heart.

*Probably his only moment of selflessness.*

Matt was the one that gave me my first taste of revenge when he set the stage for me to murder my foster parents. My payback for the years of abuse. So as much as I despise Matt, a part of me is thankful for him.

"Thirty minutes? Tribune Tower?" he suggests.

"Fine."

Hanging up, I toss the phone over to the passenger seat. Hearing his voice makes me even more anxious to leave this town. To run far away from this place and from everything I know.

I start heading back towards Michigan Avenue, and once I've parked the car, I walk over towards the Tribune Tower. The streets and sidewalks are flooded with businessmen and tourists. Making my way through the crowds, I cross the street and wait for Matt.

My attention is on a street performer who's playing an old Otis Rush number I recognize on the saxophone. As people walk past him, dropping dollar bills and coins into his open sax case on the ground, I get lost in the smooth melody. I watch the man, and wonder about him. He's old and grey, dressed in tatters of worn clothes. His dark skin is aged with deep wrinkles, and even though his knuckles are worn and ashy, they move with grace along the keys. By looks alone, you'd think he was lonely and sad, but the sway of his head as he plays is a sure sign of happiness. But how does one, who appears to have nothing, find joy? I want to ask him how, but I stumble on my feet when I'm knocked off balance, only to find that I'm now in Matt's arms. He grabs me from behind and turns me around to face him. With a hand on my back and the other holding my hand, he moves me in a slow dance to the music.

His sly grin rakes at me, knowing the pleasure he's taking in having me this close to him. If it weren't for the mass of people around us, I'd push him off of me. The last thing I need is to cause a scene, so I allow him to lead me to his liking while keeping my eyes downcast.

"Don't look so miserable, Elizabeth. People are watching us."

Biting down, I muster up a weak smile and raise my head to meet his eyes. They're dilated dope black, but that's nothing new. It amazes me that this druggie I've known since I was a freshman in high school hasn't wound up overdosing.

Pulling me in closer, he rests his cheek against the side of my head, whispering in my ear, "You miss him?"

*Yes.*

I don't answer as I focus to keep my composure in front of him, but inside I can feel my wounds ripping deeper.

His hand wraps further around me, tugging me in close while we continue to dance on the bustling sidewalk in front of the Tribune Tower.

"If you're worried, don't be," he continues softly. "I took care of it."

When I pull my head back to look at him, confused by what he means, he adds, "I made it look like a deal gone bad. Cops questioned me, and I confirmed their suspicions."

"Why?" I ask, wondering why he would want to protect me.

"To ensure your loyalty."

A fury of heat ignites my neck with the realization that this punk sleaze was able to undermine and trap me to him.

"What do you want?"

35

"I'm not ready to collect on my investment right now," he responds with a grin I want to knock off his face.

"You're a sick fuck," I sling at him. "Using Pike for nothing more than a transaction."

"You're one to accuse of using. I watched you use him since we were kids."

"You don't know anything about our relationship," I snap in defense.

"I know that he loved you and sacrificed everything for you."

"And here you are, pissing on the both of us."

"You should be thanking me for keeping your ass out of prison," he throws back at me, and then mocks, "What was Pike anyway? Number three? Four?"

"Fuck you. He was my brother."

Gripping me tighter, the saxophone continues to fill the air around us as Matt dips me and seethes under his breath, "No. Fuck you, Elizabeth. He was my best friend and you killed him, and for what, I have no fucking clue because he never did anything but give you everything you ever wanted."

He then pulls me back up, and I feel like I'm about to explode in hate at this piece of shit who doesn't know a goddamn thing about the truth of me and my brother. He has no idea what the two of us endured and how it fucked us up for life.

When Matt kisses my hand, I realize that the music has stopped.

"Don't stray too far, kitty. Remember your place in this equation. I'll let you know when I'm ready to recoup the debt you owe me," he jeers before turning his back to me and walking away.

I watch as he disappears into the sea of people, thankful

that he has no clue I'm about to hop on a plane to Scotland. If he thinks he can use me as a pawn, I won't do anything to dismantle that thought, because pride is a faulty wire that will ultimately burn you.

four

THE CRACKLING OF *the fire fills the room. Darkened in the dead of night, the only light coming from the nearly extinct embers. I've been hiding away in my home office all week, panicked and on the search for anything to weave my way out of this fucking mess.*

*Knocking back two Xanax and a hit of whiskey, I pick up the phone. My fingers tap incessantly against the bocote desktop as the ringing pierces my ears in this silence that's consumed me.*

*"Hello?"*

*"It's me."*

*"Everything okay?"*

*Rolling back in my chair, away from the desk, I pinch the bridge of my nose and bite against the oncoming headache. "She's on her way to Scotland."*

*"How do you know?"*

*"Because I'm still hacked into her accounts. I just thought you should know."*

*"Thanks," is all he says before hanging up on me.*

# five

I GRIP THE ratty, red-headed doll more tightly while everyone sleeps around me, forty thousand feet above soil as the giver of my doll lies six feet under. While I was packing, I found the gift Pike had given me on my tenth birthday stuffed in a box in my closet. I remember him being embarrassed about the doll, having stolen it, but I loved it. And I loved him for being the one person who truly cared about me at a time when I was so alone. This doll was the only good memory of that birthday, because shortly after he gave it to me, I was forced to face the demon in the basement. The demon that would utterly destroy me and mold me into the monster I am today.

"Would you like something to drink, dear?" the flight attendant asks softly.

"No, thank you."

With my mind racing, I can't settle down to sleep. I keep replaying these past few months in my head. Over and over. I miss Pike, but it doesn't even compare to the ache of losing Declan. I hate that in his last hours his perception of me was tarnished. All I wanted was for him to believe I was good and pure, the way he always saw me, but in the end, he discovered it was a lie.

That dossier touched the hands of the men in my life, but it was Declan's hands that hurt the most. It took me a while to open up that file to see what exactly was in it, but when I did, there's no denying the facts from fiction. Declan knew I was a liar, a foster kid, a con artist. It kills me to think about how he must've felt when he realized the truth about me, because all I wanted was to love him, comfort him, and make him feel safe with me.

Who am I kidding though?

I could never love the way a man like that should be loved, but I was willing to try.

*"Tell me what you're feeling,"* I remember him saying as I allow my mind to drift back.

*"I hate this,"* I said. *"I hate every moment I'm not with you. You're all that I want, and I hate life for not being fair to us. And I'm scared. I'm scared of everything, but I'm mostly scared of losing you. You're the one good thing that's ever come along for me. Somehow, in this fucked up world, you have a way of making all the ugly disappear."*

*"You're not going to lose me."*

*"Then why does it feel like it's slipping away?"*

*"It's not. I promise you, it's not. You're just scared, but you have me now. I'll take all that fear away, every piece of it that you carry around. I'll take it away. I'll give you everything you deserve from this life. I'll do what I can to make up for all your suffering."*

I couldn't ever dream of a better man existing, and I never wanted to fall in love with him, but I did. It was wicked and vicious and utterly beautiful, and it was mine. For a moment, he was mine.

And now . . .

He's dead.

And so am I.

His blood is deep inside of me—I made sure of its home—but it isn't enough to save me. Nothing is enough, and the anguish is boundless. There's no release, no cleansing, no Pike to take it all away. I've lost my vice to relieve the ache, to give me my escape, to numb me. It's overpowering, a red river of loathing, a debilitating and suffocating stabbing in the core of my very essence.

It breeds inside of me and my body chills in anxiety. A shrill ring echoes in my ears.

Bleeding, screaming, a tourniquet around ventricles pleading for relief.

Memories of his words strangle me, a noose tightening around my neck.

*"We could have a life." "You love me, right?" "I know what I want, and that's a life with you. I'll do whatever it takes to get that."*

I can't breathe.

"Excuse me," I stutter breathlessly as I stumble in a rush to the lavatory.

Locking the door behind me, I brace my hands on the sink and stare into my hollow eyes. I attempt to inhale slowly, but my body doesn't allow it. A sheen of sweat coats my pale face, drained of blood, and the hunger inside of me needs to be fed. I need to expel it before it kills me.

My fist takes a life of its own, balling up and slamming itself into my sternum.

Again.

Again.

Knuckles pounding against frail bone, and with every in-fliction, the ringing in my ears dulls and my lungs begin to fill with much-needed air. I punch myself again and again and again, over and over, busting capillaries with each violent blow. Warmth spreads through my wounded flesh, and when my cheeks heat with tears, I fall back onto the toilet, my hands pressed against the wall of the tiny bathroom as I pant from exertion. My mind clears, but I'm confused by what just happened and why it brought me relief—pleasure, really. The tormenting sadness is gone, freed by the pain I just unleashed on myself.

*That was the moment I discovered my new drug. It no longer came in the comfort of Pike or Declan. No. It came from the devil's hand—my hand—and in that moment, I felt a sense of power in my ability to stave off the misery with a blissful brutality that births an endorphined high.*

Sighing in refreshed relief, I stand and right myself in front of the mirror before lifting the hem of my top to see the destruc-tion on my body. When I observe the blood pooling beneath my skin, swelling in pink glory, I smile in pride. Contusions mar my skin in reward, and I'm pacified.

*This* is pain I can deal with. No longer do I have anyone to lean on to alleviate this discord inside of me. All I have is myself. So with a sickening delight, I enjoy my moment of assuagement before returning to my seat to cradle my doll.

LANDING, CUSTOMS, BAGGAGE claim, and rental car. Here I sit in the parking lot, on the other side of the world from where I just came from.

Alone with no plan, no direction.

I sit awkwardly on the right side of the car, wondering if I'll be able to drive without killing myself or someone else. *No time like the present.*

"Here we go," I murmur to myself and then shift the car to pull out of the parking space.

As I leave the airport and start driving through Edinburgh, the scenery astounds me. Declan wasn't lying when he said the landscapes were breathtaking. Freezing rain falls from the dark, grey sky over the Old World city. Stone buildings from another lifetime line the streets, and I'm in awe of the historic beauty. Horns honking pull me away from the sights, and I quickly yank the steering wheel when I realize I'm entering a round-a-bout the wrong way.

"Shit," I screech while waving my hand in apology to the other drivers I nearly sideswiped. Driving on the opposite side of the car, opposite side of the street, has me tense and thrown off.

Turning out of the circle of death, I resume cautiously until I find a place to stop to get a bite to eat. I'm drained from traveling, and when I walk into the quiet restaurant, the hostess sits me at a table towards the back of the small dining room.

"Water?" the woman asks, hair the same shade of red as my own, piled up in a bun on top of her head.

"Please."

"Flat, sparkling, or tap?"

"Flat," I answer and then watch as she walks away, dazed in my unfamiliar surroundings.

These people are clueless to the world I just left behind, to the people I destroyed, to the beast I am. They sit, chatting quietly, very different from the loud and boisterous American manners, and I settle in the hushed atmosphere, looking over the menu.

"Here you go," the waitress says in her thick Scottish accent as she sets the carafe of water on the table after pouring a glass for me. "What can I get for you, lassie?"

Unsure of the menu choices, I tell her, "Something warm and savory."

"You're American?"

I smile and nod, and she then suggests, "Rumbledthumps."

"What?"

"Traditional Scottish dish. Will warm you up from the cold weather."

It takes a few extra seconds to decipher her words through her accent. I never had difficulty understanding Declan, but this woman's native tongue is coated much heavier than what I'm used to hearing.

"Thank you," I respond, handing her the menu, and after I take a long drink of water, I pull out my phone to attempt to get a game plan together.

Once I gain access to the internet, I type in the name of the estate Declan told me about. I remember him telling me it was outside of Edinburgh, but I can't remember where exactly. All I know is, I need to see the house. I need to know it's real. I need to see what could have been mine if only I'd run with him when he asked me to.

Pulling up the search engine, I type in:
*Brunswickhill Estate Edinburgh Scotland*

It takes only a few seconds for the property to pop up on several different realty websites. I click on the first link, and when a picture of the estate pops up, my stomach sinks. Sitting here, I don't breathe as I stare at the home Declan begged me to live in with him. I swipe the screen with my finger to view the other pictures. One by one, I see what was so close to being my life—my fairytale. It's just as he described: a Victorian mansion set within immaculate grounds covered in lush greens, flowers, trees, and the grotto. I recall Declan telling me how much I would love the grotto that's built from clinker.

*Why didn't I run with him when he asked?*

Scrolling down the page, I note the realtor as being Knight Frank.

After taking a few minutes to read the online brochure of the estate and looking through the rest of the photos, my food arrives. I take small bites of the potato dish, trying to find comfort in the richness, but my knotted stomach makes it difficult to enjoy. Beneath my skin, wounds slowly split.

Setting the fork down, I start searching online for the public records on the house. It takes a little while, but I finally find what I've been trying so hard to hide from. But it's here in black and white, right under my fingertips. The words informing that the bank seized the estate, and the date this occurred was only a few short weeks after Pike killed Declan. I can still taste his blood from when I took my last kiss.

I read further to find that it didn't take long for the place to resell to a private buyer using an undisclosed trust. I've come to know through Bennett that this isn't an uncommon occurrence among the wealthy. But regardless of the new ownership, I still want to see it. I mark the address and pull up the directions to find it's located about an hour away in Galashiels. Taking one last bite of food, I get the attention of the waitress so that I can pay and be on my way.

# Six

"SLEEP WELL?"

"Yes," I reply to Isla, the innkeeper, as I pour myself a cup of hot water from the kettle sitting out in the main dining room.

As I was driving through town last night, I came across this little bed and breakfast and figured it would be a nice place for me to stay while I'm here. Isla greeted me when I arrived, and despite being halfway across the world in a foreign country, something about her demeanor set me at ease. She welcomed me, settled me into my modest room, and quickly excused herself, which I was grateful for. I was beyond exhausted and fell asleep as soon as my head hit the pillow.

"So what brings you to Gala?" she asks.

Dipping a teabag into the mug of water, I'm not sure how to answer. I'm so used to lying and hiding my real self that honesty seems alien. Truth is, I'm not even sure I remember the real me anymore. And then I wonder if I ever truly did. I've been faking it for so long. The last time I remember really feeling in place within this world was when I was five years old. It's like the second my father was stolen from me, so was my identity. And when he died, that identity did too, and all I was left with was a shell of what used to be me. I tried filling the emptiness with hopes and dreams, but that was a waste of time. Then I turned to Pike, using him to fill me with voidance and comfort.

And then there was Declan.

"Are you okay?" Isla questions with concern in her eyes, pulling me out of my thoughts.

"Mmm hmm," is all I can manage around the agonizing block in my throat. After taking a slow sip of my hot tea, a desperate need to find myself takes over, and I do something I haven't done in a very long time.

I tell the truth.

"I lost someone close to me. I came here to feel closer to him."

"Oh, dear," she sighs. "I'm so sorry to hear that."

Her aged eyes are filled with sympathy. Through look alone, she speaks in silence, and I can see understanding and a pain of her own.

"I apologize for being too honest. I didn't mean to make you feel uncomfortable."

"Nonsense. If a woman my age can't handle a little honesty . . . well . . . she hasn't truly lived then."

"I suppose." And she's right. Hell, I feel like I've lived a thousand years on this earth. I doubt you could say anything that would shock me at this point. I bet there isn't a pain that exists that I haven't felt.

"Will you be staying long . . . ?" she begins and then falters her words. "I'm so sorry, hun. It was late when you arrived and your name is failing me right now."

*It was in that moment, with that elderly lady who seemed to have answers to questions I had yet to discover, where I made a choice. I thought I had nothing left to lose, but that wasn't fact. You see, somewhere deep inside of me was that five-year-old girl. She held the identity I lost so long ago, and I wanted it back.*

"Elizabeth," I tell her. "And I'm not quite sure how long I'll be staying."

"Well, Elizabeth, it's nice to have you here. I won't take up any more of your time. If you need anything, please let me know, okay?"

"Thank you."

I take my tea and head upstairs to my room to unpack and freshen up. After I'm dressed and have settled my belongings in their proper places, I look at myself in the easel mirror that's set in the corner of the room. Ivory slacks, taupe cashmere sweater, nude pumps. Clothes I acquired while living my con. They scream Nina, but I'm at a loss as to what is Elizabeth. Who is she really? It's been so long since I've been her. I feel like I left her that fated day when my father was arrested. I've lived most of my life in a tomb, hiding from the afflictions of this world, until I became Nina.

And now, I'm a hollow illusion—a druxy dressed in gossamer.

I tuck a lock of my wavy red hair behind my ear before grabbing my keys.

With the address to Brunswickhill punched into the car's navigation, I follow the highlighted route that weaves me through the narrow streets up a winding hill. It doesn't take long to hit Abbotsford Road, and I know I'm close.

But not to *him,* only to his ghost.

My eyes sting with unshed tears as I round the bend and see the green sign on the stone gate wall that reads *Brunswickhill.* I'm locked on the sign as my chin trembles and my soul bleeds from the inside, filling me with the poison I feed from.

It's real.

This place—the place he wanted to give me—it's really real.

Pulling the car off the side of the road, I don't realize how tightly my fingers are wrapped around the steering wheel until I let go and feel the ache. When I step out of the car in front of the wrought iron gate that hides my could-have-been palace, the phantom of death hangs over me.

Loss is consuming.

Emptiness is overwhelming.

Sadness is everlasting.

My feet move on their own—closer. I breathe deeply, praying for the scent of him to fill my lungs that don't deserve it, but crave it. It's nothing but sharp ice though. Frigid as my hands grip the cold metal of the gate, tears begin to fall from my already-swollen eyes.

The fissures of my heart begin to rip and shred—burning, stinging, piercing agony erupting. My knuckles whiten as my grip strengthens, and the misery and regret explode in a vile rage. Jerking my hands, shaking the gates, I lose myself in a maniacal outburst. I scream into the bleak clouds, scream so hard it feels like razors slicing through my larynx, and I welcome the pain, pleading for it to cut more deeply.

Slamming the gate back and forth, metal clanging, ice severing my flesh, I sob. I make it hurt coming out. Bitterly cold tears stain my face as my body takes on a life of its own.

I want him back.

How hard do I have to cry to get him back?

Why did this happen to me? To him? To us?

I just want him back.

"Come back!" My voice, shrilling in the air. "Please! Just come back!"

Thrashing around, drowning in wails, my body tires. My hands are frozen, continuing to cling to the bars of the gate as I fall to my knees. I feel my core chipping away while my body heaves. Desperate to catch my breath against my pounding heart, I close my eyes and lean against the wrought iron. Soon, my deep gasps turn into childlike, desolate whimpers.

I just want someone to hold me. To touch me and tell me it's going to be okay. That *I'm* going to be okay. I want my brother, my daddy, my love—I'll take anyone just to get some relief. So I sit here on the cold concrete and cry—alone.

Snow drifts down, weightlessly, falling over me as time passes. The whistling wind through the trees awakens me to the dropping temperatures, and I don't even know how long I've been sitting here when I look up and through the gates. Wiping my tears, I stammer to my feet and try to get a better look at the property, but it's hidden behind the trees. On the other side of the gate, the drive winds up a hill and through a mass of snow-covered trees, and beyond that is a mystery.

But I know.

He told me all about the house, the grounds, the flowers, the glass conservatory.

I look around to find a way in, but the gates and stone wall are nearly nine feet high, and there's no way of climbing over.

What's the point anyway? It's not like anything's waiting for me on the other side. I'm not even sure why I'm still here, and when I look down at my reddened, almost maroon hands, bloodied from the ice cuts, I know it's time to go.

"DEAR, ARE YOU all right?"

"Just slipped on some ice while shopping," I lie as Isla notices my dirty, wet slacks from where I spent most of the day sitting on the snowy ground. I know I look ghastly, and the part of me that's trained itself well wants to poise up, but the weakness in me begs to slump its shoulders and take the embrace I know Isla would be willing to give. I don't know which way to go.

"You're a terrible liar, lassie," she says as she takes my hand and leads me over to the dining room table and sits me down.

She rushes into the kitchen and quickly returns with the kettle as well as a cup and saucer. I watch as her frail hands pour the hot water and dunk in a tea bag before setting it down in front of me.

I don't refute her accusation that I'm a liar. I'm too emotionally drained to play games, and then she remarks, "Your eyes look like they hurt."

And they do.

I've cried more in these past few weeks than I have in my whole life. Pike taught me how to shut off my emotions, act like a machine so that no one could hurt me, and he taught me well. But the strength it takes to turn it all off is beyond what I feel I'm capable of at the moment.

My eyes are a constant shade of pink, and the salt from my tears has burned through the tender skin that surrounds them.

Makeup only irritates it and stings, so I go easy with the powder in my feeble attempt to look as presentable as possible.

But I have to wonder why I'm even concerned about how I present myself. I'm thousands of miles away from America. I'm no longer pretending or fighting because I've already lost.

I don't want to be Nina anymore. I don't want the stupid life of Mrs. Vanderwal. It's over. There's nothing left of it because everyone is gone. Maybe, just maybe, I can stop fighting, stop the lies, stop fearing and hiding. For the first time since I was eight years old and left to decay in Posen, maybe now I can finally breathe. I just wish I knew how. It's been almost twenty-one years of suffocating, and when I look over at Isla and see the years marked in the wrinkles of her face, I give her a little more truth.

"I went to the home he used to own."

She reaches across the table and places her hand on my arm. "You said you lost him. What happened? Did he leave you?"

"Yes," I choke out, trying to hold back my tears. "He died."

"Bless you, dear. I'm so sorry."

Swallowing hard, we both sit for a while before she breaks the silence and tells me, "I lost my husband eight years ago. Nothing can compare to the pain of losing the man you give your spirit to. When you put everything you have—everything you are—into the one who promises to take care of you, you become transparent and utterly vulnerable to that person. And when he's taken away, so are you, and yet here you remain, left to continue living your life as if you have something to live for."

"Then why go on living?"

"Well," she starts, looking over to the fireplace mantel where a menagerie of picture frames line the wooden structure. "For me it was for my family. My children. It took a while, but eventually

I found the strength to pull myself together and live for them."

I scan the array of family portraits and candid snapshots, and when I turn back to Isla, she smiles, asking, "Do you have children?"

Her question hits me hard. I'm not sure how to answer because it wasn't that long ago that I did have a child. A baby. A tiny baby growing in my womb, and now that womb is empty. So, I keep my answer simple, "I don't have any family. It's only me."

"Your parents?"

Shaking my head, I repeat, "Just me."

Instead of telling me how sorry she is about this fact, she does her best to encourage. "You're so young. You have time in this life. For me, I was an old woman when my husband passed on, but you . . . you have youth on your side. You live for that. You're beautiful; you'll fall in love again, and you have time to create your own family."

"I don't think I'm strong enough to fall in love again." I'm also unworthy and undeserving of love after everything I've done.

"Maybe not now. It takes time for wounds to heal, but there will come a time when you'll be strong enough."

I'm smart enough to know that not all wounds heal, but I nod and give a weak smile before standing up. "I should get out of these wet clothes," I say and excuse myself from the room.

After a hot shower, I tend to the cuts on my hands and then wonder why I even bothered to do so as I pick up a bottle of sleeping pills from my toiletry bag. The pills lightly pad against each other as I roll the bottle in my hand. I keep wishing for some sort of relief, some comfort, but it's been here the whole time. Right here in this bottle.

What's the point of life when life has nothing but vile hate for you?

My body is numb, a casket of waste. I feel nothing in this moment as I consider my escape. I don't want this life anymore. I never wanted it.

I'm outside of my body, standing next to a pathetic woman whose bones now protrude through colorless skin because she refuses to take care of herself. I look at her, slowly deteriorating. She stops rolling the bottle of pills in her hand and stares into the translucent orange before popping the lid off.

*"Do it,"* I encourage. *"Put yourself out of your misery."*

I know she hears me as she moves gracefully, pouring the pills in her hand and then lifts her head, staring across the room at nothing in particular.

*"Just do it, Elizabeth. Everything you want is waiting for you. They're all waiting for you."*

And then she does it; holding her hand to her mouth, she dumps the pills in and takes a long drink of water from the glass on the bedside table. I walk over to her when she lies back on the bed and run my fingers through her hair, soothing her the way a parent would a child. I meet her craving for tender affection. She looks peaceful in the stillness of the room, breathing in a soft, rhythmic pattern. I notice tears puddling in her blue eyes, but she doesn't cry, and I know she's ready.

"I just can't do it anymore," she whispers to herself and then closes her eyes as she lets go of the fight.

Sometimes, for some people, the fairytale only exists in death.

Seven

WHEN I OPENED my eyes and found myself in the same room I fell asleep in, I had to laugh at how pathetic I was. I couldn't even kill myself; instead I just gave myself one hell of a nap. And there I was, greeted by another day after a lousy botched suicide attempt.

Everything inside of me was paralyzed, yet my body still moved.

*Did you know it was possible to have feelings with no emotions?*
*You can, and I'm proof of it.*

I performed the same actions of the previous day with detachment, and it wasn't long until I found myself back at Brunswickhill. I spent hours there, sitting outside of the gates and crying for my lost love.

And the next day, I returned.

And the day after that.

And the day after that.

And even the day after that.

It's a pathetic routine I refuse to break, because for some reason, as upsetting as it is to be at the estate, it allows me to feel connected to Declan. And I need that connection because I don't have anything else to hold on to. So I cling to the forlorn fairytale that never will be.

It's a little over a week that I've been coming here, spending my days crying, pleading, bargaining with a God I don't even believe in to bring him back. Isla now looks at me with pity every evening when I return to shower and sleep. We don't speak much, but it's mostly on my part. I've allowed the wall I spent my whole life building around my heart to crumble to dust, and I've never felt weaker than I do now. Not even when I was being molested by my brother when I was just a child. Or when I was bound up in the closet and locked away for days on end.

No.

This is much worse.

I drive in silence over to Abbotsford Road, and when I round the bend, I slow the car down as I see the new owners pulling up to the gate. They haven't been around since I've been coming here. Chills run through me as I drive past the gate and follow the winding road until my car is out of their sight. I'm hardly thinking as I follow my body's movements, quickly parking the car and hopping out. Walking back to the gate, I catch the taillights of the SUV as it enters the private drive and I rush to the gates to slip through before they close completely.

Curiosity gets to me, but it's more than that. It's a feeling of ownership, as if this place is mine, because once upon a time ago, it was going to be mine, but time wasn't on my side back then. It still isn't.

I step off the drive and into the snow that covers the ground beneath. I duck behind the trees to remain unseen and start exploring the grounds. Steep hills are covered in bushes and trees that the cold weather has consumed to a barren state. If I close my eyes, I can picture the lush greens and colorful flowers that would come to life under the warm sun. The beauty is still visible though. Everything looks pure and virgin, coated in the fluffy, white powder.

Looking up, I can see the house perched at the top of the hill. My heart grows heavy, sinking down into my gut as I peer up through the trees to see the stonework of what was supposed to be my palace. I continue to weave deeper into the trees, wandering about when I come across a small, manmade, pebbled creek that winds down one of the small hills. It's covered in frozen water and there's a small wooden bench at the bottom where it rounds out into a tiny pond.

And now it hits me . . .

Taking a slow spin to take in my surroundings, nestled within this beautiful place, I realize this resembles what I've spent my life dreaming about. A small forest. Carnegie's magical forest. The thought brings me a warmth of comfort along with a cleaver to my chest because now I feel I've lost even more.

Time passes as I explore, getting lost in my head with fantasies of what could have been and memories of what was. When I get closer to the top of the hill, I can see the front of the house between the branches. It doesn't look like any home I've seen. It's grand and dignified, adorned in large pieces of stone that embody this three-story structure. A massive, tiered fountain stands proud at the center of the circle drive. It's covered in snow, but it doesn't take away from the beauty.

Shrubs line the perimeter of the house, but there are several gaping holes in the hedge, missing bushes that have probably died in the frost and been removed. Everything is so pristine except for the mess of randomly missing shrubs. I take a few steps to try and get a closer look at a small building sitting off to the side of the house when I hear a door close, startling me. Quickly turning, I stagger on my feet, moving deeper into the trees to hide.

A car starts.

"Shit," I murmur under my breath, and I know I have to quickly get back down to the base of the property without being seen.

I see the black SUV making its way down the drive, and I rush towards the gate, trying to keep my balance. There's no way I'll be able to scale the wall to get out if that gate closes, but there are hidden patches of ice I'm trying to watch out for, slowing me down.

Grabbing on to tree trunks for balance as I make my way down, I notice the SUV stop from the corner of my eye, and in a panic to get to my car, I make a run for it. I'm close to the gate, and I take a look behind me to see the SUV moving again. When I turn my head back around, I stumble, crouching over to duck under a massive branch hanging too low. My shoe catches on a patch of ice, knocking me off balance. Taking a huge step to get my slipping feet back under me, I plow down several feet, falling hard onto my stomach on the drive. My palms sting as I try to catch my fall on the icy gravel.

Not wanting to get caught trespassing on private property, I do my best to hop up to my feet.

"Hey!" a man shouts at me, but my pounding heart that beats in my ears muffles him.

I slow my step and stop, cursing myself for being so foolish.

Turning around, the man's car door is open, and when he steps out, my lungs fill to the brink of their elasticity. Everything that's been working so hard at keeping me alive soothes, and my hands fly to cover my mouth in utter shock and elation.

*Oh my God.*

Confusion and fear and anxiety swarm through my veins.

Everything stops.

Time stands still.

I can't move, can't blink, can't breathe.

My eyes scan his figure as the seconds falter between us.

*This isn't real. You've been out in the cold for too long. You're upset and hallucinating, Elizabeth. It isn't real.*

But he moves.

*He's alive! Oh, thank God, he's alive, but how?*

Something between a gasp and a cry rips out of me. I can't help the thankful smile that grows on my lips that are hidden behind my hands, and I prepare to run to him. He's alive and on solid ground, not buried in the dirt of the earth like I've believed this entire time. He's whole and beautiful, and I need to cover him in my warmth just as much as I need him to cover me. To heal this suffering that's been gnawing through my flesh and bone, straight into the fibers of my cells.

I breathe in holy relief as he steps away from the SUV.

"What the fuck are you doing here?!"

I drop my hands, stunned beyond what I can comprehend as his harsh tone slays every piece of hope my foolish heart just resurrected.

"You're real?" I question, but my words are barely audible under my panted breath. My pulse is turbulent, and I'm not sure if what I'm seeing really exists.

59

"You left me to die, you manipulative bitch!"

"No!"

*No!!*

My brain races to defend, to take away the hate that is utterly obvious in his eyes. His words are suffused in it, leaving them to poison me. A menace to once was.

"You lied." His words come quick as rage boils behind his glare.

"No!" I grapple with words that I can't seem to find in my state of shock. I want to ask him if he's real again, but the venom on his tongue scares me into justifying my actions.

"You cunt!"

"Please, no! It wasn't like tha—"

"What was it like then? Huh? Tell me what is was, *Nina?*" A knowing grin creeps upon his lips—evil—as he takes a step closer, but still much too far for me to touch. "Or is it *Elizabeth?* Who the hell are you?"

"I don't know," I murmur shamefully and then continue, "I don't know who I am. I haven't been me in a very long time." My words are like knives carving pieces out of me. They hurt when I confess, "The only thing I know I am is *yours.*"

"Tell me I wasn't your goddamn pawn!"

"This was never supposed to happen, Declan. Please—"

"What? You turning me into a murderer? That wasn't your plan all along?"

"I love you. Please. You have to understand," I plead against his wrath.

In three quick steps, his hands are on me, gripping my shoulders, swinging me around as if I weigh nothing, slamming me violently against the side of his car.

I can smell him, and suddenly, there's no more pain. His fingers pierce into my flesh, bruising me instantly, and it feels like kisses on my skin. He yanks me closer towards him before smashing me back against the car again, seething through clenched teeth, "You're a sick fuck. Nothing but street trash." He takes in a deep breath, and then adds, "That's right. I know all about you and that punk kid you ran around with."

"It wasn't supposed to end like that," I try convincing. "I fell in love with you."

"End like what? Huh?"

"The way it did."

His hands drop from my shoulders, and before I know it, he's got his hand wrapped around my neck, choking, pinning me against the SUV, and I savor the heat of him against me.

"I killed your husband," he snarls, beautiful breath bathing my face.

"I didn't want that," I gasp on strangled breath.

"What did you want?"

Looking up into his eyes, they're blurred behind my welled tears when I tell him, "You."

"I should kill *you*."

My hands cling to his wrist, urging him to tighten his grip around my throat.

"Do it." My words, an offering of atonement. "I've lost everything, and out of all that, you're the only one I would have given up everything for just to have one last touch." His grip weakens but his hand remains firmly in place, and when I watch our breaths unite in small clouds of vapor between our lips, realization crystallizes.

*My God, he's alive.*

Letting go of his wrist, I reach up and run my hand along his stubbled jaw, and the comfort in the touch flays me entirely. A disgustingly raw sob erupts from my bleeding heart. I want to crawl inside of his skin and drown myself in his blood. I want to swim in his marrow.

"Don't fucking touch me," he barks, wrenching my hand off of him.

I'm a mess though, unable to contain my emotions as they pour out of me. "I thought you were dead. For weeks I've been mourning you—"

"Get the fuck off my property, bitch."

His words cut me off. I shouldn't be stunned at them, but the snarl in his tone is startling, and I quickly shut my mouth. He then grabs ahold of my jaw, forcing my chin up as he looks down on me, and I don't recognize the devilry in his eyes. He pisses his words, "You're nothing more than a shit-stain, so fuck off. I'm done with you, understand?"

"Please . . . don't."

"Nod your little head and tell me you understand."

The urgency to explain everything to him is powerful, but I know he'd never hear my words with the hatred in him right now, so I obey with a nod. "I understand."

He lets go, not giving me a second look as he turns away and gets back into the SUV. I look at his beautiful face through the windshield. I never want to take my eyes off him, and it kills to know that I have to. He glares at me with daggers as I feel tears running down my cheeks.

"I'm so sorry," I say even though I know he can't hear me and then turn my back on my prince that I so selfishly molded into this monster.

Walking away, I'm confused. There are a million feelings and reactions, and I have no clue which one to grab on to. I don't know how to begin to process the fact that I just saw my angel of death in the flesh. I felt his heat, smelled him, heard him.

It was real.

I see Pike all the time. I even talk to him. But there's never a smell, never a temperature to his touch. It's how I know the difference between hallucinations and reality. But this is real. He's alive, but at what cost? He doesn't resemble the Declan I knew. That man was firm, yes, but he had light in him that shone through his emerald eyes. But this Declan . . . he's hard and cold, and it's all my fault. I knew pushing him to kill Bennett would destroy him, change him, take away his pure spirit.

He looks as worn as I do, his frame more slender, a lack of color in his skin. I ache to touch him, taste him, make him see that this was all a terrible mistake. That loving him was my saving grace. Make him understand how everything changed and changed from a place of honesty I never knew I held inside of me.

How am I supposed to live in the same world as him when he hates me so much?

How do I right the wrongs of my past?

How do I find a hope worth living for when my one hope would rather me dead than alive?

eight

TORMENT IS THE deep well I bathe in daily. It covers me entirely as I sink beneath the surface, feeling its particles soak into the pores of my decrepit skin. Seeping through me, it consumes, wallows, and dwells so I can feel every ounce of its torturous abuse.

Black is the color that stains my insides. Declan used to color me in vibrancy, but that's when he loved me for the lie he believed I was. I'm a sick woman. Deceit paints my rotten soul, and he now sees me for what I am.

How could I destroy a man as wonderful as Declan?

He was a good man, a loving man. His touch was firm yet tender. But now, after seeing him a couple days ago, he's so different. Callous and filled with venom. Worst of all is knowing that I did that to him. I'm the culprit. I'm the cause. I touched him and turned him into a monster.

But even as a monster, I want him. I'll take him in any form I can because I'm so thankful he's alive. That Pike didn't kill him. Glory and joy somehow illuminate this bleak heart of mine and rejoice in the flesh and blood of his existence.

Where do I go now? What do I do when all I want is what I know he'll refuse?

Another touch, kiss, smell, taste. But once I get it, I know I'll want more. It'll never satisfy, never be enough to feed the hunger I have for him. My soul is starved and he's my sacrament.

I want to skin him with my tongue, loving him with every lick.

Alone is where I sit though, here in this bed and breakfast, in this room I've been calling home since I arrived. Too scared to go back to Brunswickhill for fear of what will greet me. Declan isn't a man one can push. He thrives on utter control, so keeping my distance is the only choice I have right now unless I want to throw him over the edge. And I don't. I want him to be able to see that not all of it was a lie, that I did love him, that it was real, and that I didn't want to destroy him the way I wound up doing anyway. I need him to know that, to understand his heart was something I wanted to take care of—I still do.

Hours pass as I sit, staring out the window at the snow-covered hills, wondering what my love is doing. It feels strange to be in a world where he exists and to not know, to not be a part of that world with him when we had become so enmeshed with each other. He was a part of me—still is. He lives within me; I can feel him in my bones—breathing inside of me, keeping me alive.

*He* is all I have to live for.

I grow impatient and anxious in this room, feeling like a caged animal. I grab my coat and scarf and head down to the car. As I drive the slick streets, I wind up on Abbottsford Road without thinking. It's all I know in this town, it's all I crave. I tell myself I won't stay long, that I'll just drive past, take a quick look. But when I make the sharp turn around the bend, I slow the car down and stop.

*Was it all a dream? A hallucination?*

Looking at the gate, I wonder if I was *really* on the other side.

*Did I just want it so badly that I dreamt it up?*

I know I shouldn't be here. I know what I did to him was so awful that seeing me will only make it worse on him. I want to give him that space, the courtesy of staying away because I know that's what he wants. But I'm too selfish. I want him too much, and now that I'm here, the energy collides inside of me. I want to jump over that wall, run up the hill to his front door, break it down, storm the property to find him, hug him, cling, paw, scratch, and ravage him like the animal I am.

Tingles dance up my fingers, into my hands, and up my arms. I can't sit still.

Hopping out of the car, I rush over to the gates, grab on to them and shake them, screaming at the top of my lungs, "Declan! Please let me talk to you! Declan, please!"

My voice strains as I plead and beg for him. Tears begin to coat my cheeks as I call his name, because simply having it on my tongue and lips feels like a kiss from him. So I scream even louder, a protest of my love, and my voice shrills painfully as I call out, "Declan!" over and over and over again.

I don't stop—I can't.

I'm nothing without him. I'll die without him. He has to forgive me. He just has to. I can't live with him hating me as much as he does. So I fight these gates, screaming and crying and breaking, falling to my knees—absolutely crumbling.

I'm weak as my voice slowly gives out, and I have to catch my breath around my pounding, severing heart. Dropping my head, I weep while the damp ground seeps through the fabric of my pants.

I startle and jump up when the gate begins opening. I turn to see the black Mercedes SUV he was in the other day coming up the road. Desperate to talk to him, I run out in the middle of the street, blocking him. He slows and stops, and with my hands on the freezing hood of his car, emotions overwhelm as I beg, "Declan, please. Please let me talk to you. I love you, Declan."

My words fall out in a blubber of panicky cries as I look at him through the windshield. The car shifts under my hands when he puts it in park and then opens his door. Menacing eyes greet me once again, but I'm frantic for his attention.

"Declan, please, just let me talk to you."

"I thought you understood that I didn't want you coming back here," he snarls in his thick accent, stepping in front of me.

In quick movements, he grabs my arms in both his hands. Faster than what I can fight, Declan drags me over to my car while I cry, "Please, stop. Just give me a few minutes to explain."

"There isn't a goddamn thing you could possibly say to me."

He then yanks me around so I'm facing away from him and slams my front side over against the car, knocking the wind out of me and pinning me down. With my arms bound in his hand behind my back, he presses the side of my face into the hood with his other, needling against the ice. His body hunches over mine and his breath heats my ear as he seethes, "In case I didn't make it clear, I fucking hate you."

"You don't mean that," I whisper, pissing him off even more as he grabs a fist full of my hair and snaps my head back.

My neck stretches, sparks of pain shooting through the tendons, and the *chrrrick* of my hair, popping out from the roots, ripping flesh along with it, sears my scalp in pricks of fire. I scream, but he doesn't let go.

"You've got balls, darling. Coming here, knowing one phone call is all it would take for you to be arrested and extradited."

"Why haven't you done it then?" I question through clenched teeth, and he yanks harder, ripping out more hair from my scalp. Gasping in agony, I push him, "Tell me why."

"You think it's because I care for you? You're fucking delusional."

"Then why?"

"Because seeing your face makes me want to kill you. I thought you'd be smart and leave, never come back, yet here you are," he says.

"You won't hurt me."

The sudden force of his hand shocks me, and I scream out in pure white, heated pain. My hand flies to the back of my head, trembling as I touch the bare flesh. Tears fall, and when I turn to look at him, he's holding a chunk of my hair. I can feel the blood trickling down the back of my neck. He stares—no emotion—while my body pangs in agony, but I've dealt with pain and abuse my whole life. I've been beaten, whipped, tied up for days, and one thing I've learned: physical pain is much more tolerable than mental pain.

Bruises fade. Blood dries. Scabs heal.

Sucking in a deep breath, I bring my hand in front of me and it's covered in blood.

"You won't hurt me," I repeat, and it's now that I see the torment in his eyes. There's no doubt he's furious, but there's a void, a hollowness that didn't used to be there.

"You sucked the life right out of me. I don't give a shit about you anymore," he says and then drops the lock of my hair on the ground. "I pray you put a bullet in your head."

I let him go without saying anything as he turns to get back in his car. I bite my tongue, knowing I'll only make him feel worse if I continue to speak. I'll give him a reprieve, but I won't back down. I'll find a way to talk to him, to explain everything. I've manipulated my way around obstacles in the past; I can do it again.

After I watch him drive past me and the gates close behind him, I walk to the side of the road and scoop up a handful of snow. My body tenses in preparation for the pain, and my hand shakes as I reach back. Flinching, I slather the snow on my bloody scalp, and hiss against the sting that singes my head.

I scoop up another handful and pack it against my wound, and once my body stops quaking and numbs, I slip into my car and drive back.

"WHAT HAPPENED?" ISLA questions urgently as I'm walking up the stairs.

"Excuse me?" I respond when I turn around.

Coming up the steps, she looks worried. "There's blood all over your back, lassie."

"Oh, I . . ."

"What's going on? Are you hurting yourself?"

"No," I quickly blurt out.

"Do you need to call someone? The police?"

"No. No, I'm fine," I defend. "It's fine."

Her eyes narrow in annoyance as I avoid her questioning.

"It's not *fine*. Now you tell me what's going on or I'll call the police myself."

"No police. Please," I tell her, and decide to just lie. "It was a clumsy accident. I slipped on some ice and hit my head as I fell."

She gives me a suspicious look before nodding. "You should get yourself checked out by a doctor."

"If it starts to bother me, I will. It looks much worse than it is," I try assuring her.

Once I'm in my room, I head into the bathroom to check out the damage. The blood mats my hair, and the strands are dried to the wound. I peel some of the hair away, and it rips the forming scab causing my head to bleed again. I know I could wet a towel and clean myself up, but I relish the pain. It distracts and takes away from my annihilated heart.

The misery inside of me swells and grows, so I continue ripping the scab apart, pulling my hair, and focusing on that pain instead of my internal pain. I can't release it, but I can mask it, and so I do. When I feel the heat of blood seeping out, there's a release of euphoria that delights me. I savor this momentary distraction and enjoy the blood tickling my skin as it rolls down my neck. It's all I focus on as I sigh in relief and close my eyes.

# nine

## (CALLUM)

"DON'T FUCK AROUND, inmate. Five minutes," the guard I paid off barks as he shoves the disposable cell phone against my chest.

"I need the card."

"I already programmed the number in the phone," he tells me and then hands me a small, folded up piece of scrap paper. "The verification code."

I nod and he scowls in return. "Make it quick."

Punching in the numbers, I don't have to wait long for the call to go through.

"Hello?" my longtime friend answers. The one I planted in my son's life to ensure I have all my bases covered. A man who presents himself as a loyal entity to Declan, but whose loyalties de facto lie with me.

"I don't have long," I say.

"How the hell are you calling me? I heard you were locked up."

I was arrested before I could make contact with my associate after receiving the call about Nina's whereabouts. Now I sit, here in jail at the Manhattan Detention Complex, waiting for my case to go before the grand jury.

"I have my ways. Look, I don't have time to bullshit. I need you to move the money from the offshore accounts and put it into Declan's foundation."

"No worries," he responds obediently.

"Use his foundation to wash it and make it appear as clean as possible."

"Got it."

"I also need you to keep your eye on Declan. I want him followed. After the shooting, he's been off, if you know what I mean."

"The kid is fucked up, Cal."

"Yeah, well, that's his issue. You need to make sure my issue is the one you're protecting, got it?"

"Wrap it up, inmate," the guard snaps at me.

"That money needs to be moved yesterday."

"I'll handle it," he responds before the phone is snatched from my hand.

Ten

EATING ONE OF Isla's Scotch eggs I've come to enjoy and sipping on hot tea, I flip through a local Edinburgh publication. It's been several days since my last run-in with Declan. I've been holed up in my room, crying and feeling defeated. Wondering what to do, where to go, and how to move on in this life.

I was with Pike last night. He lay in bed with me; we haven't done that in such a long time, and I forgot how very comforting it felt. I was finally able to breathe. He spoke to me, soothed me, and in that moment he was real. My head knows it's a phantasm, but my heart refuses, so we talked, cried, and eventually he made me smile.

When I woke this morning, he was gone, but somehow I still feel him here. I remember when we were kids, and even living in the vilest circumstances one could imagine, when I was in his arms, I was okay. He was magical in that way. So was Declan. Both of them loved me and healed me in entirely unique ways.

Pike reminded me of my strength, and I showed him the

back of my head, where Declan had ripped out my hair. I told him that I continue to pick at the scab and make myself bleed to feel better, proving to him that I'm weak, that I can't handle the pain anymore, so I create my own. A pain I can control and use to mask the true ache that runs deep inside of me. But he assured me that what I'm doing is a symbol of strength. The fact that I refuse to let my emotions control me, and instead control them, is a testament to my vitality.

I decided to take his words and apply them to Declan. Instead of letting him control me and keep me away, I will take the control to get what I want. I've done it before; I can do it now. Pike is right. I've been allowing myself to crumble and feel as if I'm nothing on my own, but he reminded me that I'm not. That I've always been strong. Reminded me that even though I no longer have him as my vice, I'm powerful enough to create another.

"It's so nice to see you eating," Isla says as she walks out from the kitchen and into the dining room where I sit.

"I've been a little under the weather," I excuse my lack of presence.

She sets down a bowl of mixed berries and eyes the magazine I'm flipping through.

"I found it on the coffee table," I offer. "I was thinking about getting out of town and going into the city for a day trip."

"Have you spent any time in Edinburgh?"

"No. I drove through when I arrived, stopped for a quick meal, and then came here."

"It's a great town," she says and continues to talk, but her voice fades into the distance when I turn the page.

She's muted noise, and everything around me tunnels as I focus on the eyes looking up at me from within the grains of the paper. Dapper as always, in a vested, tailored suit, no tie, and top buttons unfastened. The very essence of Declan, unkempt in a classy way. His face, a couple days unshaven, and I can remember the way the bristles felt against my lips when he kissed me. The way I would find comfort in running my hand along his jaw.

Setting my fork down with ease, my pulse slows in admiration and shock. I hone in and examine every curve and line of his face.

That used to be mine.

No more though.

He loathes my very existence, wishes me dead, prays for it. But that filters out and what remains is the lovingly harsh way his hands felt on my body. The good of Declan takes over my thoughts, and I rush back in time to when he would look at me with his powerful eyes that told so much in the depth of emerald. They would nearly illuminate and brighten when his emotions of adoration were on high, and dull out, blackening when desire and his need to claim and control would ignite. This man is built in impermeable layers, but I was the one he allowed to seep in. I guess the same could be said in reverse because I let him in as well.

Isla's touch on my arm pulls me away from my love.

"Are you okay?"

"I'm sorry," I say with a slight shake of my head.

She nods to the photograph in the magazine. "No need to apologize. With looks like that, you can't help but become distracted."

Laughing, I agree, "Yeah."

"He used to live in Edinburgh before moving to America years back. A perpetual bachelor that the lassies would fawn over."

"You know him?" I question.

"*Of* him," she clarifies. "The McKinnons were a prominent family here, but tragedy struck and they soon found assuage in the US. But recently, Declan, the son, returned."

"Hmm," I hum, feigning nonchalance.

"He lives here in Gala, you know?"

"What happened?"

When she gives me a wondering look, I clarify, "You mentioned a tragedy."

"Oh, yes. Declan's mother was murdered in their home. Callum, his father, soon left, but Declan stayed in Scotland for a while. I think I read somewhere that when Declan finished his studies at University, he moved to the States and went into business with his father. They've both been living in America until Declan's recent return."

I want to correct her, tell her that Declan parted ways with Cal and was making a strong name for himself as an international real estate developer, but I'd rather her not know my link to him.

"He attended St. Andrews at the same time Prince William did," she adds with enthusiasm, but I don't care about the trivial anecdotes she seems to take pride in.

Anxious to be alone, I take my last bite of egg and excuse myself. "Do you mind if I take this with me?" I ask about the magazine.

"Of course not."

"Thank you."

When I close the door to my room, I sit down at the small desk near the window and open the article with Declan's photo. Alone with my love, I run my fingers over his face and pretend it's real. I shut my eyes and try to smell him, but there's nothing except the lingering fragrance of my perfume in the air.

I look back at him and then begin to read the article that the photo accompanies. I feel my smile grow the further I read. And when I discover a charity event where Declan will be the guest of honor, I know this is an opportunity that I must take full advantage of—and I will. I continue to read the piece that boasts about the charities Declan supports and advocates for.

I note the function where he will be honored is being held this Saturday evening at his alma mater, and start scheming.

AFTER READING THE article a couple days ago, I went ahead and made my day trip to Edinburgh, but not after making a few phone calls. The foundation that Declan is being honored for and has become one of the main financial contributors to is one that strives to offer valuable education to under-privileged children. Knowing there will be so many eyes on him at this event, I think it will be the perfect opportunity to talk to him. I doubt he would cause a scene, but rather be forced to be cordial for the good graces of the attendees. He'd have to stand there and listen to me. So I went ahead and became a donor myself, and the sizable check I wrote secured me a seat at the event.

As I stand in front of the full-length mirror here in my hotel room in Saint Andrews, I run my hands down the lace overlay of my navy dress. The thin material hugs my petite form, just barely skimming the floor. I wear my hair down in soft waves to hide the still-grotesque wound on the back of my head. I continue to pick at it daily, and it's grown in size. I don't want it to heal because it's the only physical thing I have to represent Declan. His gift to me, created by his own hands. He gave it to me, and I refuse to let it go. It serves a multitude of purposes: it's my vice, my pain reliever, my trophy, my reminder, my solace. My love, branded into my flesh, and I own it happily.

When I'm satisfied with my appearance, I pick up my invitation and pashmina before heading down to the lobby. The car I called for is already waiting out front, and my heart beats in anticipation as the driver opens the door for me. I've granted myself permission to be vulnerable ever since I woke up in the hospital, exhausted from the emotions I finally allowed to erupt inside of me.

But now . . . now it's time to focus.

I know what I want, and I need to do whatever it takes to get Declan to talk to me, to hear my words, and to understand and believe in what we had. To know it wasn't a lie—not all of it. To know I didn't want him to kill, I didn't want to use him or betray him, but that everything spun out of control so fast I couldn't stop what had already been set into motion.

When we arrive and pass through the gate of Saint Andrews University, I take a moment to admire the historic buildings, aged to refinement. The car jostles along the cobblestone road and slows in front of a building that's adorned with rustic, fire-lit lanterns and a red carpet lined with press photographers. It's foreign that I would attend an event alone and not know a single person, but I refuse to let insecurity taint me.

The car stops and I watch women dressed to the nines in their designer gowns and men in their kilts and fly plaids. I take a hard swallow, straighten my spine, and reach out for the hand of the usher who opens my door.

"Miss," he greets with a nod. "Will you be joined by a companion?"

"No."

"May I escort you?"

"That would be lovely," I accept graciously.

I feign my right to belong and mingle among, what appears to be, the high society of the UK—wealth and prestige. But I'm good at what I do, veiling the disgust that molds me as the vile human I really am.

Looping my arm through his, he introduces in his heavy brogue, "I'm Lachlan."

I look up at his broad, clean-shaven face and smile at the forty-something-year-old man with dark hair distinguished by flakes of silver. Putting on the charm I perfected while married to Bennett, I remark with flirtation, "And where is *your* companion?"

"I'm without as well."

"Really? That surprises me."

"And why's that?"

"Truthfully?" I question, lifting a brow to create amusement, and when he smiles and nods, I'm blunt, telling him, "You're startlingly attractive. I find it hard to believe you're not here with a little tart attached to your arm."

His chuckle is deep and rich when he responds, "Oh, but I do have a beautiful little, what did you call it?—*tart?*—stuck to my arm."

I join in his laughter. "Elizabeth."

"Elizabeth?"

"My name, it's Elizabeth. And I assure you, I'm no tart."

eleven

LACHLAN AND I are all smiles when he leads me into the magnificent ballroom, draped in luxury. The room is masculine, smelling of rich varnish and weathered books, dark mahogany walls, and the finest champagne being served off of polished antique silver trays. As a waiter passes me, I pluck a sparkling flute from the tray.

"Quick on the bevvy. Eager?" Lachlan teases, and I answer with a simple, "Parched," before taking a sip.

But I am eager. Too eager, as I dart my eyes around the room in search of Declan, but all I see are unfamiliar faces.

"Elizabeth," Lachlan starts, pulling my attention back to him. "What brings you here? I attend many of these events, and I've never seen you before."

"I'm from the US. I recently arrived here but have been staying in Galashiels."

"Gala? Interesting. It's such a small town. Most travelers stay in Edinburgh. What's in Gala for you?"

"A good friend of mine," I tell him. "He's supposed to be here tonight actually. Declan McKinnon, have you seen him?"

"That wee bastard?" he belts out.

He must see my confused expression when he explains, "Scottish humor, dear. It's a friendly boast."

"Oh."

I take a sip of my champagne while he adds, "We both attended university here," and then is cut off by a gentleman at the microphone announcing that dinner will be served shortly and to enjoy the band and some dancing.

I scan the room again, which is filled with a mass of people, chatting, drinking, and mingling. Voices are quiet, aside from the random, boisterous comments from the men. Rich with their accents, I must stand out to them as Lachlan introduces me to a few people while everyone makes their way around.

My attention is half-hearted as the time passes. Lachlan accompanies me through the dinner service, and while he's visiting with a few other people seated at our table, I finally spot Declan. He's in the back of the room, at the bar, with a woman on his arm as he converses with a couple men.

I stare.

I can't take my eyes off of him as he stands there in a kilt. Good God, he's perfection. I'm used to seeing him in a dressed down tuxedo at black tie events, but there is nothing dressed down about him right now. Proper in a black jacket, red and black kilt with a matching red and black tartan fly plaid that's slung over his shoulder, and a black leather sporran that hangs low from his hips. Down to his flashes, this man is obscenely beautiful, and I want to rip that wench right off his arm.

I notice he isn't paying much attention to the woman as he

drinks from his old-fashioned and continues to talk to the men. I want to jump up and go to him—eager to be in his presence, but I know the reaction I'll get. It's the one I fear, but expect. The one I hate, but deserve.

"Something got your eye?" Lachlan says.

I turn and smile, telling him, "I found my friend."

"Ahh," he sighs as he spots Declan at the bar.

But before I can make a move, a man steps to the podium on the stage and begins talking, starting off with gratitude for the attendance this evening. I watch as Declan makes his way over to the stage while the gentleman continues to address all the attendees.

He's so close, but he's further away than he's ever been, even before we ever met, because his hatred cleaves wounds deeply. And my betrayal spears even deeper.

Declan's name is announced as the quintessential donor to the foundation. His name is praised for his time and devotion to the charity, and the round of applause is loud as the podium is handed over to him and he steps behind it. There's no arguing his humility; I see it in his expression. He feels the attention is undeserved.

He thanks the audience, and I melt into the sound of his voice. His accent, lighter than most others in this room, seduces me as I sit here. I feel exposed, as if people can see how my body is responding to his voice. My stomach trills and my heart quickens in luring excitement. I miss that voice. Miss it whispering softly in my ear, barking his possessive words to me, claiming that I'm his property, growling when he would come. Every sound of his enraptured me the way it's doing right now.

Giving his speech about the importance of proper education for all children, regardless of social and economic stature, I continue to admire the great things he is doing to his outfit. I take in every piece of the man I have been mourning for the past couple months. I can finally look at him without him spitting his enmity at me. So for now, I worship this moment in time where I see my old, confident Declan, speaking gracefully, loving his smile when he chuckles at his small banter.

When his speech comes to an end and he presents his substantial donation to the foundation president and encourages everyone to take out their checkbooks to do the same. He's showered with admiration for his time and efforts with grand applause, which he humbly accepts.

Stepping down from the podium, he shakes hands with the many committee members, and with all eyes on him, I know this is my moment. As conniving as it is, it's the only way I can get his attention without him lashing out.

"Excuse me," I say softly to Lachlan as I stand and set my napkin on my seat.

Keeping my eyes on Declan, I make my way through the people who are now leaving the tables behind to socialize and dance. As I approach, the woman I saw him with earlier is back at his side. She's tall—much taller than my petite stature—with raven hair that's pulled in a sophisticated bun at the nape of her neck. I quickly remind myself of what Declan and I shared not too long ago, and right my posture as I step next to the both of them. When the man in front of me shakes Declan's hand and steps away, green eyes widen in surprise.

"Declan, it's so good to see you again," I croon excitedly, putting on my act in front of the small group that's gathered around him.

He falls in line with me, the way I knew he would, being surrounded by all these people. He chivalrously accepts my hand and a kiss to his cheek.

"What are you doing here?" he questions, with only a mild bite to his tone, but his face is cordial.

"Now, you know charities are dear to me," I tease in mockery with a giggle. "I'd like to make my time in Scotland meaningful."

"And how long is that? Don't you have to get back to the States soon?"

Leaning in closer to him so not everyone can hear, I say, "No. At the moment, time is a little *futile,* if you know what I mean." I then turn to his date, remarking to him while my eyes are fixed on the woman, "Declan, she's stunning."

My words, and the manner in which they are delivered, make her uncomfortable. She fidgets and responds, "I'm sorry, I don't believe we've met. I'm Davina."

"It's a pleasure."

"And you are?"

"An old acquaintance," Declan interrupts, answering for me, and I giggle, adding, "Well, that's putting it modestly."

I can see the tension when he bites his jaw down, so I quickly make my request publically, "I was hoping I could steal you away for a couple minutes. There's something I'd like to talk to you about . . . privately."

"This probably isn't the best time."

"It's okay," Davina tells him with a pleasant smile. "I need to go visit with Beatrice anyway."

Smiling up at Declan, I boast, "Perfect!"

His smile is tight as he walks past me with no eye contact.

"Follow me."

I do, keeping up with his quick stride, but when I see he's making his way outside and away from all these people, I grab on to his arm and tug back. "Here is fine."

"I thought you said you wanted privacy."

"This is private enough." I need the crowd to ensure he keeps his emotions in check.

He narrows his eyes and sneers angrily under his breath, "What the hell are you doing here?"

"I needed to see you, to talk to you, and this was the only way I could get you to listen without you losing your shit on me."

Keeping his voice low, his tone is harsh when he says, "What do you want to say to me, huh? *I'm sorry? It's not what you think? Forgive me?* Well, fuck you because there isn't anything I want to hear coming out of your mouth."

"If you'll just let me say my piece, I'll go. If that's what you want, I'll leave—disappear from your life, and you'll never have to think of me again."

Declan grabs my elbow and pulls me closer to him. His face is so close to mine, I can feel the heat of his blood pulsing through his veins. "You think it's that easy? You think I can just shut you out and never think about you again—the woman who deceived me to the point that I . . ." he pauses for a second to make sure no one is close enough to hear his next words, " . . . *took a man's life?* I'll never be able to get rid of you because you're now the demon than lives inside me."

Words slaughter deeply.

The urge to drop to my knees and beg at his feet to forgive me surges through my body. I did this to him. It was me, and the weight of that responsibility is making it near impossible to stay above ground. It's sinking me down to a hell I'm terrified to face.

"Tell me what I can do," I plead. "Because I'd do anything for you, to take any piece of this away from you."

"It's done with. It happened and nothing will take that away, but you . . . continuing to pop up . . . you're just twisting the knife you've put in my back."

"Let me attempt to take it out then."

"That was a lovely speech," an older lady compliments as she walks past us.

Declan quickly thanks her and then turns back to me. "You need to leave."

"No."

"God, you're stubborn."

"Declan, no. I want to explain."

"Not here."

"Then where?"

"Tomorrow," he suggests. "You want to talk privately? Fine, I'll give you that. Come to my house, say whatever it is you need to say, and then leave."

"Okay," I respond with a nod.

"I mean it. You leave Scotland. Go back home."

I continue to nod in agreement with his words, and confirm, "Tomorrow then?"

His jaw clenches. "Yes. And now I want you to excuse yourself from this party."

And I do. Getting what I wanted, I smile, but it doesn't feel entirely victorious for obvious reasons. Retrieving my pashmina and clutch, I say my goodbye to Lachlan and thank him for accompanying me as my escort. He offers to drive me back to the hotel, but I politely decline and accept his flirtatious kiss to my hand before he opens the car door for me.

"It was a pleasure, Elizabeth. I hope to see you around," he tells me, and I return the gesture, saying, "I hope so too."

# twelve
## (DECLAN)

"WHAT WERE YOU doing with that woman?" I ask when Lachlan approaches me at the bar. "How do you know her?"

"I don't. She was alone, and I offered to escort her. Why?"

Taking a hard shot of my Scotch, I bite against the burn. "I want you to follow her."

"Who is she?"

"Just follow her. I want to know what she's spending her days doing."

His chuckle agitates me as he responds, "So now I'm a PI, McKinnon?"

"You want to work for someone else?" I snap, setting my old-fashioned down on the bar with too much force, and repeat harshly, "Follow her."

# thirteen

I DON'T WANT to look like I'm trying too hard, so I go for simplicity, wearing a modest cashmere sweater, slacks, and a pair of flats. I keep my makeup light with a touch of sheer gloss on my lips. My hand nervously shakes as I dab on a little concealer under my eyes to cover the evidence of my lack of sleep last night.

When I left the party, I checked out of the hotel, so it was late when I arrived back here at Isla's after the two-hour drive. My mind was racing all night, anxious about seeing Declan today and wondering exactly what I'm going to say. A part of me questions what it is I'm even doing here in Scotland. Confusion is my state of mind, so I don't even attempt to reason my actions, because it's a doomed feat. All I do know is that I'm lost, and Declan is the only thing that's familiar and known.

Slipping on my knee-length, ivory pea coat, I make my way down to my car. I find myself speeding to get to Declan, but I'm worried about what will greet me when I arrive. With white knuckles, I take a few slow, deep breaths as I round the bend in the road and approach the gate. For the first time, I roll up to the intercom box and press the button. There's no answer, but the gates open anyway.

The car moves slowly up the winding road that weaves through tall, snow-covered trees. When I reach the top, I pull in front of what was once promised to be my safe haven of escape. This should've been my home with Declan; instead, he's my lost love, and I, his enemy.

Gravel crunches beneath my feet when I step out of the car. I stand, looking up at the three-story estate that's secluded up here. Majestic and alone at the top of this hill, the only sound is the wind that howls between the trees and the swirling of snow that blows from the bare branches. I look over to the grand fountain and imagine the sound of its trickling water in the summertime.

"What are you doing?"

I turn to the house and see Declan standing at the front door in a pair of tailored slacks and an untucked button-down. My heart's beat immediately responds to him, and I murmur, "Nothing. Just looking at the grounds," while I walk over to him.

He looks down at me as I walk up the steps leading to the front door, and when I get a whiff of his cologne, I want so badly to jump into his arms. To make this all disappear. To go back in time so I can do it all differently. To save him from the cliff of goodness I shoved him off of.

But he doesn't say a word as he gestures with his hand to enter his home.

It takes nearly all my strength to stay on my feet when I step inside the massive entryway. Looking up and around, everything has been remodeled in an elegant, contemporary flair of whites and ivories. The foyer spans the length of the house, and you can see straight to the back where it opens up to the large, glassed atrium. Everything is bright and peaceful, except for the man who walks past me.

I follow as cold darkness leads me into an elaborate sitting room, which has yet to be remodeled. The walls are lined in aged wooden bookshelves that hold hundreds and hundreds of books. So many you can smell the pages and leathered bindings. An antique chandelier hangs over the large seating area of leather wing-back chairs and a tufted chesterfield sofa that's identical to the one he had in the office of his loft back in River North.

Declan takes a seat in the center of the couch, offering no welcome when he speaks. "Say what you need to say."

And suddenly, everything I thought about saying last night is gone. I have no words as I look at him. I walk closer, and instead of sitting on the couch with him or on one of the chairs, I sit on the wooden coffee table right in front of him, and when I do, he leans forward, resting his elbows on his knees.

We don't speak for a while; we just look into each other's eyes. Mine filled with pain and sorrow; his filled with chilling anger. Threatening tears prick and burn, but I fight to remain strong, when truthfully, I'm a shattered little girl, yearning to cling to the solace that's right in front of me and never let go.

With a shallow breath, my eyes fall shut, pushing a couple tears down my cheek and I whimper, "I'm so sorry."

I can't bear to look at him in my insurmountable guilt for what I've done. My head drops to my hands as I will for strength, but it doesn't come. That's the thing with Declan, he's always had a way of making it difficult for me to lock up the truth of my emotions. He's the one person who was able to strip down my barricade and make me feel—truly feel.

When I finally open my eyes, he hasn't shifted. His hard face remains, unaffected by my tears.

"Say something," I whisper. "Please."

Creases form along his forehead, and his eyes look to ache, when he finally does speak, asking, "Why did you do it?"

I vow to myself to stop all the lies. To give him transparent truth about everything. If that makes me a savage in his eyes, which it undoubtedly will, then fine. Because if he's going to judge me, I at least want him to do it honestly.

"Revenge," I finally admit.

"I want the truth," he demands.

"I married Bennett with intentions of destroying him," I say, and then pause before adding, "I married him to kill him."

He releases a heavy puff of air in disbelief. "What the fuck is wrong with you?"

"I don't know . . . I don't know."

"Why?"

"What I told you was a lie. The story about me growing up in Kansas and my parents' death. It was all a lie." The guilt has festered long enough, and I crack. My words bleed from the cobwebs of my soul, and I cry as the wounds shred apart. "I don't know how to make it right, but I want to. I never thought I would fall in love with you the way I did." My words spill out through my constricted throat.

"Tell me why," he snarls. "What did he do to you that you'd want him dead?"

"He murdered me. I wanted payback."

Declan's jaw grinds, and I go on, explaining, "I was happy . . . When I was a little girl, I was happy. I lived with my father, and then one day . . ." I choke on the agony of my words. " . . . One day he was taken from me. Arrested. I was only five years old when it happened. It was all Bennett's fault. My dad was sent to prison and I was sent to hell."

I stop when I can't speak anymore and simply cry. Choking in broken gasps of air while Declan just sits here—a stone of a man with eyes of disbelief, confusion, anger. It hurts to look at him, but I do it anyway.

"I never saw my father again, and when I was twelve years old, he died in prison. Killed by another inmate."

"What did Bennett have to do with this?" he interrupts.

"Because . . . it's a long story," I exhaust.

"You owe me the truth."

"He . . . he thought I was being abused by my dad, but it wasn't the truth. He told his parents, and the authorities were called to investigate, but instead they uncovered that he was trafficking guns and arrested him. I know it sounds bad, but he was a good man and I had a good life with him." My cries erupt harder, blubbering, "He wasn't bad, he was perfect and loved me, and Bennett took it all away. In a single moment, he set fire and incinerated everything in my world. That asshole stole my life!"

Shaking his head, Declan mutters, "Doesn't make sense. None of this makes sense."

"It was his fault," I press, but his response is sharp when he moves on, "I don't want to argue your fucked up rationalizations. Tell me . . . what was I?"

"Declan, please . . ."

"Tell me. Tell me what I was!" his voice booms off the walls, demanding to know.

"In the beginning . . . in the beginning you were the pawn,"

I confess.

"More," he urges.

"Declan, you have to understand that it changed and—"

"More!"

"Okay!" I blurt out and then repeat in a softer, defeated tone, "Okay. Yes, you started as the pawn. I was going to use you to kill Bennett."

"Why not you?"

"Because I was afraid of getting caught if I got my hands too dirty."

His teeth grind as he begins to clench and unclench his fists.

"I'm sorry," I breathe. "But when I got to know you, and we connected so easily, I fell for you. You make me feel something that no one has ever been able to do. No one has ever looked at me the way you do—the way you *did*. I've had a hard life, but—"

"Don't you dare do that. Don't you excuse your fucked ways because of the life you've had."

"I need you to know that what we had, the feelings that I had for you, were genuine. I truly loved you. I still do. I was trying to find a way out of the scam. I was giving it all up so we could be together."

Pinching the bridge of his nose, he takes a moment before speaking. "I need to know something . . ."

"Anything. I'll tell you anything to make this right."

"Was it true? Bennett beating the shit out of you, was that true?" His voice strains on those words, and I hate the witch I am and having to admit, "No. Bennett never hurt me."

"You fucking bitch!" he scathes through a severed cry.

I see how deeply I've hurt him. It's all over his face and it cuts through his voice. He rests his head on his tightly fisted hands, shaking in horror.

"Tell me what to do. Tell me," I beg, needing to take his anguish away. Needing to make this whole situation just disappear.

"You can't do shit, Nina." And the instant he says my name, he winces, squeezing his eyes shut and then asking, "What the hell do I even call you?"

A muted stillness lengthens between us as we look into each other's eyes—completely demolished. Seconds that feel like hours pass.

And for the first time, although he already knows it from the file, I give him my name.

"Elizabeth Rose Archer."

# fourteen
## (DECLAN)

"ELIZABETH ROSE ARCHER," she tells me on soft words after a long span of silence.

How could Satan own such a beautiful name?

I keep my hands fisted tightly so she can't see them shaking, but the roiling fury that runs thick through my blood has me on the verge of detonation. It's all I can do to hold myself together right now. This woman, the one I loved not so long ago, is like gasoline dripping on my burning heart.

Her name was already known to me. I read it in the file I found on her husband's desk after I shot and killed him. Seeing her pictures covered in a spray of his blood destroyed all my trust in the world. It was only a couple hours later after getting home and digging into that file when I soon realized I'd been scammed. Scammed by the only person who had ever been able to seep into my heart so entirely. I've never loved the way I loved her. And to know it was all a lie, the deceit of being played, was more than I could take.

I know I murdered an innocent man, and now, hearing her crazy explanation has my mind so fucked up. How could I have been in love with someone as psychotic as her?

What the fuck is wrong with me?

"Declan, please. Say something. Anything," her tiny voice requests.

My body is a mass of tense muscles I refuse to relax for fear of what I'll do. So I keep myself locked and stern when I speak. "So he never hurt you?"

"No."

"Never mean to you?"

"No. Bennett loved me. He didn't know who I was."

"How'd you get the bruises then?" I ask, remembering how God-awful she would look, covered in horrifically grotesque bruises. Sometimes her skin would split from the swelling and bleed. The battered blood that pooled beneath her skin's surface always stained her body. It fucked me up. Rage and fury for a man I believed was inflicting the abuse, lamenting heartache for the woman I loved, and guilt from not being able to protect her. The emasculating position she put me in, knowing damn well she had me fooled. And now I sit here feeling like a pussy that got manipulated by nothing more than a runaway street kid.

"My brother."

"Brother?"

"He was in on it too. I would go to him to get the bruises."

"It was your brother who beat the shit out of you? On purpose to fool me?"

She nods her head shamefully in response.

"Jesus Christ, you're sick."

I watch while tears drip from her chin and wish they were the acid she filled my heart with so connivingly.

"I know. But—"

"Just stop," I bark. I can't take any more of this shit, but she doesn't stop.

Her words come out in a rush of panic, "When I told you I loved you, when I gave you those words, I meant them. I didn't want to use you, not at that point. I wanted out and to keep you from doing what I initially wanted you to do."

"But you didn't, did you?!"

"Everything spun out of control so fast."

"Were you happy? When you found out Bennett was dead, were you happy?"

"It destroyed me to know I pushed you so far," she counters.

"Answer my fucking question!" I belt out, standing up and searing my eyes into hers as I look down on her. "Did it make you happy?"

Her body trembles when she closes her eyes and admits, "Yes."

"So you got what you wanted?"

"No."

"No?"

She tilts her head back to look up at me, and my bones beg to impale her, to beat the living shit out of her, a punishment she'll never forget. One that would mutilate her for life.

"No. It wasn't what I wanted. It wasn't worth sacrificing you because saving you was all I wanted to do at that point."

I sneer at her ludicrous words. "You wanted to save me so much that you left me in a pool of blood to die?"

Her eyes radiate horror.

"That's right, darling. I was conscious. I felt you, your touch, your kiss. But all it took was for that guy who shot me to say *Go* for you to leave me to die. Was that your idea of saving me?"

"No, Declan," she says through her tears that never stop. "I was scared. It all happened so fast. I didn't know what I was doing. I thought you were dead!"

Her words spit venom, and I can't look at her face any more without hammering my fist into it.

"You fucking left me there to die, you bitch!" I roar, grabbing her arms with force and yanking her up, shaking her as I fume, "Your words are lies. Nothing you say makes any goddamn sense."

Rage takes over and I lose it, slinging her body around and throwing her to the floor. She crumples, falling hard to the ground. I step over, grab the bitch by the sweater and yank her back off the ground as I hunch in her face. She doesn't protest my afflictions; she takes them willingly, the same way she has the past few times I've been rough with her, and I take advantage of her submission.

Her hands clamp around my wrists as I rip her off the floor and shove her away from me.

"Get the fuck out!"

"Please!"

Her voice pierces my ears so harshly I can feel the razor of it in my gut. The pain rings sharply in my head, and I boil over in red-hot revolt, clenching her frail neck in my hand, choking her. My body burns in a pyre of grief and fury as she clings to my arm, and her touch spurs me to plunge my fingers deeper into her flesh, clamping the trachea that lies beneath, cutting off her air supply.

A hoarse gurgle is the only sound she makes as her tear-filled eyes lock to mine. They shine bright from crying, and my tendons yearn to squeeze even tighter. There's so much colliding inside of me, I can feel it in my teeth, so I grit them to keep myself from biting and ripping the skin off her.

I want to kill her. I want to punish her in the worst way possible, but when my arm begins to violently shake, her mouth and eyes instantly pop open wider, and I release my hold.

I can't kill her.

She falls to my feet, gasping and coughing wretchedly as I rake my hands through my hair.

*What the hell is happening to me?*

The touch of her hands around my ankles gets my attention. Looking down on her, she's resting her cheek on top of one of my loafers. My breathing is heavy as emotions swarm, and it's in the moment she looks up at me, broken at my feet, that I give my final word.

"Leave."

I kick her hands off my legs and walk out of the room, leaving her to show herself out because if I have to look at her for one more second, I won't be able to forgive myself for what I might to do.

This woman has ruined me.

I'm a fucking monster.

Obliterated beyond my own recognition.

And it was all for naught.

# fifteen

MAKEUP COVERS MY marred neck as I give myself a once-over before heading out. My body is wounded in delicious bruises and scabs from the man my heart still yearns for. When I look at them, it's like he's still with me—his lingering touch I feen for on my body.

It took me a while to collect myself and leave his home the other day. Hopelessness consumed every inch of existence—it still does. I was weak, curled at his feet, sobbing on his perfectly polished shoes when he kicked me away and left me lying on the ground. My words did nothing but enrage him to the point he lost control. Declan never loses control—he thrives on it, needs it to function. But I could see the chaos swimming in his eyes as they bore down on me while he strangled me.

I didn't panic because I'd gladly take a death upon the hands of true love.

My ticket is booked to fly back to Chicago. I don't want to go, but I also don't want to continue hurting Declan. He's not the same man anymore because of me. His warmth has wasted away—no spark, no light, no love.

Nothing waits for me back in Chicago aside from a penthouse of hidden skeletons. I have no home. There's no one waiting for me anywhere. I figure I'll slip into town, pack up my belongings and leave the state. No longer can I live there because I'm no longer Nina. It doesn't matter where I go though, and that thought is utterly depleting. So, I decide to attempt to escape my pitiful reality and go to Edinburgh for the day to meander around.

I drive in silence, taking in the landscape, and before I know it, I'm in the city. After parking the car, I wrap a scarf around my neck and pull my coat tighter around my body. I begin wandering around the Grassmarket with the Edinburgh Castle towering above. The cobbled, winding streets are lined with a vast array of shops from designer to vintage. I pick up a few things from various stores: soaps, perfumes, a pair of shoes, and an old necklace with a weathered lotus charm. I'm not sure why I bought the lotus necklace, knowing the sadness it'll undoubtedly bring when I look at it, but I just had to buy it regardless. I buy because I don't know what else to do.

My gut is hollow. I'm in a never-ending state of anxiety, and this is my attempt at distracting myself. It's not helping though, so I find a pub to grab a drink, and when I walk into The Fiddler's Arms, I immediately make my way to the bar. The place is filled mostly with men, drinking lagers and whiskey. I spot an empty stool and take a seat.

The bartender places a drink napkin in front of me, saying, "What can I get you?"

Taking a quick look at the tap handles, I don't recognize the names, so I randomly pick one. "Stropramen."

He gives me a nod, begins to fill the mug, and then sets it in front of me. I slip my coat off and hang it on the back of the stool, and then take a long, slow drink in hopes that it dulls out the intensity that's inside of me. I lean forward and close my eyes, focusing on the noise around me, wanting to get lost in it, and when I open my eyes, I spot familiar ones staring back at me from the opposite side of the bar.

A grin grows on Lachlan's face, and he nods to the empty seat next to me in a gesture to join, and I give him a small, inviting smile.

"Fancy seeing you here," he says when he approaches and sits down.

"Wanted to do a little shopping before I head back home," I lie, and my stomach knots at the pathetic deceit.

"You're going back to the States?"

"Yes. Tomorrow."

"Short trip," he remarks.

"I suppose."

He takes a sip of his whiskey and sets the tumbler down when he asks, "Any plans on returning?"

"Doubtful," I reply and take another drink.

I turn to look at Lachlan watching me intently. He's a stately man in his trousers, button down, and tailored sports coat. His hair is lightly gelled and styled to perfection with a dignified part.

His eyes continue to linger on me with a soft expression.

"Why are you looking at me like that?" I peacefully ask.

He takes a moment, and then responds, "You seem down."

"Just worn out. I haven't been sleeping well."

"You left abruptly the other evening after your run-in with

Declan," he states. "Perhaps that has something to do with your lack of sleep?"

"Nosey," I accuse with a playful smile.

"Just observant."

"Is that all?"

"You want more?" he lightly chuckles.

"You flirting with me?"

"You're what? Twenty-some odd years younger than me?"

I nod.

"A man like me would be foolish not to flirt with a woman such as you."

"Such as me? And what's that? What am I?"

He takes another sip of his whiskey and then leans in a little closer to me, answering, "Exquisite, my dear."

His flirting isn't meaningful, but more of humorous banter, so I know he doesn't think it rude of me when I begin to laugh.

We both take another sip through our smiles, and he breaks his mock flirtation when he says, "Seriously though, is everything okay? It looked like you and Declan were having a much too dire conversation for a party."

"Just hashing out some unsettled business, that's all. Do you always make it a habit to stick your nose where it doesn't belong?" I tease.

"Always," he boasts, and we both laugh again.

"Well, at least you're honest about it."

"Can I ask you something?"

I nod.

"What brought you here to Scotland?"

I look up at his face, and I don't see any ulterior motives in our exchange other than a man who genuinely wants an honest conversation, so I answer, "Him."

"Him?"

"I came to see Declan. I hadn't spoken to him since he left Chicago, and I guess . . . I guess I just wanted to see him."

"Lovers?"

"Again . . . *nosey.*"

He smirks at my jab.

"Does he have many of those?" I ask.

"Would you feel jealous if I told you *yes?*"

Straightening my neck, I state, "I don't get jealous."

"You're a wicked woman, Elizabeth."

"What makes you say that?"

"In my experience, women who don't get jealous do so because they'd rather get even," he says and then winks.

"Is that what you think of me? That I'm a woman of revenge?" I question in jest, but secretly, I want to know how he truly perceives me.

"You know what my mum always told me?"

"What's that?" I laugh.

"She told me that while the rest of the species are descended from apes, redheads are descended from cats."

"So, I'm a cat?"

"A minx," he notes.

I shake my head, saying, "You neglected to answer my question."

"You mean Declan?"

"Mmm hmm," I hum as I take another drink.

"No."

"No?"

"I've known Declan for a very long time. He will always

have a woman on his arm at events, but it's all a show, strictly business. I've only known him to have a couple long-term relationships, but none he was too serious about. I think they were more of convenience than actual love. Declan's a well-guarded man."

Hearing this makes my guilt build heavier, knowing that what he gave me was most likely the first time he had given that to anyone. His love, his heart, his moments of sweet softness. Having this information makes the destruction feel even more malicious.

"He's a shrewd man in business," Lachlan continues. "I can only assume that filters into his personal relationships as well, but perhaps you might have better insight into my assumptions."

"You want me to open up and divulge my personal knowledge of Declan?"

"Did he hurt you?"

"No," I state matter-of-factly, and when he gives me a sly look, I murmur in an honest moment, "I hurt myself."

I refuse to reveal that I also hurt him. I don't want to diminish anyone's perceptions of the powerful, andric man they all know him to be.

"So you *were* lovers?"

"I hate that word."

"Why?"

Turning to face Lachlan, I lean to the side, resting my elbow on the bar top when I say, "It's shallow. That word insinuates a base, sexual relationship rather than intimacy."

"Has anyone ever told you you're gray?"

"You're wanting black and white? As if that even exists. There is no black and white, right or wrong, yes or no."

His eyebrows raise in curiosity, and to lighten the now heavy mood, I tease, "Oh, come on, Lachlan. Surely a man of your age has come to recognize the world for what it is."

"A man of my age?"

"Yes," I respond, smiling, and then laugh as I add, "*Old*."

"*Old*? Didn't your mother ever tell you to respect your elders?"

"I never had a mother." I catch myself as the words fall so easily and without thinking. I immediately press my lips together and turn in my seat so I'm not directly facing him anymore.

He doesn't make any comment, and the silence is unsettling as we sit here. When I do finally turn my head to look at him, there's a hint of pity on his face. It irks me, but I remain polite because let's face it, besides the elderly lady I'm staying with, this is the first real conversation I've had in a while.

"If you're feeling sorry for me, don't."

He surprises me with his unguarded bluntness when he asks, "What happened to her?"

"You don't beat around the bush, do you?"

"What do I have to lose? You're leaving Scotland; we'll never see each other again."

"Okay, then," I respond as I turn in my seat to face him dead on, and take him up on his offer. What the hell do I care? He's right. After today, I'll never see him again. "I don't know what happened to her. I have no memories of her, so I assume her to be dead. It was always just me and my father."

"You never asked?"

"My father died before I could," I answer directly.

"Have you tried finding her?"

"No."

"Why?"

"What's the point?" I say with a shrug of my shoulders.

"Aren't you curious about where you come from? What if she's not dead like you assume? What if she's been looking for you?"

And when he asks that last question, I start to wonder—hypothetically—if the woman did exist, she wouldn't have had a chance finding me. I was a runaway. An invisible child. And then I was Nina Vanderwal. How would she have ever found me when I've made it impossible?

All I have of my mom is an old photo of her. For a while, I used to think about her a lot, wondering what she was like, if she was anything like me.

"It's never too late, you know?" Lachlan says, and I let his words float in my head.

I've lost everything, but what if . . . what if I haven't? What if there's a chance that I have something left in this life? Is it worth trying to find? Is it worth believing in hope when that dream has failed me countless times? Can I take another disappointment?

Questions.

I have hundreds of them.

Looking back to Lachlan, I want to protect myself, but I'm so lonely. Lonely and in need of comfort, in need of a reason to go on. Because as I stand now, I'm beginning to seriously wonder why I'm still here—moving, breathing, living.

"Why do you care?" I ask the man who shouldn't because I'm not worthy of it.

"There's something about you," he says with all seriousness.

"But you don't know anything about me."

"Doesn't mean that I don't want to," he admits before adding, "All friendships have to start somewhere. Let me help you."

But I've never had friends. I stuck to myself in school while everyone else picked on me. Pike was my only friend, not just from childhood, but also as adults. And let's face it, the so-called friends I had when I married Bennett were just for show.

So I accept his offer, and with reluctance about what I'm agreeing to, I give a small nod.

"Okay then."

# Sixteen

I'VE BEEN PACKING ever since I got back from Edinburgh. Now that all my belongings are ready to go back to the States, I sit on the floor beside the bed I've been sleeping in for the past few weeks since I arrived here at Isla's. My mind begins to drift back to the conversation I had with Lachlan earlier today. It was weird. A mention of my mother is something that never happens. It's a part of my life that rarely creeps to the surface. But it's there now, and I'm not quite sure how it happened.

There were times in my childhood when I would miss her. But what I was missing wasn't real; it was simply a creation of my imagination. I've never known what it was to have a mom. More than anything, it's always been my dad that I ache for and miss wholeheartedly. But when Lachlan offered to help find my mother, I agreed. I don't know why. My acceptance of his offer came without much thought at all. Maybe I'm just so lonely that I'm willing to grasp on to anything at the moment.

Warmth slips down my neck, extinguishing my train of

thought, and when I bring my hand to the front of me, it's bloody with dark flesh under my nails. It's then I realize I've been mindlessly picking at the scab that still remains from Declan. It's grown in size. I reach back and begin to dig my nail into the soft, gummy exposed flesh, and a searing pain slices my scalp.

And finally, my mind is depleted of all thoughts as I go numb.

My eyes fall shut, and I drop my head forward, letting it hang. Fingers that work nimbly find an unpicked edge of a scab, and I grip it between my fingers. A moment passes before I swiftly yank, pulling the scab off along with new, uninfected flesh, enlarging the wound even more. Exhaling a lungful of air, my core tingles in delighted release when I feel a new onslaught of warm, thick blood oozing down the delicate skin of my neck.

Exultation is stolen in an instant when the door to my room opens, and I see Declan's horrified face.

*Am I dreaming?*

He's frozen for a moment before stepping into the room and closing the door behind him. I don't move as I look up, stunned.

"Christ, what happened?" he gasps, but he isn't looking at me directly.

I follow his focus as my eyes land on my crimson soaked hand that rests on my lap. His legs disappear from my periphery while my vision blurs on my weapon, and then it's gone. Covered in a warm, wet towel.

Touch.

Declan's hand works deftly as he dabs gently, cleaning the blood.

Touch.

My heart's beat reacts, delicate pumps soothe my tormented

chest into a lull of lucidity.

Touch.

No longer a hateful, punishing touch; just a touch.

Lifting my eyes to his face that's pinched in puzzlement, he flips my hand palm-up and then over again.

"Where's the blood coming from?"

I don't speak, and when he catches my eyes with his, his voice is fervent, "Nina, where's the blood coming from?"

*Don't call me that.*

Ache splinters when he calls me Nina, tightening my throat in a menagerie of emotions. A collision so unmanageable, my body doesn't know how to react, so it remains numb and silent as Declan begins to move his hands over me, pulling up the sleeves to my sweater, trying to find the source of the blood.

Lowering my head, I lose myself in skin-to-skin contact, and when his hand finds the back of my head, I go limp, falling into his lap. I lie on the floor, like a baby, with my head on his knees and silently blink out tears. I don't know if they're happy or sad tears. All I know is that they are tears that welcome my answered prayer of solace.

His fingers are tender as they move to nurse me. I rest in a ball, curled at his mercy. His pants dampen beneath my cheek, salting the wool fabric.

*If wishes were granted, this would be mine. I wanted to remain in his lap forever. To never lose that feeling because he was everything in that moment. Gentle and loving. Lying there, I felt like a child. Like a little girl being taken care of by her father. And although he wasn't my father, somehow he carried pieces of that man inside of him. It wasn't something he was even aware of, but I was. I saw it and felt it every time I was in the presence of Declan. He held it all: lover, protector, fighter. He was the ultimate fairytale, and I would have done anything to make him* my *fairytale.*

"What have you done to yourself?" his voice murmurs above me. "Sit up."

He helps me from his lap, and we sit face to face when he instructs, "Lift your arms," and when I do, he slips the sweater off of me.

Blood stains the back of the top, and he continues to clean me up before spotting my luggage and pulling out a clean shirt that he then puts on me.

Letting go of a deep breath, he sits in front of me while I remain by the side of the bed. Some of my blood colors his knuckles as I watch him drag his hand back through his thick hair. I observe the details of his movements, the way his chest rises and falls with each deep breath he takes, the way a lock of his hair falls over his forehead in dishevelment, the lines of torment that crease his face, the dark lashes that outline and brighten his green eyes that are pinned to mine.

With my trembling hand, I reach up and lightly touch his face with the tips of my fingers. He doesn't flinch or move when I do this, something I thought I'd never be able to do again. And then I mutter my first words on a hushed breath drenched thick in heartbreak, "I thought you were dead."

His throat flexes when he takes a hard swallow. "I know you did," he responds, voice strained.

"Your father . . ." I start, struggling to keep my words alive. "He told me . . ."

"It was a lie."

"Why?"

"I didn't want you looking for me."

Truths are blades. But I deserve every cut that comes my

way.

"Your head looks really bad," he notes. "Why? Why are you doing this to yourself?"

I reach back to touch his gift that burns in my flesh, and I'm embarrassed when I answer him with honesty, because I refuse to hide myself from him anymore.

"I didn't want to let it go?"

"It's grotesque, Nina."

"Please. Don't . . . don't call me that."

He drops his head, saying, "I want to hurt you."

"I know."

"My hands itch with the need to rip you apart. I crave it," he confesses and then shifts his eyes back to mine. They're dark and bitter, dilated in vehemence.

"I deserve it."

"You do," he agrees.

Pulling my knees to my chest, I wrap my arms around them, hugging myself.

"Why are you here?"

"I needed to know something . . ." His head drops again, and the utter agony in his voice when he continues wrecks me. "The baby . . ."

A broken whimper forces its way out of me.

"Was it even mine?"

The last thing I want to do is hurt Declan more than what I already have. I want to lie, tell him yes, tell him he was the only one I was sleeping with, convince him of my love.

But I can't.

I don't want to hurt him with the truth, but I also don't want to comfort him with lies.

"I need to know," he urges.

His eyes shine bright with tears I know threaten him, and I cowardly shake my head.

He takes a push back, widening the gap between us, and leans his head against the dresser.

"Why?"

"I wanted it to be," I tell him as I begin to cry from what was stolen from me.

"So it was Bennett's baby?"

"I don't know."

Confusion strikes his face. "What does *that* mean?"

God, I hate this. Hate that I keep deepening the wound. Tears soak my cheeks as I stall.

"What do you mean *you don't know?*" he presses.

"Because . . . b-because . . ."

"Say it."

"There was someone else."

My words ignite a fire within him. His neck is tense, reddening in anger. With elbows on knees and white-knuckled fists clenching hair, I know he's about to blow.

"It's not what you're thinking, Declan," I say in my attempt to explain the fucked up relationship Pike and I had.

"Besides me and Bennett, you were fucking someone else?"

"Yes, but—"

"Then it's exactly what I'm thinking!" he seethes.

"No. It wasn't like that. It wasn't . . ." *God, how the hell do I begin to explain this?* "He was . . . This is going to sound crazy, I know, but it isn't."

"I fucking hate you."

"I love *you!* Not Bennett. Not Pike. *You!*"

115

"Wait." He pauses for a moment, and then continues, "That name. That guy . . . I went to see him. Found his name in the file your husband had on you."

"Yeah."

"This shit is so fucked up. I can't even get my thoughts straight."

"Pike's my brother," I reveal.

"What the hell is wrong with you?"

"My *foster* bother," I clarify in a rush. "He's my foster brother."

"The same guy that was beating you?"

I nod.

"Do you know how sick this is? How sick *you* are? Fucking three men?"

Wiping my eyes, I move to sit on my knees. "I'm so sorry. I know it sounds messed up."

"*Sounds?* No, Nina, it *is* messed up. You need serious help, you know that?"

I don't bother correcting him when he calls me Nina.

He stands up, looking down on me in fury. "I can't believe I fell for something as disgusting as you."

"It wasn't like that," I say in a panic. "I didn't like him like that. There were no feelings attached. It was the opposite of what you're thinking. I used him so I didn't have to feel. He was a vice. That's all sex was with him. A vice to numb me."

"Numb you from what, Nina?"

"From life!" I cry out. "From everything!"

"Everything? Even me?"

"No. Not you. Once I realized how I felt for you, I never touched him again. I couldn't, because your hands were the only ones I wanted to be touched by. But I was already pregnant; I just didn't know it."

He paces the room, enraged.

"Declan, there's so much you don't know. So much I never told you because I couldn't."

"You could, you were just too selfish."

"Okay, yes. You're right. I was selfish. Selfish and scared. But you loved me, right?"

"I don't know who the fuck you are! Tell me. Tell me who you are because I'm so goddamn confused right now!"

"I don't know," I whimper and then stand with him.

"You do know."

"I don't. I want to know. I'm trying."

"What does that even mean?"

"*I don't know!*"

Pacing a couple more times in determined strides, he finally gives up and walks to the door.

"I can't do this shit anymore."

And then he walks out, not even bothering to close the door behind him.

Sobs explode out of me—loud and vulgar. I don't expect him to understand or to even want to. I'm sick; I know that. I knew I'd never have him again, but it doesn't make the pain any less awful when he walks away from me.

"Elizabeth!" Isla calls out in urgency as she rushes into my room.

I instantly catch myself, swallowing back my sobs and wiping my face. "I'm fine. I'm so sorry for the disruption," I say thickly as I weakly feign composure.

"Stop that!" she scolds as she takes my hand and walks me

over to sit on the bed. "Are you okay, lassie?"

"I'm fine. Really."

And with the pitying look on her face, I know she isn't the slightest bit convinced.

"What was the McKinnon boy doing here? You never mentioned knowing him when we were discussing him the other morning."

"I'm sorry, Isla," I state calmly now that my breathing is steadying.

"Sorry?"

"I do know Declan, I just didn't want anyone to know."

Her thumb strokes the top of my hand, looking over me, and finally concludes, "It was him. He's the love you lost." She doesn't question, only states what she's figured out.

I nod and apologize once more for pretending to not know who he was the other day.

"I'm confused though. I thought you told me he died?"

And now I must lie, because I can't possibly tell her the truth.

"I guess it was easier to pretend him dead. The thought of living in a world where he existed without me was much too painful."

With a tilt of her head, her brows tug in sorrow for me.

"I'm sorry I lied to you."

Shaking her head, she affirms, "Don't be. You're heartbroken; it's understandable."

"But it's not excusable."

"It is, dear."

We sit for a while as she continues to hold my hands before adding, "He seemed quite angry."

"He is. But if it's all right with you, I'd rather not discuss it."

"Of course not," she responds. "Is there anything I can do? Anything I can get you?"

"Thank you, but I'm fine."

"Okay then. Well, I'll leave you be. Good night."

"Good night," I say as she walks out of the room and closes the door behind her.

I remain on the bed, unmoving, and alone with my thoughts. Exhaustion presses down on me as I turn my head to the side and eye my luggage.

*Maybe I could stay a little longer.*

I know I shouldn't. I know I need to need go and erase myself from Declan's life so he can move on and heal. It's a lost cause trying to explain all of this to him. But maybe it doesn't even matter, because in the end, he's right. I'm fucked up and none of this makes any sense.

# Seventeen
## (DECLAN)

"WHAT ARE YOU doing here?" I ask when I pull up beside Lachlan's car sitting outside the gates to my house.

Holding up a file, he calls out, "Property closing. I need you to sign."

Christ, all I want is to be alone with a bottle of Aberfeldy. To try my best to relax and calm the nerves that Nina has so intensely provoked.

Lachlan pulls in behind me and follows me up to the house. I'm on edge, still unable to even think about what just happened and the things she told me. If I allow myself to go to that place in my head right now, I'll completely lose my shit. So when I get out of the car, I exert control and compose myself.

"You couldn't have emailed this to me?" I complain as we walk inside.

"They won't accept an electronic signature."

Flipping on the lights, I head back to the library to go over the final contract on the property in London I've been contending to acquire.

"You have any plans on selling this place?" Lachlan asks, and when I take a seat on the couch, he sits opposite me in one of the chairs.

"Why?"

"It's pretentious."

"Fucking dobber," I breathe under my breath.

"I heard that, you bastard."

"Good."

I've known Lachlan since our college days. He was working on his PhD while I was working on my master's at Saint Andrews. We were both a part of the OxFam Society and worked on many campaigns together. We've remained linked because of his relationship with my father. When Lachlan was my age, he worked in wealth management at one of the top firms in London, where my dad keeps his investments. Lachlan was his advisor for many years before he opted for a less demanding position and started advising small companies independently.

While I was still living in Chicago, I knew I'd soon be back here. Since I was already involved with purchasing the property in London, my father put in a call, and now Lachlan works solely for me. He handles my business finances and also a children's education foundation I've had for many years now.

"Everything should be as we discussed with the bank," he tells me as I read through the document.

"Looks good." I sign the papers and slip them back in the file. Handing it over to Lachlan, I say, "Life's about to get busy."

"Good thing?"

"Very. After Chicago, I'm ready to dive into this project."

"You ever gonna tell me what the hell happened?"

Standing up, I don't respond. Instead, I walk across the room to the liquor cart, pull the crystal stopper from the decanter, and begin pouring myself a glass of Scotch.

"Declan?"

"Drink?"

"No," he responds. "So, tell me. What happened?"

"Nothing to tell."

I take a sip, relishing the twenty-one-year-old single malt. I allow the smooth smoke of the Scotch to settle on my tongue before swallowing. I appreciate its offering as it makes its way down, heat spreading through my chest.

"She leaves tomorrow, you know?"

"And your point?"

The boyish, smug look on his face grates me, along with the way he relaxes himself into the chair.

"She's stunning."

Tossing back the glass of whiskey, my face pinching against the burn, I set the glass down, and the clank of crystal against glass reveals my frustration.

"Remind me again why I'm friends with you."

"Look, it's apparent there are hurt feelings between the two—"

I stop him mid-sentence, snapping, "What are you, my fucking therapist? Don't pretend to have insight into something you clearly know nothing about."

"I spent the afternoon with her. She's easy to read."

I laugh as I walk back over to the couch. "That woman is anything but easy to read. Trust me. Don't let her fool you. And what the hell are you doing talking to her? I told you to watch her, not befriend her."

The mere idea of Lachlan spending time with her and not knowing what's being said or what their interactions are like rubs a raw spot in me. To not know, and the fact that it bothers me so much, it's infuriating. It's the way she was able to claw her way inside of me and burrow into the one vacant spot no one has ever been able to find makes me hate her even more. She's a cherub of martyrdom, and I, her willing victim. Willing because, as much as I want to, I can't let the red-headed sadist go. I doubt I'll ever be able to because of the mark she's left on me. I'm the unhealed remnant left in her destructive wake.

"She wants me to find her mother," he eventually tells me, cutting the silence.

My eyes dart to his. "What?"

"I offered."

*Why the fuck is she giving parts of her truth to him that she hasn't given me?*

"Isn't that fantastic!" My cynical words come out loudly. "Do me a favor, try obeying my orders next time. *Follow* her and cut the friendly shit."

"No need to follow. Like I said, she leaves tomorrow," he informs as he pushes himself off from the chair. Standing in front of me, he shrugs on his coat and grabs the file. "I'll deliver the documents."

Leaning forward, I prop my elbows on my knees as I listen to his loafers echo down the foyer.

"I want to know when you find her mother!" I holler.

"Will do," he calls back before the sound of the door closing grants me much needed isolation.

Slumping down into the couch, I rest my head and stare

up at the ceiling, replaying the evening. Everything about it is a Gordian knot. And not just the words that were spoken, but the wound I gave her that she's successfully mutilated. I remember ripping the hair from her scalp and the pleasure it gave me to punish her. But her reaction was not what I expected. She didn't as much as yelp at what must have been blisteringly painful. She simply stood there as tears dripped down her face, yet she wasn't crying, not like you would think.

But tonight, when I walked in on her and saw the blood, my only reaction was to help her. Taking care of her and cleaning her up makes me sick, now that I think about it, but in the moment, all the turmoil faded. It was when she started to speak that it all came crashing back. It flooded the room, drowning me in its weight when she told me she didn't know if the baby was mine.

That fucking baby.

All I wanted was that baby. I never knew I wanted one so badly until she told me she was pregnant. Instantly, my soul split and begged to have a son or daughter fill me. I would close my eyes and dream about it.

The news birthed a surge of overwhelming protectiveness inside of me, and I would have done anything for the two of them the moment she told me she lost the baby.

And I did.

It happened all too fast.

Walking away from Nina as she fought the nurse's restraints . . . Speeding through the traffic . . . Grabbing my pistol from the car's console . . . The chill of the metal against my back as I tucked it in my pants . . . Pulling into The Legacy's garage . . . Back entrance . . . Elevator . . . Fury running thick through my veins.

Doors open, I walk.

Foyer, living room, hallway.

Door.

Head and heart pound. Ears ring. Blood boils.

One hand on gun, the other on door.

Open . . . Aim . . . BANG.

I can still smell the gunpowder, see the look of fear in Bennett's eyes, hear him gurgling and choking on his own blood. I killed a man—an innocent man—point-blank. His last words, a plea for me to not do it, still haunt me. But I did it anyway because I thought him to be the man Nina manipulated to me. I believed he killed my baby, and for that, he would die.

But it was a lie.

I shake the visions from my head and walk over to pour myself another glass of Scotch. It's my pathetic attempt to quiet the demons in me.

The conundrum I battle with is the idea that Nina is the vile one, and that somehow I'm good. But I'm not. I'm a killer. She didn't pull that trigger—I did. I don't want to bathe in the same evil as she, but I do.

It was her that screwed with my head, twisting truth with lies, creating me into this monster. But a monster I am, just as she, and I allowed. Whether I intended to or not—I still allowed it.

But it isn't just what I did, it's what she did—or didn't do. Leaving me to die. Not doing anything to help me. Yet tonight, she vowed she loves me and wants to do everything to save me from the path she put me on. How could she say that when she left me with two bullets in my chest, bleeding out on the floor of my loft—bullets fired by her brother?

God, her brother. The brother she was fucking.

All he had to say was *Go* and she went, never coming back for me. I've been lied to and manipulated by many, but her betrayal has debilitated me, ripped my heart out, riven to obliteration. Raping the soul entirely. Who knew her hands could hold so much turpitude?

Everything combined is impossible to digest. The contradictions she throws out do nothing but spur confusion and animosity. My mind craves clarity on the situation, but I doubt I'll ever get that because I doubt her sanity. Yet, the mere mention of her leaving tomorrow evokes a thrum in my chest, and that shit bedevils me the most.

# eighteen

*I'VE BEEN TRYING my best to play the part, cooperate with the authorities, and feign my innocence, but shit is looking bad. Cal's been sitting in jail, and it's only a matter of time before they come after me. I can trust that Cal is keeping a tight lip, otherwise, I would've already been arrested. But he knows firsthand what can happen if his loyalty is compromised.*

*Needless to say, with everything I stand to lose, if they uncovered my involvement in the gun trafficking and my other crimes, they'd fry me. I'm a dead man walking at this point, but I'm not a man who's going to sit back and watch his dynasty collapse. Pawns are beginning to fall, so I need to move fast.*

*The private charter is set to leave at 3:00am; everyone has been paid off and given the run-down. They know I own their tongues. My new identity is packed in my briefcase, bags are ready to go, and the car should be here shortly.*

*With a stomach filled with boulders of anxiety, I walk through the dark house to my bedroom where my unknowing wife sleeps. Eeriness looms as I walk into the room. She lies there, peaceful, completely unaware of the world she walks around in daily. Unaware about who I really am. What I really do. But if I'm going to do this, I need my family. There's no other option because they mean everything to me. So with that, I risk it all—because they're worth it—when I sit on the edge of the bed and gently nudge her awake.*

*She stirs, and when she begins to open her eyes, I take her face in my hands and kiss her. There's no preparing for this life, the one I've chosen to live for nearly thirty years. But never in those thirty years have I been under surveillance like I am now.*

*"What's wrong, honey?" she questions, pulling away from this uncharacteristic affection.*

*Remaining as calm, clear, and concise as possible so that she doesn't freak out on me, I say, "I need you to sit up and listen to me very carefully."*

*"You're scaring me."*

*"Don't be scared. Everything is going to be okay, but I need you to listen closely because I don't have much time."*

*She sits up and gives me a nod with fear-glazed eyes.*

*I take her hands in mine. "I'm leaving the country," I start when she interrupts me.*

*"What?"*

*When I place my fingers over her mouth, I stress, "I need you to not ask questions because I won't be able to answer them. I'm begging you to trust me and know that I will do everything to keep our family together. I love you, but there's a part of this business that isn't legal. I've done some things, and now I run the risk of losing my life." My words are partial truths, but mostly lies because there's no point in laying it all out there. It would only put her in danger.*

*Her eyes widen and her face creases in confusion as she slowly shakes her head.*

echo

*"This is what I need from you."*

*"I don't . . . I-I . . ."*

*"Take a deep breath, hun," I gently instruct. "You trust me?"*

*Her nod comes instantly, soothing some of my worry.*

*"Good. I need you to trust me. Never doubt me or my love, understand?"*

*"Of course."*

*"If anyone asks about me, you tell them you don't know where I am. You haven't heard from me or seen me since we got into an argument over my commitment to this marriage. That if you had to guess, I'm simply hiding out in a hotel to avoid coming home."*

*"Why would I—"*

*"Trust," I say, cutting her off. "No questions because the more you know, the harder it is for me to protect you."*

*"Protection from what? F-From who?"*

*Cupping her cheeks, I affirm, "No one will ever separate us, hurt us, destroy us. I need you to just stay put and lay low. Don't talk to anyone unless you have to. But whatever you say, you do not know where I am."*

*"W-When will you be back?"*

*Leaning in to rest my forehead against hers, I whisper, "I don't know."*

*She then begins to quietly weep with her hands on my cheeks.*

*"You love me, right?"*

*"Yes," she responds.*

*"I need you to know that when I come back, we won't be staying. We'll have to leave the country. It's not something that's negotiable."*

*"What about our life? Our family and friends?"*

*"There won't be a life if we stay."*

*Her body trembles while she clings to me, muffling her cries against my shoulder.*

*"I don't have much time," I tell her softly, trying not to upset her more.*

129

*"What does that mean?"*

*"I'm leaving now—tonight."*

She pulls away, and with broken, tear-filled eyes, she tells me, *"You have to give me something. Some assurance that you're going to be okay, that you're going to come back."*

*"There isn't anything I wouldn't do for our family. I will always protect what's mine. I will be back."*

And with that, she kisses me with urgency, pulling herself on top of my lap. She tastes like salt as she cries through her loving affection, gripping tightly on to me.

I band my arms around her, reminding, *"I love this family more than life."*

*"I'm so s-scared. I d-don't even know what to think right now,"* she whimpers, and I wipe her tears.

*"I know, hun. I know, and I'm sorry. I never wanted to drag you into this. But I have to go."*

*"No. Wait,"* she clips out. *"Maybe I can help you. If you just tell me whatever trouble you're in, maybe there's a way out. Something I can do to hel—"*

*"I promise you, I've calculated everything. Remember what I told you: we argued, and I left."*

We have one last kiss when I get the call on the untraceable cell I purchased, letting me know the car is here.

And then I'm gone as the car makes its way to the charter that will take me to Scotland, undetected and off the grid.

# nineteen

I'M A SELFISH woman for what I'm about to do, but I can't stop myself. All my luggage is packed in the trunk, but before driving to the airport, I need to say goodbye. I know my words hurt him last night when he came to see me. The more I spoke, the angrier he became and eventually stormed out. But I can't be left with that. I can't have that be our last interaction. I know I'm only thinking of myself right now, but I simply have to see him one last time.

Pulling up to the gate, I push the call button.

"Go home, Nina," his voice says.

"Declan, please. I'm going home. I'm heading to the airport now, I just want to say goodbye. Can you please give me that?"

There's no response, only silence. I wait, and when I'm about to shift to reverse, the gates begin to open. Releasing a sigh of gratitude, I start the drive up the winding road. After I park the car, I take another long look at the house. I try not to think too much about the could-have-been's because they're just never-be's. I still find it odd that the shrubs that line the house are scarce in areas. Big, gaping holes when everything else is pristine, even under all the snow.

"It's freezing out here," Declan calls out to me from the front door where he stands.

"The shrubs look sad," I tell him.

"The shrubs?"

"You're missing a lot of them. Did they die?"

"You could say that," he responds. "Can we get out of the cold?"

Giving him a weak smile, I walk over and enter his home. Declan closes the door and moves past me, and I follow, but today he leads us into the kitchen.

"I was just making some coffee," he says as he pulls the kettle off the stove. "I think the old housekeeper left some tea in the pantry if you'd like a cup."

His politeness is unexpected, catching me off guard.

"Umm, okay. Yeah, that would be nice," I say, stumbling nervously over my words.

I walk around the large center island, and take a seat on one of the barstools. I watch him move about the kitchen, pouring the boiling water into the French press, and then the rest in a teacup for me.

Looking around, I take in the surroundings. The kitchen is tucked away from the openness of the house. It's an eat-in kitchen with a large, farm-style table that sits in front of three, floor-to-ceiling windows that overlook the beautiful grounds. The room is brightly lit from the snow outside, and the windows are slightly fogged over.

"Here you go," he says, and I quickly turn back around to

the cup of tea he's set in front of me.

I stare down, watching the ribbons of steam float up and disappear. I'm reminded of the many mornings I would sit at the bar in Declan's loft, sipping on tea while watching him cook breakfast. He always looked so sexy in his long pajama pants and white t-shirt that hugged his broad chest. I could watch this man infinitely and never tire.

The memory of what used to be pangs in my chest as I sit here, and when I look up, I see him standing in front of me on the opposite side of the island.

"Declan," I say on a faint whisper. I let his name linger in the air between us for a moment. "I'm so sorry."

Setting his coffee down, he braces his hands on the granite countertop, letting his head drop. I give him silence, and let it grow as I keep my eyes pinned to the most amazing man I've ever known. His soul knows no boundaries of beauty.

When he finally raises his head and looks at me, I tell him, "If I could go back, I'd do it all differently."

"You can't go back, Nina. And what's done is done."

"I know," I admit with defeat.

"I wish I could go back too, but you can't turn your back on the choices you willingly make, and in that moment, I chose you."

"Do you regret that?" I ask on words that ache.

Before he can answer, his cell phone rings, distracting him from me.

"I have to take this," he says, and I nod as he steps out of the room to answer the call.

I swallow hard past the emotion lodged in my throat. Leaving the tea, I go stand in front of the windows. The chill from the glass makes me shiver as I watch the snow drifting down weightlessly to the ground. Looking over to the left, I can get just a hint of a glimpse of the grotto, and decide to get a better look from another window in the house.

Slipping off my coat, I lay it over one of the kitchen chairs and make my way out into the main hall of the house. I can hear Declan's voice coming from the library. I wander down the grand hall toward the glass atrium when I pass a set of stairs. With curiosity, I begin to climb the steps that lead to the second floor. With my hand still on the banister, I look up to see the stairs continue to a third floor.

I explore, opening doors and walking down the various corridors that lead to bedrooms, bathrooms, and sitting areas. Everything on this level has been remodeled and finished in greys and stark whites. I then see a massive set of white double doors with intricate carvings in the painted wood. The handles are like ice in my hand when I open the doors to what I discover is Declan's room.

My loss is overwhelming as I look at the large bed that sits in the center of the room. I'll never know the feeling of being wrapped up in those sheets. Declan's right: you can't turn your back on the choices you make, and sadly, I made all the wrong ones and lost him in the process.

I take a step into what feels like forbidden territory and look around the room. Its many windows brighten the space that's painted in a hue of dark grey, which contrasts the white crown moldings, and the fluffy, white down that lies atop the large, black leather, chesterfield sleigh bed. There's a sitting area off to the side with two black armchairs and a chaise, all leather chesterfield as well.

Mindlessly, I walk across the plush carpet and over to the

bed. I allow my fingertips to ghost along the white fabric as I mourn the loss of what was once within my reach.

"What are you doing in here?" His words are clipped and irritated.

I look at him over my shoulder before I turn to face him. My mouth opens to speak, but I can't find my words.

"You shouldn't be in here," he tells me.

"I just . . ."

"Just what?" he questions as he starts to slowly make his way over to me in purposeful strides.

"I don't know. I just needed to see this. Your home, this bed . . . *you*."

"Me?"

"Yes, Declan. *You*," I say. "I miss you."

"You don't miss me."

"Every day. I do. I miss you every single day."

His jaw ticks, and with darkening eyes, he says, "You miss what I no longer am."

"Don't say that."

"Why? Too much responsibility for you to bear? You want to ignore the fact that your lies altered my life in the most unforgiving way?" His voice grows coarser with each word spoken. "You want to stand there and be forgiven for what you did? Like you're some sort of victim in this?"

"I don't expect forgiveness."

"More lies," he grits through clenched teeth as his hands fist at his sides.

"No."

"Then why do you keep saying you're sorry over and over again?"

He grabs ahold of my shoulders, and my voice stutters, "I-I don't know, b-but I don't expect for you to forgive me for what I've done."

"Then why say it?"

"M-maybe . . . I don't know . . . Maybe hope."

"Hope? For what, Nina? For me? For us?"

"Maybe," I tremble as my emotions grow with his anger.

"You want hope where hope doesn't exist."

Fighting against the sadness is doomed when my chin begins to quiver as I say, "I'll always hope for you."

"After all this, you want me?"

I nod.

"Then tell me," he demands with intent.

My words come easily. "I want you, Declan."

His hands drop from my shoulders and land on his belt. With punishing, black eyes boring down on me, I hear the light clinking of metal as he undoes the buckle. My pulse explodes in a rush of hammering beats that knock hard against my ribs in anticipation. But at the same time, my panicked heart flutters when he yanks the belt out from the loops of his slacks.

I stand here, unmoving, and simply watch him. He takes the back of his hand and runs it down my cheek to my neck and then my shoulder. In a flash quick move, he jerks me around, crossing his forearm over my chest, and pinning my back to his front. My hands grip the sides of his thighs, balancing myself on shaky legs.

"Tell me to stop. Tell me to take my hands off you," he says with his lips pressed to the shell of my ear.

"No."

Fast hands yank my arms behind me, and he binds the belt above my elbows. His restraint is unrelenting, pinching my shoulder blades together. I gasp at the sting of the leather biting into my flesh, and then yelp out when my feet are suddenly kicked out from under me, and I fall hard on my knees. But before I can cry out against the burning pain that's radiating up my thighs, Declan grabs my hair and shoves my head facedown into the bed, making it hard to breathe.

*You've heard of the theory of atonement, right? Making a restitution to mend what's been broken. I was willing to be whatever vessel Declan needed me to be so that he could deal with his pain. This was my punishment, my meager attempt to right the wrongs, but what came next would test my limits of love for him. How far would I let his destruction go? At what point would I draw the line? Did I even have limits when it came to Declan? It was in that moment, bound and on my knees, that I would soon find out.*

Gasping for air, I scream out when he twists my hair in his hand, ripping open the scab on my scalp. My body tenses as he violently grunts with each movement; he's so different from all the other times in the past. I sense it all around me, the putrid hate.

He lifts off of me and shoves my pants and panties down to my knees, and my heart freezes in terror when he spreads my ass cheeks open and spits on me.

*Oh God, no!*

His hand grips my shoulder for leverage, and every muscle inside of me constricts when he brutally forces his cock in my ass, ripping me in the most grotesque way. I shriek in sheer agony, my cries bouncing off the walls as he growls with each abusive thrust.

I do everything I can to wrench my body away and fight him, but he's taken away my strength and power. I'm at his mercy, and he's a dark rage of unholy wrath as he takes the one part of me I never wanted to give.

Gone is Declan's control, the awareness of how far he's pushing me.

My screams are muffled when he lays a fierce hand on the back of my head, shoving my face further into the mattress. I wail and gasp, thrashing my body against his merciless pounding. The next thing I know, he shoves his hand into my mouth, all four fingers, prying my jaw open and pulling against my cheek. The fire that sears my flesh and the corner of my mouth is ruthless. It's his way of shutting me up because every attempt I make to scream or cry results in gagging on my own saliva.

*Stop! God, please, no! Stop!*

With my head turned to the side, drool running out of my mouth and down my cheek, I dart my eyes to look up at Declan, and what I see scares the shit out of me. He's completely depraved, a wild beast attacking me, and the pain multiplies as he shreds me. My body ricochets back and forth as he continues to pound into me. Each thrust is painful, unwanted, and takes me right back to the basement I spent so many years in being raped and molested. My mind can't even process what's happening as a blanket of darkness consumes me.

I close my eyes, praying for this to end, and the next thing I know, I'm taken back to the only other time this has happened. I'm twelve years old, bleeding for the first time, and Carl's pissed because Pike can't get hard to fuck me in the ass. I'm naked, and Carl has my face shoved down on the cold concrete floor. His grunting fills the basement as he rapes me from behind. Blood rolls off my back from the lashings he gave me with his belt. His fat belly slaps against my hips as he rips me open, splitting the tender flesh.

My screams go unanswered.

My body begins to heave and convulse when I come into the present. No longer is Carl raping me, but Declan. The voices in my head are screaming for him to stop as he continues to sodomize me, but it's all I have since he has my jaw wrested open, gagging me, and making it impossible for me to fight back.

*"Shut it off, Elizabeth."*

My eyes pop open when I hear Pike, and he's here. Tears fall when I look into his consoling eyes. He's right here with me, on his knees beside me. He runs his fingers through my ratty hair and attempts to soothe me.

*"Just look at me, okay? I'm here with you. You're not alone, but I need you to turn off your feelings right now."*

I fight to relax my body while Pike continues to talk to me and stroke my hair. And soon enough, in a matter of seconds, my muscles slacken and my breathing slows. My eyes are locked to my savior.

*"That's it. No one can hurt you if you can't feel,"* he reminds me. *"I'm here with you, Elizabeth. Just keep your eyes on me. It'll be over soon."*

I nod at his words and trust in them. I keep my focus and never let my eyes stray from his as Declan forces his domination on me. In mere moments, he flexes above me, filling me with his cum. His body hunches over mine as he groans out in pleasure. Or is it anger? Then I notice his hand is no longer shoved in my mouth, but instead, holding my hand.

*Why is he doing this?*

My head fills with a haze of swirling thoughts and memories that are unrecognizable. I'm dizzy in the wake of what just happened as my head lies in a puddle of saliva, tears, and snot. The mixture, the evidence of my fight, coats the side of my face and cakes in my hair.

*"You're okay,"* Pike assures me . . . and then . . . he's gone.

I don't even get a chance to grieve his loss when Declan pulls his cock out of my ass. I wince against the pain when he does this, but I'm frozen, bent over his bed, unable to move from the shock. I can feel the delicate tissues swell in a blistering heat of rawness.

"Jesus Christ," I hear him pant from behind me, and he quickly releases his belt from my arms.

I remain in place as I listen to his footsteps, followed by the click of the door closing, and it's then I finally take in a breath of air. My body slides off the bed and onto the floor where I lie with my pants and underwear still shoved down around my knees.

Destroyed.

Humiliated.

And in a sick way . . . loved.

twenty

CHILLS WRACK MY clammy body as I lie here on the floor of Declan's room. The room that was supposed to be ours, housing our bond and love for one another.

It was never supposed to be *this*.

But it is.

My thoughts are scattered and confused.

*What just happened?*

My body trembles in the aftershocks of the trauma it just endured and the memories of my childhood. I fight the vomit that sours the back of my throat as my gut bubbles in disgust.

But you want to know the most fucked up thought running through my head right now?

Here it is . . .

*I still ache for him. For his love, his touch, his breath upon my skin.*

And then I think about him holding my hand. *He held my hand.* It's nothing new for him—he's always held my hand when we orgasmed. It's his one tender gesture that would remind me, that no matter how rough he chose to be with me, that I could trust in his comfort to always be aware of me and take care of me.

*Does he still feel that way?*

Bracing my hands on the floor, I push myself up to sit, and my ass stings as I shift. Biting against the pain that shoots through me, I stumble up to my feet. I reach down and pull my pants up. Wobbly on my feet, I walk over to the en suite bathroom, and when I flick on the light, I get a glimpse of my ashen face.

I touch my reflection in the mirror. Somehow, it feels safer than to touch my actual face. There's always a disconnect in one's reflection, and right now, I need that distance. But the reflection I see is *me* at age twelve. I look at me—at her—and my heart begins to pump harder, fiercer, sadder.

Her blue eyes are filled with a pain she hides from the world, and I want so badly to reach through the glass and save her from the life I know she'll endure. I know that deep down she's buried a small light of hope, and it kills me to know it's just a wasted dream. This sweet, little, red-headed girl is destined for a life filled with anguish and despair, and there's nothing I can do to save her. Her future is inevitable, written in the stars, and bound to the solidity that the fairytales she dreams about don't exist. They never did.

Tucking my fingers in a tight fist, I feel the tingles in my palm. Everything clouds around my head in a swarm of shit memories and thoughts.

*I'm stronger than this. Don't break; I'm stronger than this pain.*

But maybe I'm not strong. I just allowed Declan to fuck me the same way Carl did, and I barely even fought him. I succumbed to him like the trash I am, gave him a piece of my worthless body for his selfish use.

*SMASH!*

A hundred eyes stare back at me, sad, pitiful, loathing eyes. *My* eyes. The clinking of broken glass falling onto the marbled sink is a song of despair, but it's ruined with my panted breaths. I look into the broken mirror and I hate what I see. I hate what I am. I hate it all. And I want to hate Declan for what he just did, but I can't. I can't, and I hate myself even more for that fact.

I deserved it. I deserve even worse.

If this is his way of punishing me, then I'll suppress the need to fight him. I'll bear it and take it without enmity.

Concentrating on calming myself down, I turn on the faucet and cup my hands under the cold water. My knuckles sting as the water flushes the split skin. It takes my blood and runs red down the drain. I allow the coolness to numb the wound.

After taking a few sips from my hands and rinsing my mouth out, I start opening the drawers and cabinets to find a couple bandages to cover my knuckles. Once I have the band-aids in place, I undo my pants to clean up. Flinching when I wipe myself, I look to see the toilet paper streaked in blood from his assault.

I splash a little water on my face, and finger-comb my hair, before I open the door and take slow steps through the bedroom. I'm timid and nervous about walking out of this room, about facing Declan, about what will happen next. Making my way down the stairs, I don't see him, so I head to the kitchen where I left my coat and the keys to the car.

I stop when I see Declan leaning over the counter. I don't move. I don't make a sound. His back faces me as he's bent over, leaning on his elbows with head in hands. The rise and fall of his shoulders is noticeable as he stands there, slightly disheveled in his tailored slacks and untucked button-up.

When he senses my presence, he shifts his head to look at me and I notice his reddened eyes. The shame is written all over him, staining him in humiliation, but I'm the only one who should feel it. Not him.

He pushes back from the counter and stands up, facing me, and when I take a slow step into the kitchen, I'm overwhelmed with the need to give him honest pieces of me. To open up with truths he's never heard before. To finally let him inside of me.

"Being with you has been difficult," I admit, my words trembling. "It takes me to the extremely dark place of my past."

"Then why me? Why not choose someone else?"

"Because," I choke out as the tears flood my eyes. "B-Because you always held my hand," I weep. "For some reason, that simple touch made it okay. Made me feel safe. I've never had that touch before."

He doesn't respond to my words as he looks at me with tormented eyes.

So I stand here in front of him and tell him the truth as I continue to cry through the shame of who I really am. "On my tenth birthday, my foster dad forced my brother to molest me while he watched and jerked off." Admitting my disgust for the first time in my life suddenly makes it all too real. Tears fall from my cheeks as I bear my disgrace in front of my love. "I was only a kid. I didn't even know what sex was until I was lying underneath Pike on a filthy mattress in the basement."

"Christ," he breathes in horror at my words.

"After that day, I found myself in that basement nearly every day for years. I couldn't believe in heaven or God when I was being forced to do things people want to pretend don't exist. But what happened to me made me believe in evil. And that the devil is real and lives inside the savages of this world."

Declan turns away from me, resting his hands back on the counter and dropping his head. His breath heavy as I add, "My foster dad . . . he had a thing for belts as well. He got off on stripping me naked and whipping me until I bled."

His fists ball tightly at my words.

"You used to frighten me when you'd use your belt on me. All I could think about were all the beatings I was forced to endure as a little girl."

"Stop."

"This is the truth," I sob. "This is what I never wanted you to know about me. I'm ugly and nasty and dirty and—"

"Stop!" he shouts.

I watch the muscles that rope his arms flex with tension. His eyes are pinched shut, and I startle when he slams his one fist into the solid granite with a guttural outburst.

I'm paralyzed, scared to move, completely exposed, and mortified. Never have I opened myself up like this. I never had to with Pike because he was there. A witness. A participant.

With his eyes still closed, he says in acrimony, "Do you have any idea what it's like to love the person you hate?"

*Love? God, he can hate me all he wants if he still loves me.*

Opening his eyes, he takes a couple steps toward me. "Because I do hate you. More than anything on this earth. I hate you with every pump of blood my heart proffers. I want to punish you in the worst ways, make you suffer and hurt. But God help me . . . I love you."

It's what I've been longing to hear, to know he loves me. But his words are filled with lachrymosity. Whatever may come of us, this love he has for me will always be tinged in venom. But even in the lies of before, it was corrupt. Cursed from the very beginning—and I was the culprit.

"But then . . ." he starts, " . . . you tell me these truths. The truths I wanted from the beginning that you hid from me, and I feel like a bastard for wanting to hurt you, but I *still* want it. I still want to make you suffer."

"I deserve it," I murmur.

"Why did you continue to do it?"

"Do what?"

He struggles for a moment when he clarifies, "Why did you continue to have sex with your brother as an adult?"

Embarrassment heats my neck, and I feel so filthy having to expose this. Hanging my head in shame, I keep my eyes downcast as I answer, "At some point, when we were kids, we started sleeping together in private. In his bed. It wasn't forced, and in those moments, he'd make me feel okay."

"*Okay?*" he questions in confusion, and when I hesitantly move my eyes to look up at him, I say, "I always felt gross and worthless. But something about Pike made me feel clean. He made me feel loved and safe. He was all I had in the world." I begin to choke on my words, telling him, "And he did love me. He always protected me."

"He raped you," Declan spits through gritted teeth.

"No," I defend. "He didn't. He was being molested himself long before. Carl, our foster dad, he forced Pike to do that stuff to me."

"He didn't have to do it. He made the choice."

"He knew if it wasn't him, that Carl would do it himself. I was safer with Pike."

echo

"But Carl . . . did he . . . ?"

I nod. "Yes. It took a while, but eventually he did." And then I admit, "The first time was when I was twelve. He raped me the same way you just did."

Instantly, Declan has his arms around me and I'm crying. He grips the back of my head and cradles me tightly against his chest. His hold is strong and hard but warm. I band my arms around his waist, clinging to him.

He's everywhere, all around me, encasing me in the safety of his touch.

*Home.*

When I begin to settle my emotions and calm myself, he whispers in my hair, "I'm sorry. I lost control on you."

"It's okay."

"No. It's not okay," he declares when he pulls away to look at me.

"It is. I hurt you. I'm so sorry, Declan. You will never know how sorry I am for what I did to you. I deserve every punishment."

"I don't want to be that man."

"You're not. You're *nothing* like that man," I tell him. "There were times my mind went to that place with you, but you're not like that. I've always felt safe with you. I've always been certain that you'd never really hurt me."

"But I do hurt you. And I like it. And I want more of it."

"Then take it. I'll give it to you. I'll give you anything to make you feel better. If it's my pain and suffering you need, then have it. It's yours."

His hands tighten on me as I speak, and with brows knit together and a locked jaw, he grunts in frustration when he releases me from his hold. Raking a hand through his hair, he growls, "What the fuck is wrong with you? You shouldn't want this. You shouldn't want me. What right-minded person would subject themselves to this?"

"I never claimed to be right-minded. I know I'm screwed up. I know I'm so far beyond damaged I'm irreparable. But I also know that you won't find the same amount of satisfaction in punishing anyone but me."

"Why do it then? Is it to make yourself feel better for what you did?"

"Partly."

"And the other part?"

Taking a few steps over to him, I say, "Because I love you."

"You shouldn't."

"But I do. I never thought anyone could have the power to make me feel as safe and clean as you do. You have the power to make me feel worthy of living. That somewhere out there, life just might have a purpose for me."

"Then why leave me? Why didn't you stay and call the medics? Why did you leave me to die?"

It's in his words I hear the heartbreak I caused.

"I told you. I was scared. Everything was happening so fast, I didn't know what to do. I panicked."

He releases a slow sigh and takes a moment before speaking again. "I'm sure I already know, but I need to hear it from you."

"What is it?"

"I know Pike is dead. And I know he died the same day he shot me."

I swallow hard when he says this, and I already know his question before he asks, "Did you have anything to do with his death?"

My chin begins to quiver, and when I can't hold on to my emotions any longer, my face scrunches as I confess, "I will never forgive myself for what I did. I loved him so much."

"I need to hear you say it," he says sternly.

Fighting back my tears, I take in a deep breath and let go of it slowly before giving him the trembling words, "I'm the one who shot him. I killed him."

"I want to be mad at you. I want to throw it in your face, but that would make me a hypocrite, and it's because of your lies."

"I'm sorry."

"Stop apologizing!" his voice rips when anger takes over. "I don't want to hear anything else from you. Every time we talk, the shit you say . . . it's impossible to understand and digest."

He walks back to the center island, facing away from me as he looks out the windows.

"Get out," he orders on a dead breath.

He's unmoving as I walk around him to pick up my coat and keys, but the struggle is evident within him. I want to say a thousand words, but I know better. So I keep my mouth shut and do as I'm told.

I leave.

# twenty-one

"WHAT ARE YOU doing back here, lassie?" Isla questions when I walk through the front door with my luggage.

"I missed my flight. Is it all right if I stay another night?"

"Stay as long as you like," she says when she walks over and takes one of my bags. "Were you able to reschedule?"

"Not yet. I never even made it to the airport. I'll have to call the airline tomorrow."

"Does this have anything to do with the McKinnon boy?" she asks.

Walking into the formal sitting room, I take a seat, answering, "Yes."

"Heartache is difficult."

Looking over at her sitting across from me, I give a slight nod. The day has been draining and I feel weak from what happened with Declan. With so many questions swarming in my head, I say, "Can I ask you something?" as I lean back in the chair.

"Of course."

"Do you believe that people can change?"

She takes a moment and then gently shakes her head a couple times. "No, dear."

I reflect on her answer as defeat looms overhead.

And then she elaborates, "I believe we are who we are and the essence of what we are built upon is unchangeable. But I believe we can change how we make choices. But just because we can change our behavior doesn't mean we've changed the core of who we are. It's like someone who's an alcoholic. They may rehab and make better choices, but I don't believe that inner voice and craving ever goes away. The change is solely in their choice to not drink, but they still desire it."

"So, evil is always evil?"

"Yes. And good is always good. But I trust in my faith that we are descendants of rectitude. That each of us, no matter how bad we may think ourselves to be, the core lining of us is threaded in holy fibers."

It's in her words that I'm taken back to my home in Northbrook. The memories of my father and I play in clips of tea parties, nighttime songs, piggyback rides, bedtime stories, and fits of laughter. And Isla is right . . . there was a moment in time I was clothed in nothing but goodness. I was pure and free and honest. But I was just five years old when my light was snuffed out.

The day my dad was taken from me was the day nothing would ever be the same. I lost more than just my light—I lost myself. Lost it entirely. I allowed the world to decay me. But how is anyone supposed to be strong enough to fight back against something so monumental? I was just a little girl. The only person I had in my corner was Pike, but then again, he was just a boy himself. We clung to each other because we were each other's

e.k. blair

only hope.

I thought I was making all the right choices, but as I look back in the wake of my life, it's filled with nothing but destruction. And now, I'm the only one that remains.

Well, almost.

Declan is still here, but in a sense, he was destroyed as well. His heart still beats, but not like it used to. My choices—my decisions—they're poisonous. I used that poison for power, but it backfired.

"Are you okay?" Isla's voice interjects.

"I made bad choices," I say without thought. The words simply fall from my lips before I can stop them.

"Welcome to life, my dear," she condoles. "I could write a novel with all the mistakes and ill choices I've made in my years. But I've come to realize that's what it's about. Sometimes we have to fall to know how to stand back up. Sometimes we have to hurt people to recognize our flaws and to see that we need to better ourselves."

"Did you ever find that some of your choices were so bad they were unforgivable?" I ask as regret stirs in my veins.

"Yes," she admits with her chin held high. "But even though I knew they were unforgivable, I was still forgiven."

"Who was it that forgave?"

She pauses, and when the corners of her mouth lift in a subtle smile, she answers, "My husband."

"You hurt him?"

"I hurt him terribly."

"Why did he forgive you?" I ask.

"It's called grace. When we love, and when that love comes from the purity of your heart, you give grace. You find compassion and forgive because we're all flawed. We all make mistakes, but love's devotion doesn't cast stones."

I want to believe the love Declan once had for me did come from a pure place. That there's still hope for forgiveness. That there's still a shimmer inside of him that still wants me. Because for me, it's more than a shimmer—it's a raging fire of need and desire I have for him. But after what he did to me today, I don't see this working out. Isla's words are nice and flowery, but flowers eventually wilt and die no matter how much love you give in tending to their needs.

"You look like you could use a distraction," she says before suggesting, "Why don't you settle back into your room, and when you're ready, how would you like to help me prepare dinner?"

"That actually sounds lovely, but unfortunately, I can't cook."

"Everyone can cook. All you need is someone to guide you."

Smiling at her invitation, I accept her offer, and agree, "Okay then. But I'm warning you now, I've been known to incinerate food beyond consumption." I laugh at the memory of the first time Declan tried teaching me to make champagne chicken and I charred the meal. But that laughter is tainted. It's bittersweet. My time with Declan back in Chicago held some of the best moments in my life, even though I was just an illusion of a better version of me.

"If I could teach my daughter how to cook, I can surely teach you," she tells me as we stand.

Picking up my bags, I look over and tease, "But is her cooking any good?"

"She always made the best meals."

"*Made?*" I question her use of the past tense.

"She left this world many years ago."

"How did she die?" I question, knowing all too well the annoyance of the overused *I'm sorry* people give who clearly haven't suffered a death filled with *I'm sorry's*.

"It was a senseless act of violence, but that's part of life, dear," she says, attempting to downsize the ache, but her loss is seen in the gloss of the unshed tears of her eyes. "I'll be in the kitchen," she says and then walks out of the room.

Death is imminent—I know this all too well—but no matter how much we lose, no matter how numb we become, we always feel the pinprick of the vacancy. The parts of our soul that our loved ones take with them when they leave this world are forever left unfilled. They're empty wounds that are always exposed and unable to heal.

As I make my way up to my room, I settle my things in and decide to keep myself busy to block out the thoughts that keep filtering in. Memories of this morning's defilement. The vision of Declan when I looked at him, his villainous eyes, blackened in rage, keeps finding its way into my head. He was a riled beast, taking what he wanted, forcing his power on me.

Shaking the visions away, I quickly rush out of the room to find Isla for the much needed diversion. We spend the rest of the day in the kitchen, and I find myself enjoying my time with her. We cook, share a bottle of wine, and enjoy each other's company, and I'm thankful for the distraction she's able to provide me.

But it's when I excuse myself for the evening and am lying in bed that it all immediately comes rushing back. Declan tying me up, spitting on my ass, smothering my face into the mattress, the pain of his intrusions, the sounds of his wild grunting. I shift in bed, heart pounding, and I feel the burn from his assault, and then it's Carl I see in the darkened room. I can smell the stench of his cigarettes.

Lurching off the bed, I dash to the toilet and vomit. My stomach convulses in heaves as the acidic bile stings my throat, and when I gag, it fills my nose and burns like a bitch. My eyes prick hard with tears, and another bout of puke forces its way out of my gut as my body constricts and hurls over the toilet.

When there's nothing left for my body to expel, I tire and scoot my back against the wall. I wipe the sheen of sweat from my forehead and take in slow breaths. My hands are jittery and my body is broken in a spell of cold sweats. Even if I wanted to shut myself down, I don't think I'd be able to. I don't think I'm strong enough to battle the skeletons I've spent my whole life hiding from. The skeletons that Declan awoke when he forced himself on me earlier today. Only one other person has made me feel that decrepit and filthy, and I burned him to his death. Never did I think Declan would haunt me the same way Carl used to.

WARMTH STIRS ME awake, and as I begin to move, I feel a weight on top of me. Opening my eyes, my body jumps when I see Declan holding himself above me.

"Shh, baby, it's only me," he whispers.

"What are you doing here?"

His eyes pinch shut, and he lets go of a pained breath, saying, "I can't do it. I can't stay away from you."

His words settle my heart, and I don't question him because I need him. Reaching up, I run my hand along his stubbled jaw, and when he drops his head, my body warms in peace as his lips press softly into mine. I can't control the moan that comes out of me, and I wrap my arms tightly around his neck, holding him close.

To have his taste back in my mouth soothes. The world lifts from my shoulders, and finally, I can breathe—*really* breathe. I don't ever want this to end. I need this—need him.

As our bodies begin to move and writhe together, he reaches back and pulls his shirt off. Lowering himself on top of me, he threads his fingers through my hair, saying, "Forgive me for what I did to you earlier. Please forgive me and let me fix it. Let me attempt to take it away."

I place my hand over his bare chest, and I can feel his heart crashing inside of him. I want to calm that heart just as much as he wants to erase what happened in his room, so I nod my head. That's all it takes for him to start slowly undressing me. Slipping my clothes off, along with his, he covers us up under the sheets as our naked bodies rediscover one another.

He allows my hands freedom to roam over his body—an un-Declan-like thing for him to grant me, but I take it. He runs his damp lips down my neck and along my collarbone before taking his tongue and dragging it over my pert nipple. Covering the tight bud with his lips, he sucks with the heat of his mouth, and my body bows in response to the touch.

My hands fist his hair, and he moves to my other breast. His cock is raging hard against me, and his slow movements are making my pussy ache in wetness for him.

"I need you, Declan," I pant in wanton heat.

He pulls back and looks down at me with eyes molten in lust. His hand ghosts down my body, my stomach, and when he reaches my pussy, he sighs as my muscles tremble in anticipation of what I thought I'd never have again.

"Oh, God," I mewl when he delves his fingers into my wet folds. My hands press into his flesh, and I hang on as he begins to pump in and out of me.

I'm on fire, needing more of him, so with a strong hand, I wrap it around his wrist and hold his arm still. When I being to rock my hips and fuck his fingers to my own liking, he growls, and the erotic sound spurs my hips to buck up and fuck him even more fiercely.

"That's my baby," he encourages, and when my moans intensify as my body climbs, he pulls his fingers out of me and quickly pins my arms above my head.

I'm relaxed under his restraining hold. Looking up at him, *this* is the Declan I remember. He's in total control—dominating me with loving affection. With his hand locking my wrists above me, he takes his other hand, fingers glistening in my arousal, and slips them into my mouth. I roll my tongue and suck the taste of my pussy off of him.

He then finds my clit with his wet fingers and gently strokes on the bundle at the same time he pushes his large, strong cock inside of me slowly, so slow it borders on torture. I feel every ridge of his dick until he's buried himself deep in me.

And I'm finally home—safe in the comfort of the only man I ever want to share this with.

He holds himself still inside of me when he says, "You're the only one who's ever made me feel like this."

"Like what?"

Pulling out of me, he thrusts back in, grunting, "Like this," as he fills me deeply.

My body arches off the bed as he elicits carnal moans from

deep in my womb, and I spread my thighs even wider for him because I need more.

Dragging his cock out of me again, he slams his hips down into me, while asking, "You feel that?" hitting my sweet spot deep inside.

"Yes," I breathe.

"Tell me," he demands as he drives himself back inside of my body, now pumping in and out with purpose, mending us together.

My eyes falls shut as I let him take me over, giving him my body entirely for him to have and use however he wishes.

"I love you," I release in the breaths of air we now share.

"Tell me again."

My skin tingles in radiant pleasure, warmed in passion.

"I love you, Declan."

I begin to lose myself, bucking my hips to meet each of his thrusts. I can feel his cock growing thicker, harder, hotter. His hold on my wrists tightens, but it only makes me feel safer.

"Open your eyes," I hear him say, and the moment before I do, I smell it—stale cigarettes and piss.

My body locks up when my eyes open and it's Carl looking down at me, fucking me with his disgusting dick and breathing his putrid breath all over me.

JOLTING AWAKE, MY eyes pop open to be greeted by another snow-filled night. Another bad dream possesses my subconscious. This is the third nightmare I've woken from tonight. Gone are the nights of exploring with Carnegie, my caterpillar friend.

He's been replaced by morphed scenes of Declan loving me and by dank basements, urine-stenched closets, and the visions of Carl jerking himself off as he watches me.

I take my time to quiet my rapid-beating heart before I lie back down. I focus on the snow that collects on the window. Some of it melts, tuning into trickling rivers that slowly make their way down the glass. I burrow down into the blankets, trying to warm myself, and when I roll over from the moonlit snow, it takes a moment for my eyes to adjust.

It's after I blink a few times that I see him, and I hold my breath, wondering if I'm imagining this—imagining *him*.

# twenty-two

HE SITS ON the chair a few feet from the bed I'm lying in, leaning over with his elbows propped on his knees. I know he's really here when he lifts his head and looks at me, the moon illuminating his green eyes. My head remains resting on the pillow, and I breathe in deeply.

*Why is he here?*

Neither one of us moves or speaks; we simply watch each other in the dark silence. I want to move though. My body begs to crawl onto his lap, to have him dominate every one of my senses. The dream I just woke from felt so real. It's all I want, to be in a place where we can have moments like that together. But the dream turned to a nightmare so quickly, and I know it's because of Declan that it did.

How can I crave this man who now torments me? What is it about him that makes me want to forgive him so easily, to not even question him?

I notice the creases that line his forehead and his brows that cinch in the despair we both feel.

"What are we doing?" His voice, a quiet rasp filled with oppression.

Sitting up, I never take my eyes off of him, but I don't know what to say. I wish I had an answer for him, but I'm just as confused. He has my emotions bouncing all over the place and colliding in a war inside of me.

I lose the contact when he drops his head down into the palms of his hands, and his voice is a soft murmur, "What've I done?" and I don't know if he's talking to me or simply to himself, but I remain quiet as he continues. "What've *you* done? I don't know what's going on here . . . what this is between us . . . what this is inside of me."

"It's a battle between heart and mind," I whisper, and when I do, he looks up at me.

I watch his face tighten in grief, the feeling thickens the room, and it takes him a while to speak again, but when he does, the words are drenched in shame. "Are you all right?"

When I don't answer him, he exhausts on a breath, "That's a stupid question."

"Declan . . ."

"I'm sorry. What I did . . . That wasn't . . ."

"Stop," I tell him when his voice begins to crack.

"What happened to you as a child . . ." His hands clench as he fights with his building emotions. "It fucking breaks me."

"Don't do this."

But he doesn't even acknowledge my words as he goes on, "And then what I did to you . . . I don't know how I lost control like that. Seeing you in that room . . . That was supposed to be *ours*. You don't know how badly I wanted that. How much I wanted to take you away from the husband I thought was . . ."

He lets his words drift, and I want to cry, but I don't. I know he doesn't want to see my tears, so I keep myself focused, but I'm dying on the inside. To sit here and listen to his words that are masking cries of his own is awful. This is a man of abundant discipline and authority, so to hear him so broken down, so weak, it destroys me.

"How do I get past a deceit of this magnitude?" he eventually questions.

"I wish I knew. I wish I could go back. But I can't. I don't even really know how to explain this all. I want to be honest. I want you to know the real me, to know the truth, but it's so hard. Because the truth is so gross and twisted, you probably wouldn't even believe it, because people don't want to believe that life can be that horrifying. I'm a fucked-up human; I know this. I don't know what it is to be a rational person, but you make me want to learn. You make me want to try."

"His eyes were open," he says out of the blue, and I'm confused as to what he's referring to, but then he adds, "After I shot him. I saw photos of you on his desk. I gathered them up along with the file, and when I looked down at Bennett's bloody body, his eyes were still open."

He says this and I remember that Pike's eyes were the same. I'll never forget how haunting they looked.

"He knew who you were."

"I know," I say. "I heard him in the hospital. He was having me followed; he knew you and I were together."

He then stands, walks over to the bed, and sits down next to me. He doesn't touch me, although I wish he would.

"I hurt you today."

"I'm okay," I whisper.

He then looks down at my knuckles that are wrapped in band-aids. "My shattered mirror tells me otherwise."

"Bad memories."

"Did it happen a lot?" he asks on a voice that's barely even a whisper. Like he's afraid his words will break me, and for the first time in a long time, I feel like they possibly could. That I'm not as tough as I used to be.

I give him a nod, but it isn't enough for him when he urges, "I need you to tell me."

I hesitate, licking my lips, wanting to give him the honesty he's asking for but also terrified for him to know.

"Tell me, Nina."

"Please . . . don't, don't call me that."

"I'm sorry," he says, looking away from me. "It's all I know you as."

"Look at me." He does. "This is me. This is what I want you to know."

"Elizabeth," he murmurs, and I nod, affirming, "Yes . . . Elizabeth."

"Tell me then, Elizabeth. Because I need to know you, to figure you out."

"Yes," I respond. "It happened a lot. It was dirty and gross and—"

"What did he do to you?"

I swallow hard, scared to say the words. My hands fidget nervously, and when Declan sees, he covers them in his own.

"I've never told anyone," I confess. "Only Pike knew, and he was there. I didn't have to say a word because he saw it all."

"I told you about my mum, remember?"

"Of course I remember."

"I opened up to you about something I had never spoken about to anyone. I gave you that piece of me. A piece that makes me embarrassed and ashamed."

I remember seeing his tears when he told me he cowered under a bed while he watched a man shoot his mother in the head. A shot that killed her. He thinks himself weak and a pussy—those are the words he used. He made himself vulnerable to me, so I'll give him what he's asking for, something I've never given anyone.

"It started on my tenth birthday with him forcing Pike to have sex with me. He would take us down to the basement. There was a dirty mattress he kept on the floor. He'd watch us while he sat in a chair and jerked himself off. Most of the time he would get up to cum on either Pike or myself." Saying the words turns my stomach, and I can already feel the wave of nausea come over me. "We would be down in that basement at least four times a week. A couple years later was when it switched and Carl started touching me."

I stop and drop my head. I can't bear to look at Declan anymore when I start to feel the filth crawl along my skin. Tears burn the backs of my eyes as I try to keep them at bay, but they come anyway.

"Don't look away from me," he tells me when he tugs my chin up to face him.

With my head up but my eyes closed, I say, "It's humiliating."

"I don't care. I don't want you hiding from me. Look at me and trust me enough to give me this truth."

So I do. I open my eyes, and while tears continue to fall from my eyes and drip off my chin, I tell him everything that happened in that basement. How Carl would rape me, sodomize me, piss on me, beat me, and whip me. How he'd cum on my face and laugh at me while he'd wipe it off with his finger and force me to lick it. How he'd piss on the mattress and shove my face in it, force me to finger his ass while he'd beat himself off. How it didn't take long for him to turn me into a machine because it's what I had to become in order to survive.

I sob as I give him this sick part of me, and explain why I started having sex with Pike by ourselves. Explained how it soothed me and provided an escape for me. I rip myself open and let the rot fall onto Declan's lap as I reveal my twisted childhood to him.

He listens, never interrupting, but encouraging me to go on. His eyes are wide in disbelief and pity, and I know he will never look at me the same way again. He now knows the reality of my pathetic existence. The worthlessness of my body, the one he used to look at in amazement and admiration. He'd call me perfect, beautiful, and flawless.

But now he knows the truth.

This body was never something he should've valued. Anyone would be foolish to value the pile of shit it is. It's simply a capsule—fancy wrapping paper—that conceals everything I'm made of . . . sewage.

"Why didn't you ever say anything?"

"Because I was scared if I did, I'd lose Pike. I feared going to another abusive home and being alone. Pike was all I had; I didn't want to be without him," I try to explain.

"He used you."

"Who? Pike?"

"Yes. If he loved you like you claim he did, he would've

pushed you to get help, to get you to a place that was safe."

Shaking my head, I refute, "It doesn't work like that. And he did love me. He gave his whole life to me. I was always safe with him."

Declan bites down hard causing his jaw to tick, and I tell him, "You won't ever change my opinion of Pike. I don't expect you to understand, but we were just kids. We did what we could to survive. Whether you believe it to be right or wrong, what's done is done, and looking back won't change anything."

"I wish I could take it away."

"You can't," I say weakly. "Just like I can't take away the pain in your life. I want to. I want that power more than you know."

Sitting in the darkness, making my confessions and opening myself up, I wonder why Declan remains unmoving by my side. My desire to crawl inside of his head, to know the thoughts he hides in there is strong. His expression is hard to read as he looks at me. The hush in the room is unsettling, yet peaceful. I was starting to wonder if he would ever be able to be in the same room as me without punishing me.

"I should go."

He stands up from the bed, and when he does, I lie down. I watch him turn back to me, and in a sweet gesture, he pulls the covers over my body and then braces his hands on the mattress, hovering over me.

"Stay."

"Why?" I breathe.

"I don't know why. Just don't go back to the States just yet."

He pushes off the bed and walks to the door. I'm sad when he leaves—lonely and empty. His scent looms in the air, and I take a deep breath to capture him in my soul. Lying here in the dark, I feel haunted by the demons I just released.

And now he knows the fallacy of it all.

As for me, I've just sliced through my deepest scar tissue and reopened the wounds of desecration.

I battle with my heart to shut down, to turn into the machine that protects me from that which is destined to destroy me. Between the memories that just rebirthed inside of me and the loss of Declan's presence, the mass of emotions is too much for me to even think about right now.

So I cloak myself in armor and delight in stupor.

# twenty-three
## (CALLUM)

I WAS OFFERED a plea deal when my attorney came to see me yesterday. Since my part in all this was simply being a man of the books—the white-collared crook—they want me to rat out the bigger names to the operation. The thing is, I don't have many names. The men that do the runs are worth a lot more to the Feds than I am, but I'm not privy to that side of the business. The one name I *am* privy to is the one I know they want the most.

The king of the cartel.

But to cross paths with him would be a death sentence. I've learned that lesson. So I played dumb, kept his name shrouded in my arsenal. If I nark, I'm a dead man. It's much safer for me in here—locked behind steel and iron.

No one messes with me much. Money buys safety, and I've got an endless source and people on the outside that make sure the steady stream keeps flowing. What isn't available to me is being taken care of by Lachlan, whom I'm now calling.

The guard keeps watch outside of the laundry hall where I now work four days a week, earning a pitiful eleven cents an hour.

"Cal," he greets when he finally answers. "How are you?"

"How the hell do you think I am? Did you take care of the money?"

"Yeah. All done. There was an event recently that was held for the charity, so it was easy to filter into the accounts."

"And Declan?" I ask.

"What about him, sir?"

"Any suspicions from him?"

"No. He's been distracted these days."

"How so?"

"A woman. Elizabeth Archer. She appeared in town recently. He's been having me follow her."

I don't bother to ask why. Time isn't my friend at the moment, but I can only guess that boy will probably forever be fucked up when it comes to trust. He never told me anything about the shooting—who did it or for what reason. But I know it all boils down to Nina Vanderwal. All he told me was to feign his death to her if ever we should cross paths and that he wanted me to keep my distance from him. I agreed, and he disappeared back to Scotland to live in that estate he bought years back. I can't figure that kid out or why he wants to wallow alone in practically the middle of nowhere.

I've yet to have anyone make contact with him, and as far as I know, no one has. He's unaware that I'm sitting in jail for crimes he knows nothing about. Crimes I've been committing since he was a little boy.

"She's staying in town close to him," Lachlan adds.

"In Gala?"

"At the Water Lily."

*What the fuck?*

"Declan was there?" I ask, wondering if he knows what was kept from him.

"It's where Elizabeth is staying. He was there the other day for a couple hours in the middle of the night and then returned home."

I'm not given the chance to respond when the guard slams the door open and shouts, "Time's up, inmate!"

He snatches the phone from my hands and disconnects the call.

"What the hell happened to five minutes?" I sling in hostility.

"Price influx, bitch. It's gonna cost you more next time."

Grabbing my arm, he leads me out of the laundry room, and even though my bones burn to knock the living shit out of this pussy, I keep myself in check because I can't be getting thrown in the block. I need to continue to have access to that fucking phone or find a way to get my hands on my own.

First thing I need to do is find out who this Elizabeth woman is that has my son going to the Water Lily. So I wait in my cell until rec time and then make my way to the phone bank where I can make my call.

"Cal, baby," Camilla's voice sighs into the phone.

I thank God that the values of this woman are slightly shady to accommodate being involved with a man who's facing up to twenty-five years in a federal prison.

"How are you holding up, love?" I ask.

"I miss you. Trying to take care of everything on my own is drowning me."

"I know. I'm sorry. I need to see you though. I need you here this weekend."

"Of course. You know I never miss a visit. Is everything okay?"

"Yes. I don't want you worrying about me," I tell her. "It's just important that I see you." I urge my words because what I need her to do for me isn't something I can mention on these monitored calls because of the names involved.

"Callum," she softly scolds, "You're in jail. How can I *not* worry about you?"

*"Ninety seconds remain."*

"Fuck!" Bracing my hand against the cinder block wall, I bark, "Did you send the money into my account?"

"Yes, but you know how slow they are."

"I need you to call about it because I'm all out of time. I won't be able to call you until I get that money."

"I promise, Cal."

*"Thirty seconds remain."*

"God, I hate this," she cries. "I miss you so much."

"I miss you too. I'll see you in a couple days."

"I'll be there. I love you."

"Love you too."

Walking into the quad, I take a seat in front of the TV that's playing an episode of Jeopardy. I look to my left and watch a couple of illiterates shout out their answers, and I find them to be more entertaining than the actual show.

"Hey, puta."

My body stiffens when the words slither across my ear and the coolness of what I imagine to be a razor blade pierces the flesh of my back.

"I'm talking to you, esé," he says, sitting behind me with his face hovering by the side of mine as he talks quietly into my ear so as to not arouse attention.

"What do you want?" I keep my voice even and hard.

"Your boss wanted me to relay a message for him."

"My boss?"

"That's right. He don't want you actin' a jit. Sayin' things that don't need to be said. Mentioning *names* that don't need mentioning." He digs the blade into my skin, and I bite back against the sting as he sneers, "You don't need to be reminded about your vieja, no?"

I snap my head to look him dead on, and he backs off, slipping the blade down his sock quickly. My blood boils, and the rage that brews inside takes an effort to keep under control.

The guy smiles, dismissing his threats in exchange for a light chuckle, saying, "Whoa, mi amigo. Relax."

"Relax? You mention my *vieja,* and you expect me to relax? I don't need a reminder, and I'm not your amigo. Next time you talk to my boss, you remind him that loyalties lie thick, sometimes in a pool of blood."

He gives a curt nod, taking in my words, and then I add, "You threaten me again, I'll turn you into a prag and stick a brinker on your ass."

He laughs, stands, and before walking away, shakes his head, saying, "You surprise me, blanco." And then, with a smile, adds, "I'll let the boss know we're good."

"You do that."

"I HAD TO lift my bra, Cal!"

"What? Why?"

"Apparently, I look more suspicious than the garbage I was standing in line with," Camilla whispers under her breath and then takes a scan of the room to make sure no one else heard her. "It was utterly degrading."

Sitting at the small table, across from the woman who's loved me for the past year, I'm pissed at the scum that got to see my doll's tits when I haven't had the privilege since they arrested me. She's mortified and angry and completely out of place. She always stands out like a sore thumb when she visits me, dressed in her designer clothes, but that's my Camilla.

"I miss you, love."

"The waiting is killing me. I know it isn't fair for me to say that when you're locked up in here, but I feel like I'm in a constant state of anxiety," she says.

I haven't told her about the plea deal that was put on the table because she'd have me do anything, throw whoever they wanted under the bus, just to get me back.

"The case will be taken to grand jury soon enough. That's the first step. But in the meantime, I need you to do something for me, okay?"

"Okay."

"First, any update on the Vanderwal murder?" I ask since you can't get the guards to turn the TV to any of the news stations.

"The whole company in under investigation, but for what, the public isn't aware of yet." She releases a heavy sigh, leans forward, and grows emotional. "What am I supposed to do, Cal? It's only a matter of time before this all hits the press. Everyone will know; our names will be smeared all over the place."

"My words are safe with you, right?"

"You don't even have to question that. Of course they are. They always have been. I love you and will do anything for you, you know that."

"I just needed to hear it again. This place messes with my head," I tell her, but I know I can trust her. She's unlike any woman I've ever loved. She may be twenty-three years younger than me, but she's a fighter. After my arrest, I came clean to her about the illegal activity I'd been involved with. I told her everything and she didn't disappoint when she offered to tell the authorities whatever it was I wanted her to. This woman would lie, cheat, and steal for me, and I love her even more for that. So as she sits here, prim and proper against the trash of the city's misfits, I smile inside to know she'd probably fight dirtier than most of them, and she'd look simply gorgeous doing it.

"What about his wife? Has she been in the news?"

"No. The coverage is so limited at this point. The police are keeping a tight lip while the case is being investigated."

I give a nod, and then she adds, "Honey?"

"What is it?"

"Have you thought any more on calling your son? Don't you think he should know?"

Clapping my hands together, I rest my forearms on the table. "Not yet."

"I could call him."

I shake my head, saying, "Lachlan mentioned a girl he's been spending time with in Gala. Elizabeth Archer. Can you remember that name?"

"Elizabeth Archer," she repeats. "Yes. Why?"

"I need to know who she is and what interest she has in my son. Lachlan told me she's only been in Scotland for a short time. I couldn't get too much information because the call was cut short."

"Who do you think she is?"

"Don't know. But someone shot Declan within days of Bennett's murder, and he refused to mention who. There's a link in this somewhere; I know it."

"This is so unfair," she voices. "I mean, you never hurt anyone. I don't know why you're sitting here in jail and not the others who are involved. Why don't you give up their names?"

"You know why, Camilla. We've already talked about it. These aren't the types of people you turn your back on. This business is much bigger than me. And knowing the amounts of money I've been laundering and the lives at stake if someone were to blow the whistle, I'd be killed."

"I know we've talked about it, it's just . . ."

"Look," I say, wanting her to not get wrapped up in the emotions of it all. "For right now, just focus on taking care of yourself. Focus on figuring out who this girl is that's spending time with Declan. I don't want you getting hung up on things that are out of our control right now, all right?"

Nodding, she yields, "All right."

# twenty-four

*STEPPING FOOT ON foreign soil feels freeing. I'm relieved of the weight I've been bearing on my back, and it's a welcome change to be able to walk around without constantly looking over my shoulder.*

*I arrived here in Scotland yesterday, and after getting my first night of solid rest in a long time, I woke up this morning, revived.*

*But now, it's business.*

*Finding her is my ticket to freedom.*

*So when I open up my laptop, I start searching with the two names I'm already aware of that she uses: Nina Vanderwal and Elizabeth Archer.*

# twenty-five

"HELLO?" I ANSWER when my cell rings.

"Elizabeth, it's Lachlan."

His voice disappoints. Ever since Declan came to me and asked me not to leave, I've been hoping to hear from him, but so far, nothing.

"Hi."

"I was wondering if we could get together. I have some information about your mother."

A slight jolt of adrenaline rushes my body. Or is it anxiety? Fear, maybe? I don't know what it is exactly, but it awakens something inside of me, and I ask, "You found her?"

"Yes. Do you have time to meet me?"

"Are you in town?" I ask, knowing he lives over an hour away in Edinburgh.

"I can be. You just tell me what works for you."

"I can come to the city."

"Are you sure?"

"Yeah," I respond. "It'll be nice to have a little change of scenery."

Honestly, I just need a distraction. I spent all of yesterday moping around after having Declan here the night before. The tangled mess of this situation is driving me to madness. Trying to deal with the wound I opened the other night is proving to be too much for me to cope with.

And when one wound opens, so does another.

With the rousing of the shame and disgust of my past that I'd forced to lie dormant for so long, I needed a vice to help me grapple with the war inside of me. So I did what I'm becoming good at, and when the tranquility of blood running down my neck faded, I hammered my fists into my thighs. I wasn't sated until I could finally see the blood pooling beneath my skin. Mutilated alabaster.

I hang up with Lachlan after I jot down his address and grab my scarf and coat. I head out and make the drive to Edinburgh. When I turn onto Merchiston Gardens, I'm greeted with beautiful Victorian homes.

"Did you have any problems finding it?" Lachlan asks when he opens the front door after I pull up to his house.

"I'm in a foreign country," I tease. "I always have problems when I drive here."

He laughs, and as I approach, he remarks with jest, "Well, you appear unscathed, and the car still looks to be in one piece."

"Lucky car," I respond with a wink before stepping into the foyer.

The walls are bathed in rich taupes, ivories, and wines with hardwood floors and large bay windows. The house is airy with lots of natural lighting.

"Lovely home."

Walking past me, I follow Lachlan through the house to a formal sitting area.

"Can I get you a drink?" he offers.

"No, thank you." Slipping off my coat, I drape it over the couch and take a seat with Lachlan sitting adjacent to me. "Impressive."

He laughs, saying, "You're being generous. One could say I was slumming it when compared to the likes of your man's Brunswickhill."

"My man?"

"Isn't he?"

Continuing the light banter, which tends to come easily between the two of us, I say, "Well, for anyone who knows Declan, you're instantly aware that no one stakes claim on him. He operates on the contrary." Crossing my legs, I chuckle, adding, "Total control freak."

"Try working for him."

His words perplex, and I question, "You work for him?" and when he nods, I note, "You failed to mention that."

"You failed to ask."

"Is there anything else I've failed to ask that I should be aware of?"

"Oh, yes," he exaggerates in humor. "But where's the fun in transparency?"

"Man of mystery."

He smiles, and I laugh.

"So, tell me, Lachlan. What is it that you do for Declan?"

"I manage his finances among other things. And what about you?"

"Me?"

"What do you do for a profession?"

His question perturbs, and I deflect, "I prefer to dabble instead of commit to a singular entity."

"Entrepreneur?"

"Isn't that just a fancy word for *unemployed?*"

"Which do you prefer?"

"Honest and straight forward," I tell him. "No reason to dress up the truth because when people realize the crudité is just a veggie platter, they feel cheated and the culprit looks like a fraud."

He laughs, but little does he know, *I'm* the crudité here. I'm a distorted hyperbole. At least that's what I *have* been. I'm trying to shed the guise because I need a solid ground of understanding to figure out who I am. What are the true fibers from which I'm woven?

And then I remember why I'm here, and I wonder, *Am I ready for this? Do I really want to know?* He told me he found her, the mother I've never known, and a multitude of questions begin to rain down: Did she ever love me? Did she love my dad? Why didn't she want me? Did she know my dad was in prison? Did she know I was in foster care? Why didn't she come for me? Why didn't she save me? How could she just dispose of me?

"Are you okay?" Lachlan questions, his voice thick with concern.

I flick my eyes up to him, realizing I let my mind drift and pull me away.

"Yes. I'm sorry." I shift, and leaving the humor behind, I say, "I'm a little uneasy."

"How so?" His voice mellows with the change in mood.

"Wondering if I want to open this door that's been closed my whole life."

"We don't have to do this," he tells me. "If you've changed your mind or you want to wait . . . it's up to you."

"Seems weird," I remark. "Sitting here with you—practically a stranger—and yet you know about my mother when she's nothing more than a question mark for me."

"She doesn't have to be a question mark. But if you're not ready . . ."

"I thought I was. Now I'm not so sure."

He stands up, walks over to the credenza, and picks up a manila envelope. My eyes follow him as he moves to me and sits by my side. Placing the envelope on my lap, he says, "I don't believe there's a right or wrong choice here, but if you do find yourself wanting to open the door to the mystery, it's all in there."

I run my hands along the paper that separates me from my mom, and my apprehension grows. It's the conundrum of whether this envelope holds hope or dejection. Will this lead me to answers or just create more questions? And do I even care? It's not like she means anything to me, *right?*

And then I wonder why I never did care enough to learn about her. Maybe it's because Pike was enough for me to fill that void of family. I mean, he never could fill the void of my father—nobody has the power to do that—but Pike did become my family. He was my protector and comfort, and I didn't feel like I needed anyone else because he was enough.

But now he's gone.

And so is Declan. Even though he keeps me around, he no longer belongs to me. But did he ever?

These few weeks since everything came crashing down, my

loneliness has grown to a point of neediness. And now a part of me feels like I need this, whatever it is that's inside of this envelope.

"Tell me, Lachlan, are your parents still alive?" I ask in melancholy, confused about my feelings, wondering if there's anyone else here on this planet that can relate to me.

"Yes."

"Big or small family?"

"Big."

"Close?" I question.

"Yes."

Sad warmth creeps along my cheeks, and I take a moment to push the feeling aside before speaking again. "I never had that."

He doesn't respond, but what is there to say?

"Would you like a distraction?" he offers, and I sigh in exasperation, "Please."

His smile is friendly as it grows, and he takes my hand, guiding me to stand.

Handing me my coat, he says, "Let's get out of here."

He then takes me to Caffé e Cucina where we indulge ourselves with cappuccinos and kouignoù amann, which Lachlan promises I'll enjoy, and the French pastry doesn't disappoint.

We spend a leisurely few hours getting lost in conversation. He tells me stories about his time with Declan at St. Andrews, as well as a few funny tales from his own childhood in Scotland. I ask questions about the culture, as does he about life in the States. It surprises me to find out he's never been to the US. I tease him about eating beans for breakfast, and he teases me about the fact that getting a thirty-two ounce soda, or as he calls it, *fizzy juice,* is a commonality in the States.

Lachlan provides me with a good afternoon, doing exactly as he said he would by giving me a distraction. I haven't spent much time with him overall, but it's nice to feel like I have friend here, someone I can talk to and laugh with. Lachlan makes it easy for me to feel relaxed in his presence, and I enjoy our friendly banter.

But now, the joviality is gone as I sit here, back in my room in Gala. Since I returned, I've been sitting here with this envelope, debating on whether or not I should just throw it away, trash it, burn it. Or should I open it and read it. I asked Lachlan, since he knows what's enclosed, if it was worth me reading. His response was vague, telling me that people find comfort in various ways, and only I could make that decision.

*And I did. You see, as much as life had failed me, as much as I wanted to pretend I didn't waste my time on hope anymore—I still hung on to it. And that evening, sitting in my quaint room at the Water Lily Bed & Breakfast in Galashiels of Scotland, I made my decision and allowed that hope to bloom inside of me. I thought that maybe, just maybe, I had a mother out there that wanted me but could never find me. That maybe the envelope held the key to my maternal Godsend. But what I learned next frightened me, and let me tell you, I wasn't a woman who frightened easily.*

The first thing I see when I pull out the contents from the envelope is a mugshot of my mom. I recognize her face from the photo I've always had of her. But in this picture, she looks wrecked with a blotchy face and ratty hair. I stare into her eyes, eyes that look like mine. Along with the mugshot are a stack of court documents, a birth certificate, and a contact printout for Elgin Mental Health Center.

*The State versus Gweneth Archer* catches my eye when I begin to read. Her name's Gweneth. She's always had a face from the one picture I have of her, but I've never known her name until now. I start scanning the court documents, and my stomach begins to twist when I hit certain words. With jittery hands, I flip through the papers. My heart rate picks up in shock and confusion as my eyes dart back and forth, unable to focus on the sentences.

*Defendant . . . Child Neglect . . . Abandonment . . . Illegal Sale of a Child . . . Communications Fraud . . .*

Disbelief consumes me as I read the words. I grow frantic as I continue to scour through the papers. I will my eyes to focus on the words, but I feel myself on the verge of flipping out.

This can't be real. This can't be true.

*Mental Illness . . . Postpartum Depression . . . Manic Depression . . .*

I keep reading, and with each word my mind fights to process, I come unhinged. The room begins to tunnel around me, and my chest tightens, making it difficult to breathe.

Prosecutor: *"Mrs. Archer, did you negotiate the sale of your two-month-old daughter, Elizabeth Archer?"*

Defendant: *"Yes."*

A hysterical explosion of tinnitus ricochets in my head, piercing, shooting an unrelenting blast of pain. My hands clutch tightly to the papers as my vision teeters in and out of focus. I squint, determined to read further, but I'm fading out fast when my eyes scan: *Not Guilty by Reason of Insanity.*

The papers drop, scattering across the floor as my hands shoot up to my ears in an attempt to mute the high-pitched ringing, but it's coming from inside my head. It's splitting my skull as it builds. The welling of every emotion inside of me creates an unbearable pressure, and I need release.

I can't take it.

It's so loud, so painful, too alive, too much.

*Oh my God! She sold me.*

Shuffling over my own feet, I have no balance as I move across the room. I can't hear anything aside from the squealing in my ears. I stumble and catch myself from falling, gripping on to the closet door handle. Gasping for breath, my eyes blur, and I begin crying—sobbing—wailing—screaming.

*She never even wanted me.*

Standing in the doorway to the closet, I grab on to the doorframe and hold tightly as I drop my head. My vision diminishes in a wild haze, and it's too much to contain. I can't handle the overwhelming hysteria inside of me anymore.

I can't do it.

I'm going to rupture.

I can't do it.

I can't.

Lifting my head, I dig my nails into the wood, splintering it with my forceful grip. In quick motions, I reel my head back, grit my teeth down, and use every ounce of force inside of me as I violently slam my head into the doorframe. Drawing back, I bear down and do it again, smashing my forehead into the solid wood. My vision bursts in pops of light.

There's a pounding knock on the door, but it sounds miles away.

Thick, warm blood runs down my forehead, over my eyes and nose and cheeks. My body gives out and slides down to the floor. The ringing dampens and my body tingles in gratification as the blood oozes from my gashed head.

I faintly hear the door handle to my room ricketing back and forth, and then there's banging.

"Open the door!"

I can't focus on the voice yelling outside my room as the ringing returns to my ears, and the words I just read run back through my mind. Leaning my head back, my eyes begin to burn with the mixture of my tears, blood, and makeup. The sounds that engulf are out of control and torturous.

The banging grows louder, and I move my eyes to focus on the door.

"Open the fucking door!"

I don't even flinch when I hear the crashing and splitting of wood as the door is being kicked down because I'm too far gone. I'm lost inside myself and nothing feels real anymore.

Another kick, and I watch in a daze as Declan storms over to me.

"Oh my God!" I hear a woman shriek, and I know it's Isla, but I keep my attention solely on Declan.

"Jesus!" he panics when his hands come to my face, but it all seems like a dream.

I can't even feel his touch; my body singes in radiant tingles, but somehow the flesh is utterly numb.

"I need wet towels!" he shouts, and the ringing inside me settles to a low, monotone hum. It's incessant.

"Should I call a medic?"

"No," he snaps at Isla before dabbing the wet towel to my face.

I feel nothing though.

*Is my heart even beating?*

I know it must be when I finally feel the pressure of touch, but it isn't from Declan. I roll my head to the side, and Pike is here with me. He takes my hand in his and holds it tightly.

"You're here."

*"I'm always here."*

"Yeah, darling. I'm here. What happened?"

I faintly hear Declan's voice, but it's almost an echo as I concentrate on Pike.

"I miss you so much," I say as I begin to weep through a new slew of tears.

*"Talk to me."*

"I'm right here, Elizabeth. Don't cry."

"She never wanted me," I choke out.

*"Who?"*

"Who?"

"My mother. She sold me."

*"Fuck her. You never needed her anyway."*

"Shh . . . Just breathe, okay?"

"I need someone though. I'm so alone," I say to Pike.

*"You're not alone,"* he insists and then nods his head towards Declan.

I briefly look over, and his hands are still on me, pressing a towel firmly over the top of my head. When I look back to Pike, I admonish, "He doesn't want me. He only pities the pathetic waste he now knows I am."

"Elizabeth, what are you talking about?"

*"He cares for you. Why else would he be here right now?"*

"How could he care about me after what I did?"

*"Love is love. It doesn't just vanish."*

"How can you be so sure about that?"

His hand squeezes mine, soothing the chills that now start to wrack me and leans over to whisper softly in my ear, *"Because even though you shot and killed me, I still love you with every little piece of my heart. I still want to give you the world."*

e.k. blair

"How can I be sure of what? What are you talking about?" Declan's distant voice questions me, thinking I'm talking to him.

"Is she going to be okay?"

"She's fine! Please go and give us some space, will you?"

I barely hear Declan and Isla, but my eyes never leave my brother's as more tears fall. How can he still love me when I'm so unlovable?

"I'm so sorry," I cry. "I want to take it back so bad, Pike, but I can't! I don't know how."

"Darling, look at me. Who're you talking to?"

"Tell me how, Pike. How do I go back and fix this?"

*"You can't."*

The finality of my choices, knowing they can't be undone, is a horrendous weight I carry with me now. A weight I doubt I can carry for much longer.

"Elizabeth, look at me! Focus!"

*"Look at him, Elizabeth."*

"He doesn't love me. It hurts to look at him."

*"He hides it, but if you look close enough, you can see his cracks."*

"But what about you? I want you to stay. I want you back," I plead like a small child begging for something that's impossible, but I beg anyway.

*"You have me inside of you. I can't get any closer than that."*

"God dammit, look at me!"

*"You're scaring him,"* he tells me in a calm voice and then urges one last time, *"Look at him, Elizabeth."*

And when I do, one touch is exchanged for another. My hand grows cold as my face warms under Declan's touch, and I begin to sob uncontrollably at the switch.

# twenty-six

## (DECLAN)

"I'M SO SORRY," she wails, but she isn't looking at me. "I want to take it back so bad, Pike, but I can't! I don't know how."

*Did she just say Pike? What the fuck is going on?*

"Darling, look at me. Who're you talking to?" I ask as I press the now blood-soaked towel on Elizabeth's head, trying to clot the bleeding. But it's as if she doesn't even hear me when she continues to talk to nobody.

"Tell me how, Pike. How do I go back and fix this?"

"Elizabeth, look at me! Focus!" I yell at her, needing to get her to snap out of whatever hallucination she's having.

"He doesn't love me," she goes on. "It hurts to look at him."

*Fuck, what's going on with her?* She's scaring the shit out of me with her cryptic eyes and this arcane conversation.

"But what about you? I want you to stay. I want you back."

"God dammit, look at me!" I yell again, grabbing her shoulders and shaking her.

Slowly, she finally turns her head and raises her eyes to mine. My hands now cradle her face, and after a couple blinks, she crumples over and starts bawling—completely broken. I hold her as my heart pounds in turbulent beats, confused as shit.

The adrenaline in my system slowly wanes as I sit on the floor with her. Her blood is everywhere, and I still don't have a clue as to what the hell happened in this room before I kicked down the door.

Her body suddenly jolts, hands cup her ears, and her face pinches as she releases a ghastly scream. Horror storms through me, and I grab her shoulders to pull her up.

Her eyes are clenched shut as she cries out, "It's so loud! Make it stop!"

"Make what stop? Tell me what's going on," I urge.

She reaches her hand back behind her, and as I'm trying to get her to open her eyes and calm down, I'm horrified when I catch her clawing at her scalp. She writhes, hissing in an agonizing breath. Urgently, I scramble around her, grabbing her arms to restrain them behind her back. She struggles to get loose, but I tighten my hold when I see the grotesque scab that she's dug her nails into and ripped off.

*Fucking Christ, this girl is having a complete breakdown.*

"Stop fighting me," I demand harshly.

But she doesn't stop as she cries out, "It's so loud. Let go of me!"

"Breathe. Stop fighting me and just breathe."

I then let go of her arms, but quickly pin them to her sides when I band my arms tightly around her chest, taking control over her. It's harder for her to fight me and jerk around from this position, but she keeps trying. So, I hold her until she begins to tire, all the while, doing my best to keep an even tone as I continue my attempts to soothe her, repeating over and over, "It's okay . . . You're safe . . . Breathe."

When her body weakens, losing the tension, and sinking back into me, I release my firm hold on her. She's quiet and pulls in long, deep breaths. I don't know what the fuck is going on with her, but I do know she's losing her shit. The fact that she's hiding away here and inflicting these attacks on her body is beyond disturbing. One has to wonder if she's suicidal. And the fact that I just caught her having a full conversation with someone that doesn't even exist anymore is insane.

I don't know what to do, but I know I can't leave her alone here. God only knows what she'll attempt next. So, I stand and gather all the papers that are strewn on the floor, then scoop her up into my arms. Her blood is all over me and streaked down her face. Her body folds into me, and I get her the fuck out of here.

"Is she okay? Where are you taking her?" Isla asks in worriment as I make my way to the front door.

"She's fine. I'm taking her to my place."

Walking out into the biting chill of the night, I put her in my SUV. She doesn't speak; she's completely absent. I strap the seatbelt around her and start heading to my house.

While I drive, I pull out my cell and make a call to a friend of mine whose wife is a doctor. I stress to my friend the urgency of the situation, and after he explains what's going on to his wife, she agrees to meet me at the house.

Once we make it back to my place, I carry her in my arms upstairs to get her in the shower and cleaned up. She's totally withdrawn as I begin to remove her clothing. When I have her stripped down, I'm appalled by what I see.

She's covered in a vast array of bruises: blue, purple, green, yellow, brown. They're all over her chest, stomach, and thighs— blotches of muted colors.

"Did you do this to yourself?" I ask, but she doesn't respond. She keeps her eyes downcast and doesn't utter a word. "Look at me."

But she doesn't.

I duck my head to try and catch her eyes, but I get nothing but desolation. Turning on the water, I strip my clothes off as well and then help her into the shower. She stands, unmoving, as I wash her. The water turns red as it runs over our bodies, taking the blood down the drain.

I keep moving to distract myself, but after we're both clean, everything slows. Standing under the hot water, I see a girl I've never seen before. She's severed and lost and weak. She's nothing like the woman I met in Chicago—*Nina*. And I begin to wonder how different these two people truly are.

*Who is Elizabeth? Is she anything like Nina? Strong? Snarky? Funny? Smart? Who is this girl standing in front me?*

I run my hands over her cheeks and cup her jaw, angling her head up to me. Her eyes shift to mine, and as I look into her, I murmur, "Who are you, Elizabeth?"

She blinks, no expression to her face, and after what feels like hours, she finally responds in chilled words, "I'm nobody."

And as mad as I am at her, as much as I hate her, as much as I want to celebrate her downfall, I have the urge to convince her that she *is* someone. I want to remind her of all the reasons I fell in love with her, but who's to know if those reasons were just products of her deception. I need a ballast of understanding with her, but I don't know if that will ever come.

And what would I even do if I got it?

There's so much I want to say, so many questions, but I know this isn't the moment for any of that. Turning off the water, I grab some towels, tying one around my waist before I get her wrapped up.

I lead her to the bed and sit her down, saying, "Stay here. I'll be right back with some clothes."

I rush to my room to toss on my sleep pants and a t-shirt before returning with a pair of my boxers and a shirt for her. I get her dressed and lay her down in the bed. She remains quiet; I don't even attempt to speak when she rolls onto her side, facing away from me. I know she's got to be physically and emotionally drained, and I want to let her rest, but I also don't trust her to leave her alone right now.

So while I wait for Kyla to arrive, I pick up the envelope that contains the papers I took from Elizabeth's room and take a seat on one of the chairs in the corner of the room by the windows. I pull out the sheaf of documents, and start riffling through them to get them in order before I start to read.

The information contained in the court documents is unsettling, and I can't believe what I'm reading. I spend the next half hour going over her mother's testimony where she admits wanting to terminate the pregnancy when she learned about it, but her husband begged her to keep it for him, so she did. But that after the baby was born, she grew depressed and started having thoughts of harming and even killing Elizabeth when she was an infant. How she felt her husband loved their daughter more than her. And eventually, how she secretly handled the selling of the baby to some guy she met through friends who lived in Kentucky.

The intercom buzzes, alerting someone's at the gate, snapping me out of my engrossed thoughts.

Setting the papers down on the side table, I walk over to the bed and am shocked to see she's still awake as she stares out the window blankly.

"Are you okay?"

No answer.

"I need to run downstairs for a moment," I tell her, but still, no returned response.

Before I walk out of the room, I push the button on the intercom to open the gate and then head downstairs to meet Kyla.

"Thank you for coming on such short notice," I tell her when she enters my home.

"Alick stressed how important it was for you to keep this matter private."

"Yes. The last thing I need is for some reporter to start digging around if it were to be mentioned I was at the hospital with a woman."

Her smile is warm, and when she touches my arm, she says, "You and Alick have been friends for years, and although you and I don't know each other that well, I want you to know that you can trust me."

"Thank you."

"Before I check on the girl—"

"Her name's Elizabeth," I interrupt, my stomach still knotted tightly from reading about her mother.

"Before I examine Elizabeth, can you tell me what happened tonight?"

"I received a call from a friend, letting me know she would be learning something that would probably upset her."

Her brows rise in confusion.

"The details aren't important, but needless to say, she didn't take the news well. After I ended the call with my friend, I rushed over to where she's been staying, wanting to check in on her, and when I arrived, she had locked herself in her room. She was screaming like a maniac and crying. I kicked the door down and she was covered in blood. She must have smashed her head against something. There was blood everywhere. She had calmed a little and began talking. I thought she was talking to me, so I was responding to her, but she wasn't looking at me. And then she mentioned someone else's name," I tell her, not wanting to reveal too much detail. "She must've been hallucinating, and then it was like her whole body was in pain and she started complaining about a ringing in her head."

"Has she had episodes like this before?"

"I'm assuming, but I don't know for sure. When I brought her back here, I put her in the shower, and her whole body is covered in bruises. It's like she's been beating herself. I know she has this wound on her head that she's been picking at."

"Is she on any medications that you know of?"

"No. I don't know."

"It's okay," she assures and then asks to see her.

I lead her up the stairs and into the guest room where I left her. I stand off to the side while Kyla walks around the bed to talk to Elizabeth.

"Hi there. I'm Dr. Allaway. Can you tell me your name?"

I look on, waiting for some sort of movement, but there's no shift when I hear her weak voice answer, "Elizabeth."

"Last name?"

"Archer."

Kyla sets her medical bag on the nightstand and begins asking Elizabeth a series of questions about the evening's events. Kyla helps adjust Elizabeth in bed and sits her up with a stack of pillows behind her back. They begin talking, and Elizabeth's voice sounds hollow as she explains about her mother, and I can tell by what she's saying that she doesn't know the extent of the facts like I do. She probably just read a few words and got herself so worked up, she exploded.

"Was there anyone else in the room with you and Declan?" she questions, knowing I had mentioned witnessing her talking to someone that wasn't there.

I lean against the wall, silent, with my arms crossed over my chest when I catch her eyes glossing over with tears.

She nods, and Kyla asks, "Who else was there?"

"My brother," she answers weakly.

"Can you tell me where your brother is now?"

"I'm not crazy," Elizabeth immediately defends.

"No one said you were. But I need you to be honest with me so that I can help you."

"You can't help me."

"Will you let me try?" she offers. "We don't have to talk about your brother right now if you don't want to, but would you let me take a look at your head?"

Kyla begins to treat the wounds on her forehead and also the one on the back of her head. She then moves to examine the bruises on her body along with taking her vitals. While she does all this, she continues to talk to Elizabeth, and soon she reveals, "Sometimes when I'm really upset or stressed, I see my brother. He talks to me and calms me down."

Once she is finished, she writes a prescription for a mood stabilizer and as I walk her out, she tells me, "I'd like to see her again, but I'd like her to also visit with a psychiatrist. Like I said, I don't know much about this case or the patient's family history, but my first thought is that she's most likely dealing with an untreated depressive episode with some congruent psychosis."

"What does that mean?"

"There's no doubt she is terribly depressed right now, but that coupled with seeing and hearing things that don't exist along with her erratic behaviors raise quite a few red flags. It's actually a good sign though that her hallucinations seem to be related to her distress."

"I've never known her to be this unstable though," I tell her, thinking back to the time we shared in Chicago. She was always so pulled together and witty. Sure she would have these moments of sadness, but nothing like this.

"It's not an entirely uncommon reaction and most often it surfaces under times of extreme stress," she informs. "She also has a slight concussion from her head trauma. Nothing serious, but I would strongly suggest that you make sure you are waking her up every two to three hours, okay?"

"Of course."

"I'll email you a list of doctors I would recommend for her to visit when I get to the office tomorrow."

When she puts her coat on, I hand her back her bag, saying, "I cannot thank you enough for this."

She smiles and gives a nod. "If you need anything else or notice any changes in her, please call me." I watch as she walks to her car, and before she gets in, she reminds, "And get that script filled."

"Drive safely."

Walking back inside, I immediately pull out my cell and call

Lachlan.

He picks up on the second ring. "Hello?"

"What the fuck were you thinking calling me *after* you gave her the information on her mother?" I snap.

"Is everything okay?"

"I told you I wanted to know as soon as you knew, not after you met with her. If you're finding it difficult to follow my very simple instructions, maybe you'd be better suited to work for someone who doesn't give a shit about attention to detail."

"It was a complete oversight on my part; I apologize."

"You knew what the fuck was in those court documents, and your *oversight* was in complete negligence."

"Agreed."

"How the hell did you get your hands on those documents with the case involving a minor anyway?" I ask.

"Luckily I know someone who knows someone that I was able to pay off in exchange for papers," he explains, and then asks, "She read them?"

"Yeah, she read them."

"Is she okay?"

"Not of your concern. I think you're forgetting that your priorities are with me. I want you to stop following her because it seems you're sidetracked, and I don't want another *oversight* on your part," I berate and then disconnect the call.

When I turn around, I stop in my tracks when I see Elizabeth standing at the foot of the stairs.

"You were having me followed?"

# twenty-seven

"DO YOU BLAME me?" he says after I question him.

And he's right, I can't blame him. How can I expect him not to be suspicious of me?

His face is soured in frustration as he walks towards me. He brushes my shoulder as he passes, saying, "Go to bed," and then heads up the stairs.

"Why am I here?"

He turns and looks down to me. "Because I don't trust you to be alone with yourself." He begins walking back up the stairs, and a few steps later, adds without making any eye contact with me, "The doctor says you have a slight concussion, and I'm to wake you every couple hours. You should get some rest."

"Why are you so cold? You're so on and off," I question, confused by this push and pull he has with me.

"Certainly you don't need reminding, do you?"

I watch as he ascends, and I'm left alone in the silence of his home. His demeanor shifts in a snap, and I can only assume

e.k. blair

that whoever he was just talking to on the phone is the cause for that sudden snap. I don't worry about being followed because I deserve the distrust.

Making my way back up the stairs, I notice the door to his room is open and quietly pad over. When I look in, he's lying on top of his perfectly made bed. His hands folded behind his head, ankles crossed, and staring up at the ceiling. I'm allowed a moment to absorb him before he senses my presence.

With his body remaining still and his eyes fixed to the ceiling, he says without any inflection, "Get out of my room."

His tone is even, but I can hear the animosity deep within. So I go to the room he's put me in and crawl under the sheets. There's a disconnection inside of me, no doubt due to the extremities of this evening. Maybe I should be embarrassed that Declan saw me coming completely undone like he did, but I'm numb to emotion right now. My body is depleted, and to dissect this whole situation would take more energy than I have. So I roll to my side and stare out of the large windows at the full moon that lights the night's ink and slowly drift away.

WHISPERS CATCH ME, wrapping their sweet timbres around my heart, and gently pull me out of my slumber.

"Elizabeth," his soft rasp calls to me. "Open your eyes."

Fingers comb through my hair, and the touch sends a sparkling shiver through me, warming me from the inside and rousing me awake.

Declan sits on the edge of the bed, hand cupping the side of my head as he looks down upon me. And he's so beautiful, I question if I'm still dreaming.

"Are you feeling okay?"

Exhaustion is all over me, and as much as I want to stay up with him, my eyes drop. I'm able to answer his question with a nod before sleep takes over.

LIGHT FILTERS THROUGH my lids, and when my eyes flutter open, I see Declan moving about the bathroom. When he emerges in the doorway with a glass of water, he flicks the light off, darkening the room. I'm in a haze as his shadow moves closer to me, and when I feel the bed dip, my arm instinctually reaches out for him.

"Here," he says. "Take these."

Dropping a couple painkillers in my hand, I put them in my mouth and then take a sip from the glass of water he gives me. My head falls back to the pillow, weighing a thousand pounds and throbbing with an oncoming headache. I release an appreciative hum at the fact Declan was a step ahead of me in knowing I would need the pain relief. And with my eyes closed, the haze thickens, and I sink into darkness.

GASPING HARD, I'M knocked out of a dead sleep as my body shoots up. Eyes flash open wide and I clutch my chest, panting loudly. My head is clouded with sleep as it strains to catch up to my alert body. Looking around my unfamiliar surroundings, I panic. Everything is disoriented.

"Elizabeth."

My attention flies to the doorway of the room where Declan is standing, and it's then my confusion dissipates into clarity.

"Are you okay?" he questions as he walks over to me and sits down on the bed.

"Yeah," I tremble.

"What happened?"

"I don't know. Bad dream, I guess."

We sit, facing each other, and I notice he's no longer wearing his shirt, and the moment my eyes catch it, I choke on a strangled breath.

It's there, on his chest—my disgrace.

The unmistakable proof.

The reality of my fraudulence.

My focus is locked on what remains from my twisted game. It mars his perfect body.

Two gunshot wounds branded on his left pec, tainting his chest in my scum.

My pulse quickens, and when he looks down to see what has me so shaken, my heart reunites with the anguish from when I thought I'd lost him forever.

My hand lifts, and he doesn't stop me when I reach out and brush my fingertips over the bullet wounds. The raised flesh that hides the deep scar tissue beneath splinters me to the core.

I keep my eyes on his chest as he allows me this touch, and when my chin starts to quiver, I force my words out around the lump lodged in my throat, and the tears slip. "I thought you were dead."

And in an unexpected move, a tender gesture I never thought I'd get again, he cups my face and licks my tears. My hands grip tightly to his wrists as he cradles my cheeks. Closing my eyes, I lean into his mouth as he swallows my salts.

In an unrushed moment, his lick eclipses into a silken kiss that erupts a wondrous rekindling inside of my womb. Whether I believe his emotions to be real or not, I pretend that they are, because I want his love so badly. I want to believe his lips are genuine and they mean exactly what my heart yearns for them to mean.

I calm as we now share the same breath. My hands still cling to his wrists because I need the support of his strength in this moment. Opening my lips with his, he sinks his tongue deep inside of my mouth, claiming and binding us together.

His taste is home—familiar and delicious.

My body begins to swim in bliss when he lays me down on my back, and my legs fall open for him. He's incredibly hard, pressing himself against me. I whimper as his kisses become more intent. His lips begin to move fervently, rapturing my mouth, and I meld to him, allowing him to take take take. I'd give him my last breath if that's what he desired.

He's my body's epitaph.

His intensity grows and we're nothing but wild heartbeats, frantic breaths, bleeding lips, broken souls. We cling, grab, and claw our way to incomprehensible closeness. His mouth finds the curve of my neck, and I writhe in pleasure as he bites me, marking my flesh, breaking through the delicate tissue, bleeding me out for him to taste.

He growls deeply, chest vibrating against mine. Reaching down, he grabs the hem of my shirt and pulls it up, but quickly stops. Bracing himself above me, he looks down at my stomach, and when my eyes move to see what's pulled him away from me, my gut turns. I've mutilated my skin, gifting it with monstrous bruises.

Declan drops his head, the tips of his hair brushing along my stomach. The moment my hands touch his head, he snaps up and pushes himself off of me. I sit up and instantly miss him as I watch his sudden change. His eyes narrow then pinch shut as ache penetrates his face.

What he's able to mend inside of me so quickly, he shatters even faster.

He stands and walks away, depleting the goodness he just filled me with. But before he leaves, he turns back, and says, "You breathe deceitful fumes; I can taste it when we kiss."

And then he's gone, leaving me an empty mess, not wanting to think about the war that's going on inside of him, because that war will always cast back to me, and I can't deal with the responsibility of that burden in this moment. I'm too weak.

WHEN THE SUN begins to shine through the windows, I wake. My head is already throbbing as I stretch and sit up, tired from being woken up all through the night. I had a hard time falling back to sleep after kissing Declan, and when I walk to the bathroom, my darkened eyes confirm.

I rummage around but find no toiletries. All my belongings are back at Isla's. I shiver from the chill in the house as I make my way to Declan's room, but it's empty.

"What are you doing?" he asks, startling me, and when I turn around, he's walking up the stairs with a mug in each hand.

"I woke up, and . . . I was just looking for you. I wanted to freshen up, but there was nothing in the bathroom."

He hands me one of the mugs, and I'm instantly greeted with a fragrant floral spice from the tea he made for me.

"Umm . . . thanks," I mumble when he moves past me and into his bedroom.

I don't know whether I should follow him, so I stay put, but I don't have to wait long for him to return with his leather toiletry bag I remember from his loft back in Chicago.

"Here," he says as he hands it to me. "You can use my things."

He then walks into my room, and this time, I follow. He takes a seat in the sitting area by the windows, and I go into the bathroom, closing the door behind me. I open his bag, pull out his toothbrush, and take comfort in using it along with his deodorant. I brush my hair, careful not to rip off the bandage the doctor put over the scab on the back of my head.

When I walk out, he's made himself comfortable, looking pulled together in slacks and a crisp, charcoal button-up. But I can see the exhaustion in his eyes as well. I walk over and slip back into bed, covering up in the warm blankets, sitting against the upholstered headboard. I take a sip from my cup of tea and look over to Declan who's flipping through a stack of papers.

"Are those . . . ?"

He raises his head and says, "I wanted to know what upset you, so I took them from your room."

"Did you . . . I mean, have you . . . ?" I fumble with my words as my anxiety picks up, remembering what I read.

"I figured it would be best to talk about this and deal with it head on instead of it taking control over you."

Shaking my head, I tell him, "I don't want to talk about it,

Declan."

"Why?"

Putting the tea aside on the nightstand, I wilt down in the bed and give him my honest thoughts. "Because it hurts too much. Because talking won't change it. Because my life is already too screwed up for me to handle."

He sets the papers down on the coffee table in front of him, leans forward, and says, "Ignoring it is only going to make it hurt worse. That's your problem, Ni—Elizabeth." Shaking his head at his near slip, he looks back to me and continues, "You hide everything, and when you do that, you give those things power over you."

"I don't."

"You don't think so?"

"No," I respond, and he releases annoyance in a sigh, saying, "Then explain last night to me."

"That wasn't—"

"Have you looked at yourself lately?" he chides. "A woman who's in control wouldn't be smashing her head into a fucking wall."

"You don't understand," I defend.

"Then please, explain it to me. Make me understand why your body is covered in contusions."

His glare is sharp, pinning his frustrations to me as I sit here awkwardly. Knowing how Declan saw me last night, knowing the things I've revealed to him, I feel denuded of my armor I'm used to hiding behind. I've laid myself bare to this man, but now I want to hide again. I want to throw the façade on and lash my crude words at him. Push him out of the honesty I've been giving him.

But he sees me wanting to avoid when he presses, "I want you to tell me why you're determined to destroy yourself. Tell me why."

Shaking my head, I stutter, "I don't . . . You wouldn't understand . . . I can't . . ."

"Why hide now? Why? Just talk to me. Tell me."

But I doubt he would even understand if I told him. I barely understand it myself. As I continue to avoid answering, he stands up and walks over to me, sitting on the bed in front of me. His closeness, especially after kissing him last night, unsettles me, and I let my fear grow.

With a rigid tone, heavy with his brogue, he says, "Help me figure you out. Tell me why you're hurting yourself."

"I'm not . . ." I begin when I hear the tribulation in the cracks of his stern voice. I give in to his request because I know he deserves it. I owe him whatever it is that he wants. "I'm not hurting myself."

"I don't understand."

"It makes me feel better," I confess. "When I'm hurting, *really hurting,* I hit myself and it takes the hurt away."

"You're wrong. You're just masking the pain; you're not getting rid of it."

"But I don't know how to get rid of it."

"You deal with it. You talk about it and face it and process it."

His words are reminiscent of Carnegie's. He once told me something very similar when I spoke with him about Bennett. But the thing is, to face a pain like that takes a particular type of strength I don't possess.

"But what about you?" I accuse. "You hide."

"I do," he admits freely. "I miss my mum, and I hide from that whole fucked up situation. But it's not eating at me the way you allow things to eat at you. I'm not the one throwing punches at myself, *you are.*"

His words are caustic. They piss me off because they're true. He's right, and I hate that. I hate that I've become transparent to him. Hate that I've allowed that. Gone is the camouflage. I left it behind for atonement, for repentance.

"I don't know how to do this," I concede.

He gives an understanding nod. "I know. I just want you to talk, that's all."

"About my mom?"

"It's a good place to start."

"What's to say? I mean, I'm scared to know too much," I tell him, struggling to not break down.

"Too much? Did you not read through everything?"

"No. I was so upset, that I . . . I just couldn't read it. I couldn't focus."

He insists that I need to know, so I sit and listen to him tell me the documented facts of how and why my mother sold me to some guy she barely knew. And the fabricated story she told my father and the police that I was kidnapped when she left me in my car seat unattended while she went inside a gas station to pay.

He speaks in detail as I sit here like a stone, forcing my feelings away. I keep my breathing as even as I can as I concentrate on restoring my steel cage while he continues to tell me about her mental instability. She had extreme postpartum depression and was later diagnosed with manic depression and deemed insane by the courts, which is why she was sentenced to a state mental hospital instead of prison.

"Say something."

I keep my eyes downcast, afraid if I look at him, I won't be able to hold myself together as well as I'm doing right now. "Is she still there?"

"No. She was released after serving twelve years."

"What?" I blurt out in disbelief, finally looking up to Declan. "But . . . I was still a kid. Why didn't she come for me?"

"She relinquished her parental rights."

My thoughts begin to collide in my head, and when I turn my face away, he catches me. "Don't do that. Don't avoid."

"Why am I so unlovable?"

"Look at me," he demands, and when I do, his face is blurred through my unshed tears. "Your mum was sick. She—"

"What the fuck are you doing?" I scream in disbelief. "Why are you defending her?"

"I'm not defending, I'm being rational."

"You can't rationalize what she did," I throw at him. "She sold me! What if the police had never found me? But she didn't care what happened to me as long as she got what she wanted."

"You don't think it's worth making sense out of? To find any semblance of understanding?"

"Are you kidding me? No! What she did was wrong! People like her don't deserve understanding!"

"You mean people like you?" he throws at me.

"What?"

"How is what she did any different than what you did?"

His assumption that I'm anything like the woman who sold me pisses me off, and I snap, "What the hell is that supposed to mean?"

"I'm talking about *you*. Why did you marry Bennett? Why

did you make me fall for you? Why did you lie?"

"It's not the same," I state, refusing to believe I'm of the same vile nature as my mother.

"Because you wanted something to make you feel better. Because you were only thinking of yourself and you didn't care what happened to the people who came in your path or that you destroyed," he answers for me in growing rage.

His words shut me up. I don't want to acknowledge the parallels, but it's there, unmistakably. He just threw it in my face.

"She knew better," I poorly argue.

"So did you," he affirms.

"I can't forgive her for what she did."

"No one is saying you have to. I just want you to face the facts and deal with it. I don't care how you deal with it as long as you do something with the information instead of hiding from it," he says. "And yes, what she did was awful, and it makes no sense, but neither do your actions."

"And neither do *your* actions, Declan," I condemn, and he knows exactly what my words imply.

"No, you're right. I can't make sense out of the things I've done to you. But I do know enough to recognize that ever since I took a man's life, I haven't been the same. I carry an appalling amount of animosity inside of me that I don't know how to deal with."

"So we're all just screwed up?"

"To some degree, yes," he responds. "I don't want to downplay what your mother did, that's not what I'm trying to do. I just want you to face the facts and do something with it."

And I see his point, because it doesn't even take me a second thought to know I don't want to resemble that woman in the slightest. I don't want that hostility living and breeding inside of me anymore. I want to let go of the resentment. I want to let go of the blame. I want to let go of the constant fiending for payback. But sometimes we don't get what we want, and even though I want to be without it, a part of me will probably always want to hang on to it.

# twenty-eight

I AIM MY foot to land on the small patch of snow just to hear it crunch under my rain boot. The sound brings me a tiny piece of joy as I walk the grounds. The snow started to melt away yesterday when the sun finally peeked out from behind the heavy blanket of grey clouds. But today is another dank day, cold and damp.

Declan still has me here at his house. He took me back to the Water Lily to pack some of my belongings, but I'm still paying for the room because he told me this arrangement was simply temporary until I was well-rested and feeling better.

This is my second day here, and I've hardly seen Declan. He spends most of his time up on the third floor where his office is. When the sun came out yesterday, he suggested that I soak up the vitamin D, so I decided to enjoy the grotto. I spent hours inside the clinker structure. He has a small round table with two chairs set in the center under the glass ceiling. Even though the temperatures were in the thirties, the sun warmed the room where I sat and daydreamed like a little girl. As if that grotto was my palace, and I, the princess captured, waiting for my prince to save me.

And now, as I walk the grounds, stepping from snow patch to snow patch, I feel myself imagining this fabulous property as my magical forest. Winding through the trees, up small hills, passing flower gardens bedding the blooms that will emerge in the coming months, as well as benches and manmade stone and pebble creeks. I wish for one of the creeks to be the mythical Lethe that Declan and I could drink from to vanish the past into a vapor of vacuity. To eradicate the sufferings of our souls.

It's as if this is the forest I spent my childhood searching for. I used to sneak out of my foster homes during the night in a fit of wanderlust, hoping to find the place my father told me about. The fairytales of kings and queens, flying steeds, and of course, Carnegie—my life-long caterpillar friend who used to fill my dreams. He hasn't come around since that night when I turned into a caterpillar as well. He's been replaced by the corrosive memories of my past, and when I'm lucky enough, empty nights of blank space.

I find a spot up on a hill to perch myself. I sit and my pants dampen, seeping up the melted snow that soaks the earth beneath me, but I don't care because I'm at peace. I fold my legs in front of me and look down on this house that for now, I imagine is my kingdom. And when I close my eyes and lie back on the sodden ground, I believe that the man hiding away in his office at the top of the castle is my prince.

I breathe in the essence of the innocent child-like dream, and I'm five years old all over again. Dressed in my princess gown, I see my father holding the bouquet of pink daisies. His face still a crystal perfect image in my mind. Although twenty-three years have passed, I'm still a little girl, and he's still my handsome daddy who can fix anything with his hugs and kisses.

*"You're so beautiful,"* his voice whispers through the wind, and my eyes flash open when I sit up.

My heart flutters at the realness of his voice, and then I hear it again.

*"Where have you been, sweetheart?"*

"Daddy?" My voice rings high in optimism through the breeze blowing through the trees above.

*"It's me."*

Looking around, I see no sign of anyone. I know this isn't real, but I don't care. I let whatever chemical my brain is spilling take me away, and I give into the illusion.

"I miss you," I tell the wind that carries wishes coming true.

*"I miss you too. More than you'll ever know,"* he says, and I smile at the way his voice warms my chest. *"What are you doing out here in the cold?"*

"Escaping."

*"Escaping what?"*

"Everything," I say. "Being out here and exploring transports me back to a place of happiness. Where evil doesn't exist and innocence isn't lost."

*"But what about down there?"* I look down to the house as he continues, *"Why can't you find that inside those walls?"*

"Because inside those walls lies the truth. And the truth is . . . evil *does* exist, and innocence is just a fable."

*"Life is whatever you want it to be, sweetheart."*

"I don't believe that," I tell him. "I don't believe we are stronger than the forces of this world."

*"Maybe not, but I'd like to think of my little girl as someone who*

*would fight for her fairytale."*

"I've fought my whole life, Daddy. I'm ready to throw in the towel and give up."

"Who are you talking to?"

Turning my head, I see Declan standing off in the distance. "I'm not crazy," I instantly defend.

He begins walking towards me. "I didn't say you were."

But if I did what my soul is screaming for me to do, he would. Because right now, the emptiness that refills what my father just warmed makes me want to cry out at the top of my lungs for him to come back. It roils inside of me, panging on the strings of my heart, but I mask it for fear of completely breaking down.

Declan sits next to me, and I deflect, teasing, "You just might destroy those slacks, sitting in the slushy dirt with me."

He looks at me, and his expression is hard to read, but it's almost despondent.

When he doesn't speak, I ask, "Why have you been hiding in your office?"

"Why have you been hiding out here?" he counters.

"I asked first."

Taking a deep breath, he admits, "Honestly . . . It makes me nervous to be around you."

"Why?"

He pulls his knees up and rests his arms over them as he explains, "Because I don't know you. I feel like I know the character you played—I know Nina. She made me comfortable. But you . . . I don't know you, and that makes me nervous."

But before I can speak, he says, "Now it's your turn to answer. Who were you talking to?"

Casting my eyes away from him, I reveal, "My dad," and wait for his response, but what he says next surprises me.

"What did he have to say?"

Shifting my attention back to Declan, he looks sincere in wanting to know, so I give it to him. "He told me I need to be stronger."

"Will you tell me about him?" he asks, and then smirks, adding, "The truth this time."

"What I used to tell you about him, the way he comforted me, the way you two resemble each other, it was all true, Declan. The lie was the Kansas story. Truth is, we lived in Northbrook. He was a great dad. I never had to question his love for me because he gave it endlessly." Thoughts from the past pile up, and I smile when I tell him, "The reason my favorite flower is the pink daisy, is because that's what he would always buy me."

My chest tugs when the memories fall from my eyes and roll down my cheeks.

"We used to have these tea parties. I'd dress up and he'd join me, pretending to eat the little plastic pastries." I wipe my tears, saying, "I never asked about my mom. I never really thought about her because my dad was more than enough. I never felt like I was missing anything."

"You mentioned he went to prison," he says, and I nod.

"Yeah," I respond and sniff before explaining, "He was caught for gun trafficking. I was five when the cops arrested him in front of me. The vision of my dad on his knees, being hand-cuffed, and promising me that everything would be okay is still so vivid in my mind."

"So what happened?"

Shrugging my shoulders, I resign, "That was it. I never saw

him again. I went into foster care and had the shittiest of case-workers out there. He went to Menard Prison, and I wound up in Posen, which was five hours away."

"Nobody ever took you to go see him?"

"No. My caseworker barely made time to come see me, let alone drive me across the state. But she did make the time to come tell me when my dad had been killed in a knife fight."

"How old were you?"

"Twelve."

He reaches out and takes my hand, turning my palm up. His voice is gentle when he says, "You didn't answer me when I asked you this before, but I need to know." He then drags his thumb over the faint white scars on my wrist. "Tell me how you got these."

My head drops in embarrassment, not wanting to add another layer of disgust on top of everything else he knows about me. With my hand still in his, he takes his other and covers my wrist with it. When I look into his eyes, he urges, "I want you to tell me."

So, I take a hard swallow and muster up what strength I can to confine the pain. It takes me a moment, and after a measured breath, I cut through another wound and allow it to bleed out for Declan. "When I wasn't in the basement, I was in the closet. My foster dad would tie me up with his leather belt to the garment rod in the closet beneath the stairs and lock me up."

"Jesus," he mutters in disbelief. "How long would you . . . ?"

"Every weekend. I'd go in on Friday and come out Sunday. Sometimes I'd be in there during the weeknights. But during the summers, it was constant. I'd be in there three to five days at a time. He'd let me out long enough to go down in the basement, but then he'd tie me back up and lock the door again."

I feel numb when I tell him this, caging off the emotions I fear. The horror splayed across his face is hard to look at, so I keep my head down, but he picks it up. Moving closer to me, with his hands on my cheeks, he angles me to look up at him. My jaw is locked tight while I continue to hold myself together.

"Why?" he scolds harshly as he holds me in his hands. "Why didn't you tell someone? Why did you let that happen to you?"

His words rankle my nerves, but instead of blowing up at him in a rage, I narrow my eyes, and seethe, "You don't know shit. You had a home, you had a family, you were safe. So don't you dare sit here and question my actions. You don't know fear like I do. I may be fucked in the head, but one thing I do know for sure . . . I didn't *let* those things happen to me. What happened wasn't my fault, so fuck you for blaming me."

I jerk away from him and stand up, but he's quick when he meets my moves and grabs my arm. He pulls me back to him, and when I try yanking out from his hold, he tightens his grip.

"Let go of me!" I yell, but he says nothing as I struggle my arm free. I don't wait another second and start walking down the hill away from him. I don't expect anyone to understand my childhood, but to think a little girl would allow someone to debase her like I was is fucking crazy.

"I'm sorry," his voice hollers down to me, but I keep walking. "Elizabeth, stop!"

I do. I instantly stop the moment I hear his voice break. When I turn to look up at him through the trees, I exhaust in a softer tone, "I was just a little kid."

With hurried steps, he makes his way down, and when he's standing before me, he says, "I'm sorry. My words came out wrong. I'm just angry." He grabs on to me. "I'm so fucking angry when you tell me these things. I feel helpless."

"Why?"

"Because I want to take it away from you. Because somewhere inside my hate for you, a part of me still cares."

Staring up at him, I know better than to leech on to the goodness and hope of what he just said, so I ask, "Which one is it? Do you care more than you hate?"

I watch the tension strain through his eyes, and a moment passes before he answers, "No."

His honesty burns and sinks down inside of me. I question why I'm even here if he hates me so much. I feel like a game to him, but I don't even know what he's gaining from playing with me like this.

Shrugging out of his hold, I take a couple steps back from him before demanding, "Take me back to Isla's."

"No."

"It wasn't a question, Declan. I'm leaving," I tell him and then turn my back and rush towards the house, fuming mad.

I move quickly, doing my best to avoid ice patches, when I hear his heavy footsteps behind me. Looking over my shoulder, he's moving fast, but I'm too angry to face him right now, so I pick up my pace and start running from him.

"Elizabeth, stop!" he shouts from behind me, but I don't, and with each of my strides, my armor cracks.

His words just reminded me how alone I am in this world. Foolish of me to think maybe he wanted me here for the sake of wanting to be near me.

When I finally reach the house, I make my way around the back, but he catches me. His hand locks around my elbow, and when I stumble over my feet, he swings me around to face him and loops his arm around my waist. I cry out when he picks me up, lifting me off the ground.

In a flash, he has my back pressed against the side of the house, his body pinning me to the stone. With him flush against me, both of us panting heavily, I don't fight him as emotions overflow between us.

He doesn't speak, and neither do I, and before I know it, without thinking, my arms wrap around his neck. Our eyes are locked, never straying. He rests his forehead against mine, and my heart beats uncontrollably when he moves his hands to my pants. With our heads pressed together, staring into each other's eyes that reveal the unfamiliar emotions we're both experiencing, his cold fingers press against my stomach as he unzips my pants. He shoves them down, and I fumble, kicking off my rain boot, and working my one leg out of my pants as he unhooks his slacks.

The foggy vapors from our heavy breaths swim between our mouths, and suddenly, his hands wrap behind my knees, lifting me up. I lock my ankles around him, and the instant I feel the heat of his cock against me, a couple tears escape and fall down my cheeks.

He grips himself in his hand and presses into my folds, wetting his dick as he runs his burning tip through the slick warmth of my pussy. My arms cling tightly around him when he barely pushes the head of himself inside, teasing me, tugging at my opening. Clenching my thighs around him, a few more tears fall when he finally pushes himself inside of me.

I moan in carnal heat when he buries himself in my body. My heart leaps at the connection that soothes all the friction away. I'm finally pacified and free. I revel in knowing he has the antidote to clean the rot in me. I'm like the angel of martyrdom and he's the bezoar that purifies.

"Tell me you're not leaving," he says on a heavy voice that edges on violence, and I yield to him, saying, "I won't leave," because I'd do just about anything for him in this moment to keep his touch.

And with my words, he takes my mouth in a savage kiss as he begins fucking me with powerful, deep strokes. His eyes blacken in primal lust as he takes me, driving me back against the wall with each of his urgent thrusts. The sounds of my moans mixed with his heady pants fill the air around us.

His body grows rigid when he moves his hand to my throat, wrapping his fingers around my neck in a light choke. He releases a husky growl, and I can feel his cock strengthen and throb inside of me.

"Touch yourself," he orders, and I obey.

Licking my fingers first, I drag them down to my swollen clit and begin rolling them in soft circles. My eyes swim out of focus as our bodies reunite consensually for the first time in months.

His grip constricts around my throat, depleting the amount of air I'm able to take in, but I don't panic as my body finds comfort in the familiarity of his tender force during sex.

"Put it inside of you so you can feel me," he instructs, and I reach down a little further, my neck pushing against his hand as I slip my finger alongside his cock, sinking it in my pussy at the same time he slams inside of me. I pump my finger in rhythm with him. Touching us in this way, feeling the warmth of our mended bodies, slick in arousal, it's too much.

"Oh, God," I mewl loudly as I feel my walls pulse around my finger and his cock.

"Don't ever walk away from me again," he scolds.

"Never."

"You wanna come?"

"Yes," I strain around the cords of my throat that he continues to hold hostage.

And in his feat of control over me, he orders, "Ask permission."

"Please."

My body rises in a fiery storm amidst the nearly freezing temperature.

"Ask!"

"Please," I repeat in a breathless whimper. "I need it."

"Don't do it. Don't defy me," he warns, and when I reach the brink, I clamp my thighs to his hips with as much strength as I can to slow him down.

Holding on to my breath, I fight with everything in me to ward off the orgasm that's about to erupt.

"That's it," he delights in his power over me.

But I can't hold on. Looking in his eyes, I give in, "Can I come? Please, I need it."

"You want it?" he taunts.

"Yes."

"Fuck yourself faster," he instructs, and I do.

I lose all control and begin fingering myself against his cock that swells inside of me, spurring my explosion.

I come.

Hard and wild.

Every muscle in my body tightens in spasms of euphoria, bucking my hips into Declan, greedy to keep the pleasure going. And then I feel his release. He soaks my finger that's still inside of me, fucking myself while he fills me up. I don't stop moving as his cum seeps out of me, running down my hand.

His teeth grit as he keeps his eyes on me the whole time, and I watch him grunt in pleasure through the shatters of light that fracture my vision into a thousand prismatic flakes of pure ecstasy.

When our bodies slow, he lets go of my neck, and my head falls to his shoulder as I allow my body to slack against his. He holds me for a moment while our hearts calm and we catch our breath.

I wish for frozen time, forgotten sins, and never-ending love.

But I know this isn't love on his part. I'm not sure what it is, but I know it isn't that. I want it to be though, so I keep my head tucked into the crook of his neck, scared to move, because I know the moment I do, reality will resume, and his loathing for me will continue.

I wrap my legs tighter around him, wanting to prolong having him nestled inside of me, but my attempt at pushing time away doesn't last. When I feel Declan pulling out of me, I slip my finger out and wrap my hand around his still hardened cock. But he doesn't allow the contact, taking my wrist and forcing me to let go.

With my feet steady on the ground, I watch as he shoves himself back into his pants. He doesn't utter a word, and his eyes are no longer on me. And then he's gone, turning his back and walking away from me, leaving me with my pants down, covered in his cum, in the bitter cold.

Maybe I should feel used and dirty. Maybe I should hate him. Maybe I should give up and be done. But my heart won't let me. Because in the end, I know I'll always want him any way

I can get him.

I'm an epicurean for his pain.

He's my sadist, and I'm his masochist.

We're the reflection of each other's monsters.

# twenty-nine

I HAVEN'T SEEN Declan since he walked away from me, leaving me alone in the cold earlier today. But I haven't been looking for him either. I've spent most of the day roaming around the house, taking in the history, the artwork, and exploring the books in the library.

And now, as I lie on the chaise here in the atrium at the back of the house, I gaze up at the black velvet sky peppered with stars through the glass structure. With civilization sparse and the lack of clouds, you can see every star in the sky. Thousands of them, glittering in the obsidian of night, each holding wishes from foolish people and hopeful children. And I can't help myself when I throw my own up to a few of them tonight.

The house is dark, the only noise coming from the wind as it whistles through the bare trees. And with Declan's constant push and pull, he reminds me of the wind. It blows, wrapping itself around me, but as soon as I feel it, it's gone. It's uncatchable, unstoppable, uncontrollable, and as much as I want Declan, all I'm really doing is chasing the wind.

I turn my head to the shadow of Declan who stands in the open doorway. He wears only his long pajama bottoms that hang low on his hips. A warmth surges through me as I admire the deep cuts of his abs and the defined muscles that rope his broad shoulders and arms. He's so beautiful that it pains me to look at him, but I can't stop myself.

"Are you okay?" he says after a long span of silence.

I nod, but it's a lie. I'm not okay. He fucked me like an animal and left me in the cold. One minute he's caring and sweet, and the next, he's transformed—angry and silent, completely shut down and wanting nothing to do with me. And now, here he is, and I wonder what version I'm going to get.

He walks into the room, and I keep my eyes on him as he moves with ease.

"What are you doing out here? Aren't you freezing?"

"I like the cold," I tell him.

"I know you do."

His words make me want to smile, but I refrain. Moving closer, he then sits next to me on the chaise.

"Where've you been all day?" I ask.

"In my office. I came looking for you because I have to leave tomorrow for London."

"Oh."

"I'll be gone for just a couple of days."

"What's in London?"

"Business," he answers, offering no further insight, so I inquire, "Another hotel?"

"Yes. I recently closed on the land. I'm meeting a few different architects tomorrow that I could potentially hire."

"That's really exciting." And when I sit up, I ask, "When will you be taking me back to Isla's?"

"I won't," he says evenly. "I would prefer if you stayed here where I can keep an eye on you."

"An eye on me?"

He then looks away and nods his head in the direction of a small camera that's attached to one of the steel beams that connects the panes of glass.

"They're in all the rooms," he states, and it makes sense that he would have that level of security in a home this massive.

"Declan," I hesitate, feeling awkward about staying here while he's away.

"I don't trust you at Isla's. Twice I've walked in on you hurting yourself."

"But it feels weird to be here if you're not."

"You don't like it here?" he asks, and I instantly respond, "No, it isn't that. I do like it here. It's just . . ."

"Then you'll stay put until I get back."

"I don't understand you," I whisper weakly.

And with my words, he exhales deeply, turning to look away from me, dropping his elbows to his knees.

"Declan, please. Give me something to work with here. Tell me something to help me understand."

He keeps his head forward, and the tension and struggle is all over him. The muscles in his back flex, and I can see the rise and fall of it as his breathing increases. I know it's a reflection of his building emotions, I just wish I knew what they consisted of.

I want to touch him, but I'm afraid it will piss him off and he'll leave again, so I keep my hands in my lap as I simply watch.

When he finally speaks, his voice cracks, along with my

heart, as he says, "Your voice . . . the moment I heard your voice after I was shot, I did everything I could to fight my eyes open just so I could see you. I'd already read the file. I already knew you had been lying about everything. But a part of me . . ." His voice slips before he takes a hard swallow and looks over his shoulder to face me, continuing, " . . . a part of me wanted to believe I had gotten it all wrong and that it wasn't a lie. But when he said *Go*, and you did so easily, leaving me to die . . ." His face contorts with the pain he's fighting to hide. " . . . No one has ever made me feel so worthless and disposable."

"I was scared." My words tremble, not knowing what else to say. "I was *so* scared."

"I was too, and you left."

I hold my breath as I stare into his eyes that harbor the scars I inflicted. The burden of guilt that consumes me is paralyzing as I watch him expose the fragile pieces he hides so well. He's a man who is nothing but strength and control, but in this quiet moment, he reveals just how broken he is. Broken and hurt, and it's all because of me.

"When I came here," he starts again, "I wanted nothing to do with you. I wanted you dead, but then I found myself outside with a shovel, digging up the flower bushes that surround the house like a fucking maniac losing my mind."

"Why were you digging them up?"

"Because you told me you hated the color purple, and those shrubs bloom purple flowers in the spring."

And that's the dagger that impales my façade of strength. Tears pool in my eyes, and my body restrains to not completely burst into tears.

"My head has been so fucked up because I can't get you out

of it."

"When I was eight years old," I begin, needing to speak because the sound of his voice is too upsetting for me. So, I distract myself and reveal another part of my past. Another denouement for him. "I wound up being moved to a different foster home. The one that would make me believe that monsters were real. I was terrified to the core, and when I was shown the room I'd be sleeping in, all the walls were painted purple." Declan's hand finds my cheek as I continue to talk. "All the years of torture and abuse were stained in purple."

His other hand covers my other cheek, and he holds me. I don't want to lose the touch, but I need more to remedy the sour bile that ripples in my stomach. Mirroring his affections, I cover his cheeks with my hands. A rush of comfort wraps around me as I feel the crackle of his unshaven jaw under my hands. I tug him in and he comes to me willingly, touching his lips to mine. We don't move as we rest peacefully against each other.

The moment fractures when he abruptly pulls away. My hands fall from him as his clutch tightens around my face. I can feel the strain in his hands as their nerves vibrate against my cheeks. His body locks up, the corded muscles banded around his shoulders contract.

"Why?" I breathe. "Why do you turn so cold?"

He grinds his teeth, and his eyes flare disdainfully at me. "Because I don't want to be this close to you. Because I despise you. Because you're a scheming witch."

His tone stabs like an ice pick, and I wonder if it will always be this way with us. If he truly is incapable of allowing himself to ever be vulnerable with me again. Maybe he's destined to be the yearning ache of my heart.

*La douleur exquise.*

"Then why have me here? Why don't you throw me out, tell me you hate me?"

"I do hate you," he sears.

"So why touch me, kiss me, fuck me?"

"They're my sick cravings," he admits. "The hunger grows worse the more I feed it."

And the scheming witch he just accused me of being comes to life. Because with him, I want to be selfish. I want him to be mine and no one else's.

I know I'm narcissistic when I tilt my head to the side, presenting him with the soft skin of my neck, but I don't care when I invite him to take, saying, "Then feast."

"You don't want me this way."

"I want you in *every* way."

His growl is low, deep within his chest, but far from the heart that beats in deadly ways. He's a degenerate of love, but I want him regardless.

He stands and demands, "Strip. And when I return, I want you on your knees, face down on the floor and ass up."

And he just made me feel like I'm a child and taking orders from Carl. I watch as he walks out of the room, and I begin to question if it was a lie. If I really do want him in any way I can get him. Because right now, I want to barrel my fist into his dick for ordering me to expose myself in a humiliating position on this freezing concrete floor.

As much as I want to spit my acrid words at him, I know the derelict I am.

So I do as commanded.

I strip.

And when I walk to the center of the room, I kneel down. With my knees parted, I lower my bare chest onto the ice-cold floor, whimpering against the scathing chill that bites the tender flesh of my nipples. Stretching my arms in front of me, resting my cheek on the floor, I spread my knees wider, lift my ass in the air, and close my eyes while my heart beats wildly.

Presenting myself in degradation, I wait.

And I wait.

And I wait.

Time passes; I'm not sure how long I've been in this position when the muscles in my legs begin to burn and cramp. My body grows colder with each minute lost with no sign of Declan.

Shivers overtake, and when I can't hold on to this position any longer, I let my body fall to the side. Lying here naked and mortified, I finally blink out the tears as I pull my knees into my chest and quietly weep.

*Was this his plan? Was this a punishment? To shame me, knowing he wasn't going to come back for me?*

My body turns numb after a while, making it difficult to move my muscles when I attempt to pick myself up off the ground. Slowly, I pull my clothes back on while I vacillate between loneliness, resentment, sadness, and anger. All of it swarms through me, taking my energy, and depleting me to the point where I just want to disappear.

Wrapping the blanket around me, I walk into the kitchen to get a drink, and when I do, I notice a car down at the gate on the intercom monitor. The windows are darkly tinted, so that when I move closer to the black and white screen on the wall, I can't make out the person who's driving. But then the car starts to back up, and when it drives away, I begin to wonder about the life

Declan has here in Scotland and the people he surrounds himself with, if any at all. I only know about Lachlan—that's it. I wonder if he's as alone as he appears to be, and who's lurking at the gate in the middle of the night.

I don't even stop to peek in his room as I head to bed. I'm too embarrassed.

*Did he ever come back to the atrium and see me exposing my body for him?*

I shake the thought away, and when I go into the bathroom, I see he's set the bottle of pills the doctor prescribed me on the sink. I take a pill out and stare at it, wondering if I'm just like her, just like the woman who never wanted me. I wonder who the hell I am. I fear I'll never know if I stay here in this tug of war with the man who hates me.

Flicking the pill from my fingertips, it plops into the toilet water. I know if I leave here and go back to the States, I won't want to do it alone. I need Pike. I'll probably always need him because he's still all I have, and if I take that pill, I risk losing him. And I can't lose him.

"Get out," I seethe when I walk back into the bedroom and see Declan.

"I couldn't do it," he says. "I knew if I went back to you, I'd fuck you and hurt you because I want to punish you. I wouldn't have been able to resist taking all this anger I have out on you."

"I can't do this, Declan," I say in defeat. "I want to. I want to be strong enough because I don't ever want to be without you. But I'm starting to think that being here with you might just hurt worse than not being with you at all."

He walks over and sits on the edge of the bed, dropping his head.

"There too much pain in me. There's so much rage and hate, and I don't know how to get rid of it," I tell him. "I've been fighting my whole life trying to rid myself of these feelings that won't ever go away." I move to sit across the room from him in one of the chairs. "I thought getting rid of Bennett would be what I've been needing. That somehow I would feel better about this life, but . . ." I begin to cry, "I don't feel better. Nothing feels better. And then I killed my brother, and I'm not entirely sure why, but I did, and I carry that with me every day. I plot revenge and I kill and I fight and I still hate this life. I still hurt and it won't go away."

I don't even realize my eyes are closed and I'm bent over sobbing out my words until I feel his hands on my knees. I open my eyes to see him kneeling in front of me.

"But this hurts too," I add. "Being here with you hurts me, and as much as I want to hate you for all the ways you've been humiliating me and punishing me, I'm scared to leave. I'm scared I'll never see you again."

"Was Pike the only one?"

"What?" I question, confused as to what he's asking.

"You said you kill. Was he the only one?"

I hesitantly shake my head and shock streaks his face.

"How many?"

Closing my eyes, I confess, "Three."

"Jesus Christ," he mutters in disbelief. "Who else?"

"My foster parents," I say when I look back down at him, and his shoulders lax a little.

His hands slide past my knees and grip my thighs with his question, "What happened?"

"Pike and I ran away together, and shortly after, we returned

233

one night with a friend of his, and . . ."

"I want to know everything," he demands harshly. "I want to know how those fuckers died."

"Pike and his friend, Matt, they tied them to the bed and dumped a couple containers of gasoline on them," I say. "I remember standing there, watching them scream and flail around, trying to break free. Matt handed me the match like it was a gift, wrapped in the most delicate silk bow, and it was. When I struck that match and threw it on that bed, it was the greatest gift anyone had ever given me," I cry. "Those sick fucks destroyed every piece of me. But here's the really sick part, as happy as it made me to kill them, it still wasn't enough. It's never enough, Declan, because I'm still so alone. I still feel worthless and disgusting, and all I ever wanted was the one thing Bennett took away from me. I miss my dad."

Declan pulls me out of the chair and onto the floor with him as I lose myself to the emotions I'm so used to caging up. He cradles me in his arms, gathering me up completely, and pressing me tightly against him.

"I miss him so much. It hurts so bad. But then I met you. And it took me a while to see it, to see how I felt about you because I'd never experienced that feeling before. I'd never loved like I did with you, never opened myself up like that. And when I look at you, I see parts of my dad in you. The way you'd comfort me and love me. No one has ever given me that."

"What about Pike?"

"He was my brother. It was different. With you, I finally felt like I had a home. But I knew I had destroyed our love from the beginning. I knew we never had a chance."

"But that didn't stop you."

"I was selfish. I knew that no amount of time with you would suffice to make it easier for me to walk away."

His eyes only take a second to scorn. The flip is instant, like it always is with him, and I know what set him off when he spews, "But you did walk away."

I don't know what else to say, so I plead for penance in the absence of words. And as we sit, his touch on me fades as his animosity breeds. It stirs in the reticence between us, and I know our expiration date is near.

The awareness that we have this death sentence over us makes me want to do two things, but I don't know which one to choose.

Do I run away, or do I stay and watch us die a painful death?

# thirty

I'VE BEEN DRIVING *around the countryside trying to find the house the old lady at the Water Lily told me about. I was able to track Nina down once I found out she was going by Elizabeth Archer again. Made my life a little easier, and when I found out where she was staying, I was grateful when the owner was forthcoming about where I could find her. She never doubted me when I lied and told her I was Elizabeth's uncle and had been trying to get in contact with her.*

*I had to laugh to myself because when Bennett had me follow her not so long ago, she was the easiest little thing to trace. And now, exactly as I thought, she's with the same bastard she was with back in Chicago.*

*But now, I've wasted the light of day because this fucking town isn't very considerate with street signs. I round yet another bend in the road with no houses in sight. I slow down, peering out the window, when my headlights catch a small plaque on a stone wall, and it's then I see gates. Slowing more, the sign reads what I was told it would: Brunswickhill.*

*"Checkmate," I mutter under my breath as I kill the headlights and*

*pull up to the gate.*

*Stepping out of the car, I look up the steep hill, but can't see anything in the dark. No lights. Nothing.*

*"Fuck."*

*Getting back behind the wheel, I decide to just call it a night. I know that beyond this gate, they are more than likely here. For now, I'm tired as shit, but at least I have my stakeout position. And knowing there's a manhunt back in Illinois, my next steps need to be quick and deadly.*

# thirty-one

I CAN STILL feel the vibrations that ricocheted though my bones with each gunshot. The two that Pike fired into Declan's chest, and the single blast from the gun I held that took my brother from me. The sound is something I'll never forget. A bang so loud, it knocks your shoulders back, deafening and startling. And when the mark is hit, the ice your heartless heart pumps fills your veins, and you know you'll never be the same again.

Forever changed.

Forever a monster.

Each bullet leaves a soot stain on your soul that you can't get rid of, and you never forget the taste of burnt gunpowder on the back of your tongue. Each life you take brands you for eternity.

I hoped it wouldn't. I hoped the aftereffects would wither away as the echoes did. But if there's one thing I've learned in this life, it's the realization that echoes live forever. I may no longer hear the screaming demons of my past, but they do indeed continue to scream. It's a reminder that you're never truly free.

I don't know where I'm going or what I'm doing, but I don't think this is the place for me. I've been lost in my head all morning. Declan left at sunrise for the airport. When he did, I needed to find comfort and realized I left my doll behind.

I called Isla to tell her I would be stopping by to collect the remainder of my belongings. Since he took the SUV, I take his Mercedes roadster to Isla's.

As I pull up to the charming house that I've stayed at since my arrival several weeks ago, I know, that as much as it hurts, there's nothing here for me in Scotland. I never knew what it was I was looking for when I came here. The last thing I thought I would find was Declan alive, but I did. And maybe that's gift enough, to know he'll go on and that his life wasn't sacrificed because of my deceit.

The key is under the ceramic planter right where Isla said she would leave it. I walk in, and even though I've only been at Declan's for a couple of days, it feels much longer. But then again, each day with him is filled with insurmountable emotions and conversations. It's taken a toll on me, having to face my past and confess the truths I've hidden for so long. The hardest is having to see the pain Declan battles inside of himself—pain that was birthed because of me. I own it; he endures it.

I head upstairs, and after finding my doll, I begin to pack my things and focus on keeping the dread at bay. I wish I had direction, I wish I knew what I'm doing and where I'm going. It's a heavy emotion to carry, to know how alone I really am. But I fight to keep myself numb to all the questions there are no answers for.

I move faster the more my thoughts wander. Flashbacks of what's occurred in this room begin to gnaw, and when I walk over to the bed to grab my phone that I had left behind, I freeze. Below the window, parked in the street, is the same car I saw on Declan's gate monitor last night. Or at least I think it is. So many of the cars here are the same, so I can't be certain, but something in my gut sparks the paranoia.

The car is directly under my view, so all I see is the roof. Hopping off the bed, I rush downstairs, lock the front door, and make my way through the house to see if I can get a better view. Passing the windows, I find myself walking into a room I've never been in before—Isla's room. Pushing the door open, the room is dark with the heavy drapes shut. Barely parting the curtains with my fingers, I peek out, but the car's gone. The street out front is now vacant, aside from my car.

I open the drapes further to get a better look, and sure enough, the car is gone. Shaking my head, I release a pathetic sigh.

*You're losing your mind, Elizabeth.*

I take in a calming breath, retiring my batty thoughts that have no basis. I turn my back to the window and close my eyes as I laugh at myself. When I open them back up, I take in Isla's room. Scanning around, I walk over to her nightstand to look at the book resting on top. I'm running my fingers along the cover of *Madame Bovary* when I notice a collection of photos on the mantle above the fireplace. I move slowly along, looking at each picture.

"Oh my God."

Picking up the tarnished silver frame, I hold it close as I look in disbelief. I wonder if this is the foolish paranoia that remains from the car outside or if this is exactly what my eyes believe it to be.

*How did she get this? Why does she have a picture of him?*

He's younger than what I've ever seen him, a little boy, but the eyes are irrefutable. There's no mistaking what I know so well.

It's him.

But why?

The doorbell rings, startling me, and I drop the frame, cracking the glass as it lands on the wooden floor.

"Shit."

Scrambling, I pick up the small frame and tuck it in the back of my pants as I run to see who's at the front door.

Before I make it, there's a loud knocking.

"Elizabeth? You in there?"

*Lachlan?*

Looking out the window, I see it's him.

"What are you doing here?" I question when I open the door.

"Declan asked that I check in on you, and when no one answered my gate call at his home, I came here."

"He's been gone only a few hours. What trouble could I possibly have gotten myself into in such a short period of time?" I tease, but the cool metal frame in my pants is evidence I smirk at.

"What's so funny?"

"You men need hobbies," I quip as I turn my back and walk towards the stairs.

"I've been worried."

"Have you now?"

"Declan told me you had a hard time with the file," he says.

Embarrassment rouses, but I shut it down quickly. "I'd prefer to never discuss that issue again."

e.k. blair

"Of course. My apologies."

"Look, I appreciate you checking in on me, but if you don't mind, I'm just packing the rest of my things to take back to Declan's."

"Are you sure everything's okay?" he presses as if he's privy to something he believes me to be aware of.

Call it intuition, but everything about today has got me on high alert for some unsettling reason.

"Yes, everything is just fine," I say smoothly with a light smile to appease him. "The past couple days have been taxing, as I'm sure you can understand."

He nods, taking my directive to not mention the file.

"You can report back to your boss that the kid in question is taking good care of herself."

I smile at my words, and he laughs in return, agreeing, "Will do."

He turns to leave, but before he shuts the door behind him, he says, "By the way, I've tried calling you a couple times . . ."

"I left my phone here. No one calls me on it, but now that I know I have a babysitter, I'll be sure to charge it up for you," I joke.

He shakes his head at me with a smile and then leaves. I go to the door and lock it behind him before returning to my room. Tossing the rest of my things in my suitcase, I take the photo out of the frame and shove it in my bag. I don't know why she has this picture, but I want it for myself.

When my luggage is loaded into the car, I head back to Brunswickhill after returning the key to the planter. A part of me wants to call Declan to ask why he sent Lachlan to check in on me. He says he hates me, but then I see these hints of the man I

242

knew back in Chicago. The man who was furious if I was more than a minute late. The man who controlled and dominated to ease his worry. But I won't call him because I never know what it is about me that's going to trigger him to push me away.

"What the hell?" I murmur under my breath when I round the bend in the road and see the same car that was at Isla's now sitting outside of Declan's gate.

Slowing the Mercedes, I stop and wait since the other car is blocking my way. My curiosity is piqued, wondering if Declan is still having me followed, and if so, why they are being so blatant about it.

Growing impatient, I honk my horn, and when I do, the driver's door opens. I watch a shiny, black loafer step out onto the street, and a thousand penetrating emotions shoot off inside of me.

*What the fuck is he doing here?*

Nerves wrack me as I fist the steering wheel tightly in my hands. I watch him approach my car, and for a split second, I consider running him over. But truth is, I have no idea why he's even here.

So without wasting another second, I fall back into the character I know so well and hide myself in Nina's mask. Righting my spine, I forget all about Elizabeth, and open the door.

"How quickly you move on," he taunts as I stand before him.

"Nice to see you too, Richard."

"I doubt you mean that, but thanks anyway."

"What are you doing here in Scotland?"

"I could ask you the same, but I think it's pretty clear."

His words irk me as always, and I bite my response, "Cut the shit, Richard. Tell me why you flew halfway around the world."

His face flattens in a no-nonsense expression when he states, "We need to talk."

"About what?"

"Your husband."

As far as I know, Richard knows nothing about the lies and deception. He only knows me as Nina, Bennett's wife, and now widow. He's been Bennett's business partner from the very beginning, and the two of them were close. Not close enough though because I know Richard is clueless to the fact that Bennett fucked his precious little wife and that the baby Richard believes to be his is, in fact, just a pathetic bastard.

"I haven't been contacted about anything concerning the investigation," I tell him. "Are there any new developments?"

His eyes narrow, and I don't trust the hinting grin on his face. "Don't you think it's a little hard to be in the loop of information when you're operating on a cheap, disposable phone?"

My poker face is strong, but my body numbs, wondering how he knows about my untraceable phone. My words deflect my panic as I say, "Always butting your nose in where it never belongs, aren't you?"

"Like I said, we need to talk."

"Then talk."

"Inside," he states firmly.

"Why not here?"

He grows irritated, fuming loudly, "Because it's fucking cold and my balls don't like it."

He's so damn disgusting.

I hesitate on taking him inside Declan's home, but figure it's safer up there with all the cameras than down here on the street.

"Fine."

He follows me through the gate and up to the house. As I lead him in and to the library, he remarks, "You don't ever slum it, do you?"

"Is there a point to the nonsense you spew?" I sit across from him, and when he takes a seat, I say, "So what is it? What is so important that you needed to travel all this way?"

He leans forward and takes a moment before looking over at me, revealing, "I know who you are."

"Oh yeah, and who's that?"

"No use in playing coy because I know your dirty, little secrets."

His words imply threats, and I don't take well to his evasiveness. "Cut the shit and get to your point."

"He knew. Bennett had me following you when he suspected you were fucking around on him."

"It was you?"

He nods as he leans back, getting much too comfortable for my liking. I think back to the hospital, and I knew the voice sounded familiar when he told Bennett who I really was, but I couldn't pinpoint it with all the drugs they had me on.

"Needless to say, I wasn't surprised when I discovered your affair," he says condescendingly. "What *did* surprise me was when I found out you were nothing but runaway street trash."

"What's your point, Richard?"

"Why did you marry him?"

"Because I loved him," I lie. "Nothing wrong with reinventing yourself to get a fresh start in life."

"Except when the person you reinvented yourself for winds up dead."

"You're an asshole," I sling at him in mock disgust.

"I just have one question . . . who did it? Who did you have off him?"

"I don't know what you're talking about."

"How convenient, but I don't think the cops would buy it if I turned over all the information I have on you."

"You're so cute," I sneer, pissing him off. "You think your threats have an effect on me? Why don't you just tell me what you're after and stop wasting my time."

"No bullshit, cut to the chase?"

"Please."

In all seriousness, he tells me, "I need money." I laugh, and he snaps, "What the fuck is so funny?"

"*You.*" I sit back, cross my legs, and ask, "Why on earth would you be coming to *me,* of all people, for money?"

"Because I trust you to keep that pretty little mouth of yours shut if anyone were to come asking questions."

"What do you need money for?"

"You haven't been watching the news?"

"I've been a little preoccupied to be keeping up with American news."

He shakes his head with an arrogant smirk, and I cross my arms in irritation. "Enlighten me. Please."

"Linq Incorporated is under investigation. I thought you'd know that by now since your lover's father has been sitting in jail for his part in the fraud."

"What?" I question, confused as to what the hell Cal has to do with my husband's business and what was fraudulent about the company. "What fraud?"

"The company's just a front for washing money."

"Money from what?"

Richard then stands and walks across the room. When he's right in front of me, I freeze as he reaches his hand inside his suit jacket. "Guns," he states as he pulls out his own and aims it at me.

Adrenaline flushes through my system as I stare into the barrel of the pistol that's marked me as its target. I try to appear calm, but my staggering breaths are my tell—I'm scared.

"I want what was left to you in Bennett's will. You give me that and I'll disappear. You'll never hear from me again."

"I don't . . . He didn't . . ." I stutter over my words. "I didn't get everything."

"You're lying to me. I know you're the sole heir."

Shaking my head, I try to explain, "I thought I was, but . . . he changed it before he died. I didn't know until I met with the attorney."

He scowls, takes another step closer, and presses the cold steel to my forehead. I gasp in fear, clutching the arms of the chair as my heart beats in erratic terror.

My voice is pitchy when I frantically explain, "Look, if what y-your wanting is m-money to flee, I-I don't have that much for you. I mean . . . it wouldn't be enough."

"Then where is it?"

The desperation in his eyes makes me fear what he would do if I told him the truth. He'd most likely lose his shit and pull that trigger if he knew about his son being Bennett's. But beyond that, what the hell was Bennett doing with his company? Did he even know? My mind warps in confusion, overwhelmed with too many questions, that I begin to lose focus.

"Where is it?" he shouts, scaring the shit out of me with his murderous glare.

The tip of the gun shakes against my head as I look up into his furiously crazed eyes, and I begin trembling. My whole body jittery in fear.

"I-I don't know."

*WHACK!*

I scream in heated pain as I fall out of my chair and onto the floor. My hand cups the side of my head where he just pummeled his gun. The blunt force sparking a fire of light in my vision as I fight against the sharp agony that pierces through my skull.

He stands over me, pointing the gun at my face, and I wail, "Okay! Okay!" I throw my hands up in surrender.

"Stop fucking around with me!"

"I'm not!"

"Where is it?"

"It's in a trust," I reveal. "He put it in a trust I don't have access to."

Richard kneels down to one knee, hovering over me, gritting between clenched teeth, "Whose trust?"

With nerves crashing, I tell him, "A trust for his son."

"You lying cunt."

"Fuck you. It's the truth," I lash out when my anger grows at his degrading words. My emotions get away from me as my head spins in waves of turbulence. As I stare up at this man I've loathed for years, I see the wretchedness and desperation in his eyes, and I feel a little deranged as I begin to laugh at him.

"What the fuck are you laughing at?"

"He played us both," I say as my laughter intensifies.

"What are you talking about?"

"Bennett," I tell him.

"He doesn't have a son. I've known Bennett since he was a

kid. I know everything about him, so I don't know what the fuck you're talking about."

"No?" I question in mockery. "Tell me something then," I start, and pleasure blooms inside of me to be the one to deliver the truth to him. I smile and continue, "How deeply have you looked into Alexander's eyes?"

I watch as his face contorts and add, "Because if you look deep enough, you'll see Bennett staring back at you."

And when realization splays across his face, he takes a step back in shock. I know Richard adores his son. Probably more than he does his wife. So to be the one to stab this dagger of truth through his heart delights me.

I move to stand, and when I do, the giggle that slips from my lips is maniacal as I gloat, "That's right, Richard. Your precious little wife fucked my husband and they had a baby together."

"You're full of shit!"

"Bennett left everything to him. But if you think you can get the money, you're wrong. You see, Bennett was smart enough to not assign Jacqueline as the executor. He assigned his attorney."

His nostrils flare, and I lose myself in utter delirium as I continue to laugh at every fucked up part of this crazy story. The room spins around me, a blurry realm of colors and shadows, as my hearing tunnels in the reverberations of my own laughter.

"Fuck you!" his voice cuts through, but only for a moment before he swings his arm around. It all happens in a flash of slow motion, but too quick for me to stop, as he drives the gun with a force that parallels his anger into my head, knocking me off my feet.

My head clips the corner of an end table before smashing against the floor.

Light flashes behind my eyelids.

Sparks.

Diamond dust.

Clouds.

Blackness.

# thirty-two

"MMMMM!" I SCREAM from my throat behind the tape over my mouth.

My heart crashes so hard it beats in my head. Sheer panic punctures every organ inside of me, flooding my body in pure fear as I thrash around in the darkness. I jerk and kick, but my wrists are bound behind my back and my ankles are tied together in duct tape.

"MMMMM!" I force my voice as loud as I can as it scratches through my strained cords. I know no one can hear me, but I don't care.

Twisting my hands is useless against the tape that's secured in a tight restraint. Frustration boils over, pricking in tingles along my palms, and I lose control. I release another worthless, muffled scream, squinting my eyes in an attempt to amplify the sound as I flail my body around like a maniac in the trunk of the car I've woken to.

Time wisps past me as the miles collect and my panic dissolves. My body slacks, absorbing the bumps in the road as I'm being taken into the labyrinth of Richard's desperation.

I knew better than to push him over the edge like I did, but I lost it. I was outside of my head and taking joy from my lashings. But now those lashings have me tied up in the trunk of his car, and I have no way to escape.

I fill the drive trying to figure out what the hell Bennett's company was being used as a front for. Richard said guns, but in what capacity? All I can think about is my father's business. He trafficked guns; is it possible that's what Linq is a cover for? Another trafficking scheme? Surely not. But if so, is it in any way linked to my dad? My thoughts aren't logical. I mean, maybe it's coincidental.

Fuck, what's going on? Did Bennett know? I find it so hard to believe that he did. He was such a straight-edge guy, built out of strong values and always following the rules. It was sickening to watch, but that was the core of Bennett.

And how the hell was Cal involved? Maybe Bennett did know. After all, Bennett and Cal worked in a few business deals together through the years. Does Declan know about his dad? God, he seemed like such an honest guy as well, but maybe he knew.

Irritation swarms the more I think and question, but what's the use? I'm not going to dissect this on my own.

My body alerts as I feel the car slow and then come to a stop. My pulse quickens when I hear the door slam shut.

Are we in a public place? Are people around? Do I risk making noise?

Taking in slow, quiet breaths, I focus on what's going on outside, but I hear nothing. Every muscle in my body is tensed up as I wait, but nothing happens. Time continues to pass, and eventually, I feel myself drifting to sleep. I struggle to stay awake as my eyes fall shut.

I DON'T KNOW how long I've been out when I feel the car halt to a sudden stop. I wonder how far we've traveled. I hear the door shut, and it's only seconds until the trunk pops open.

Light burns my eyes, and I flinch away as Richard's hands grab on to me, yanking me out of the car. I don't even think to take in my surroundings, simply fighting against his hold, jerking my body around.

With his hands on my arms, he slams me against a solid rock wall. He knocks the wind out of me, and I gasp desperately through my nose while my throat strangles against my depleted lungs. Hunched over, I panic and choke when he grabs my hair and pulls my head up. Hairs rip from my scalp as a steel blade meets my cheek.

My eyes widen in horror as my breath finally catches. Whimpering, I close my eyes as he presses the blade into my soft flesh. My cry is muffled by the tape that still covers my mouth when I feel the pop of my skin as he slices me open.

He then presses the flat of the blade to the tape that covers my lips, saying, "If you think I have limits, you're wrong."

Bending down, he uses the knife to cut the duct tape around my ankles, but leaves my wrists bound. The blood from my cheek drips from my jaw, landing on my top.

"Walk," he commands, grabbing my arm and leading me down an alleyway.

I look around, quickly attempting to figure out where we are, but it's too dark, and the alley is too narrow. He leads me down a flight of steps to an underground area, and I remember Lachlan telling me about the vaults under the city. He told me some of them now serve as clubs or restaurants, some for ghost tours, but others simply remain empty. And there's no doubt that's where he's taking me as he moves me through a stone tunnel, damp with water, and into a fairly large room.

Taking in my surroundings, I can tell this used to be used for a business of sorts. There's electricity, built-in counters along one of the walls, a desk, and a couple of chairs. I watch as Richard walks over to the desk and lays his gun down. When he returns to me, he rips off the tape covering my mouth, and my eyes prick with tears against the sting.

"Sit down," he tells me, and I obey.

"What do you think you're doing?" I ask.

"You're all I've got. I need you to help me disappear."

"From what?"

"If the cops find me, I'll spend the rest of my years in prison."

And he's right. Richard is in his late fifties. I don't know the crimes he's committed, but the fact that he's just kidnapped me tells me he's in deep shit.

"But I told you, I don't have what you're looking for," I tell him.

"You may not, but someone who loves you does."

"Who?"

"Declan McKinnon."

I shake my head, saying, "You're wrong. He doesn't love me. He hates me."

"Yet you're living with him? I think you're lying to me."

"I'm not. You have to believe me. He doesn't love me. He keeps me there to punish me."

"Punish you for what?" he questions, but I bite my tongue, not sure how much to say.

I won't incriminate Declan, but do I incriminate myself? If I do, I run the risk of going to jail myself. So, I give him what he already knows from following me back in Chicago, and say, "For the fact that I wouldn't leave Bennett for him."

I tell the lie, but I hate it because Declan is worth so much more than anyone else on this planet.

Richard chuckles in irritation. "I don't know exactly what you were doing with Bennett, but I'm smart enough to know, *Elizabeth Archer*, that you didn't love him. So what was it about for you? What were you after? Money?"

I don't respond to him as he stares down at me. After a moment, he grabs a chair, pulling it in front of me, and takes a seat. He leans in towards me, and my head throbs in beats of aching heat from where he pistol-whipped me.

His eyes bore into me as a sly smirk creeps across his lips. His voice is low when he asks, "Or does it all have something to do with your father?"

My body pricks in chills at the mention of my dad. I tense around my hollowed chest, and wonder why he would even mention my father.

*What does he know?*

I don't say a word out of utter terror that I've gotten myself mixed up with the wrong people when I started this fucked up game. I've always been in control when it came to my charade in Bennett's life. But now all that control is gone and in the hands of this bastard, and that has me scared beyond belief. I pretend to be strong, but the reality of this situation has all confidence lost. I've been kidnapped and I don't have the first clue how to get myself out of this.

"I don't know what you want from me," I finally say, my voice coming out weakly. "What I told you about Declan was the truth. He hates me; he won't care if you hurt me."

"Then you need to find a way to make him care," he sneers before backhanding me so hard I fall out of the chair and onto the floor.

My vision fades for a moment when my head hits the concrete, and my urge to attack fumes inside, but I'm bound and useless.

"There isn't anything I wouldn't do for my family," he tells me and then steps away.

Staring up at him, my frustration multiplies, and since I can't knock the shit out of him, I attack with my words.

"Even with Bennett's dick inside your wife? Would you have done anything for her in that moment?"

"Your lies are humorous."

I don't acknowledge his denial as I continue antagonizing him, spitting my words, "Did you enjoy fucking her when my husband's cum was still inside her filthy pussy?"

He stomps back over to me, and I laugh to just piss him off even more. He grabs my hair, and immediately shuts me up when he balls his fist and punches the side of my face. Everything turns bright white, and my mouth fills with blood from where my teeth puncture the inside of my cheek.

Writhing in agony, I groan in exploding pain from my head. My skull thumps hard, and I can't open my eyes because it hurts too much. And the next thing I know, he covers my mouth again with tape.

The pain in my head increases as time passes. I've got my body pressed against the wall as I continue to lie here, and I wish he would just knock me unconscious to put me out of my misery.

When Richard walks out of the room and into the corridor, I make an attempt to break the tape as I twist my wrists, but it's not budging. I roll off my side and onto my stomach before I start grazing the side of my face along the floor. When I start to feel the corner of the tape pull away from my mouth, I press my face down harder, rolling it to try and catch more of the tape to pull it off. Once I feel the tape peel off the corner of my lips, I use my tongue to push it off, and when I can move my mouth and speak, I wait for Richard to return.

I can hear him talking to someone on the phone, but I can't make out what's being said. After a while, he returns, and I keep my voice as free from hostility as I can when I say, "It's true."

His eyes meet mine, and I add, "They did a DNA test that Bennett kept in his safety deposit box. Bennett left him everything. I couldn't believe it when I found out, but it's true."

"Tit for tat?" he says, confusing me.

"What does that mean?"

He then pulls his chair around to me and sits as I lie here, staring up at him.

"You hurt me, I hurt you."

My brows pinch together, not understanding his riddled words.

He continues, "I've got nothing to lose, and unless I get my money, you're not walking out of here alive. And from what I remember of your father, he wasn't much of a fighter, so I have a feeling your days are numbered as his were."

"Fuck you!" I snarl at him for speaking shit about my dad. "You don't know what you're talking about."

He laughs at me, revealing, "I know more than you think, little girl. You see, I knew your father."

My chest palpitates anxiously when he says this, and a thousand questions flood.

"Steve and I go way back."

I don't want to believe Richard had anything to do with my dad, or that my dad had anything to do with him. But . . . if he were still alive, he'd be right around Richard's age, so there's possibility in what he claims. But how?

"When Bennett had me following you, I started digging into your past. When all the pieces came together, I couldn't believe the Archer girl had been right in front of my face for years. I should've known you'd turn to pulling cons. At first, I thought I was your target when I was convinced you knew who I was. But when I started thinking back, I realized you didn't. I knew then it was Bennett you were after. But I still don't know why."

"Why would I be after you?" I question in terror, wondering who this guy really is.

"Maybe you blamed me for what happened."

"Tell me how you knew my dad."

"There's a lot I can teach you, you know? You were pretty good at fooling Bennett for all those years, but whatever it was you were trying to do, you moved too slowly and didn't properly assess the people you were surrounding yourself with."

"Tell me," I demand as I struggle to keep my tears back because just talking about my dad has me falling apart. He's my weakness, my softest part, and now I fear Richard has something to do with me losing him. "Tell me!"

"Call Declan."

"What? I don't have his number."

"Then we wait," he says. "I know he's in London and will be returning tomorrow. You'll call his landline then."

"Tell me how you know my father, Richard. You want to hurt me? Is that what you want? Then just tell me, because anything you have to say about him will surely be a dagger."

"That's too easy."

Richard then leaves me to be as he moves to the other side of the room and sits. I struggle to get comfortable with my hands still taped together. I lie on the cold concrete and rest my cut cheek to the ground to help soothe the ache that pulses through the gash. My head weighs heavy in an excruciating headache, and I close my eyes to drown out the cheap fluorescent lighting, but the buzzing from the bulbs keeps me agitated.

Hours pass as I drift in and out, and when the fog from all the high-strung emotions begins to clear, I'm finally able to focus. I run through everything Richard has told me, trying to figure out what the fuck is going on, when I remember his claim.

*Guns.*

# thirty-three
## (DECLAN)

MY MEETINGS HAVE been long, sitting around and listening to several architectural firms make their presentations and going over the bids for the job. This will be another boutique hotel that will cater to wealth, and above all, privacy. Lotus was my first solo venture, and it has proven to be a success in the few months it's been open. We maintain an exclusive clientele, which the city of Chicago was in desperate need of. It's full service in every luxury accommodation, selective on who's approved to book a room, and the London property will be the same.

I ring the house as I head back to the hotel for some much needed sleep. It's late, and I'm at my end.

It feels strange to have Elizabeth in my home, as if she's more than just a houseguest. She has me on mental overload. There are times I see her and I want to smash her face against a wall because my anger is too much to contain. And then there are times I look at her and I wish it could be like before with us. In those moments, I want to touch her and inhale her soft scent. I want to feel her, lick her, taste her, fuck her. I want it all, but my heart refuses to get too close to her.

She's the devil's angel.

The moment I start crossing lines, I shut down. It's not even something I consciously realize I'm doing, it just happens. One moment, I want my tongue tasting her sweet mouth, and the next, I want to rip more of her hair out.

Fucking her outside against my house yesterday was a twisted delight I selfishly indulged in. When I saw her from my office window, sitting on the ground, I saw someone so broken that I doubted her malice. In that moment, I let my guard down and got tangled up in the moment. And nothing can deny the solace that consumed me when I sunk my cock inside of her sweet pussy. Having her snug around me, Jesus, no woman has ever felt as good as her. But her warmth and comfort are merely an illusion. She's a magician's ruse that I stupidly fall for repeatedly.

She's evil and duplicitous, and yet a part of me wants her—a very disturbed part of me. Because no one in their right mind would want anything to do with the widow who injects her poison with self-serving motivations. For some reason, in knowing what a con she is, I don't want her to leave. A part of me feels sorry for her. I pity her. I've never seen a person at a lower point than she is at right now. This has to be her rock bottom because I'd hate to see what would happen if she got any lower.

Her body is branded in self-inflicted abuse. She craves the moment that she can hurt herself. I know Elizabeth is a sick woman who needs help, and the dark part of my soul wants to be the one to offer it. It's screwed up, because I also want to punish her.

When I told her to strip down last night, my plan was to humiliate her by having her perched on the ground as I had instructed. I left her to grab some rope because I had every intention of punishing her. I was walking around the house with a hard-on just thinking about it. My mind was consumed with visions of her tied up while I slapped her pussy and tits until they welted up red, picturing my cock shoved down her throat, gagging her, just so I could see tears fall down her rosy cheeks.

Even now that I know about all that she endured as a little girl at the hands of her foster dad, I still wanted to debase her like that. It's wrong; I know it, which is why I didn't return to her. I couldn't allow myself the pleasure that would just solidify the savage I fear I am—the savage she groomed me to be. But I hurt her anyway, and when I went to her room and saw the mortified look on her face, I hated myself in that moment.

There's no answer when I call, so I hang up and dial my home again.

Nothing.

She's probably outside.

I pull up the security app on my phone to log into my home system. Once it's connected, I tap on each camera to view the rooms in the house. From the kitchen to the library, atrium, bedrooms, dining room, office, roof . . . nothing. I then flip over to the outdoor cameras and check the grotto, backyard, and various cameras that overlook most of the grounds. No sign of anyone. When I tap to view the garage, I notice my Mercedes roadster is missing, which explains why she's nowhere to be seen. Irritation scathes me, not knowing what she's up to or where she is.

I hate not knowing details, especially when it comes to her. I know I'm controlling and overbearing, but it's the only way I know how to function without losing my shit.

She no longer has her old cell phone, and I haven't seen a new one, so I don't have a way of contacting her.

I decide to call Lachlan. I told him to stop following her because I didn't like how involved he was getting in her life, but I swallow my pride, and call him anyway.

"McKinnon, how did the meetings go?" he says when he answers.

"Good," I snip. "Look, I'm trying to get ahold of Elizabeth, but she isn't at home and I don't have a cell number for her."

As soon as I have her number, I hang up and dial it.

# (ELIZABETH)

A SUBTLE VIBRATION is all it takes to rouse me from my restless exhaustion. My mouth tastes metallic from the blood I consumed when Richard punched my face. I shift off my side and onto my back. The arm I've been lying on tingles and aches painfully. Looking across the room, I see Richard slumped back in a chair with his eyes closed and a hand on his gun.

My body alerts when the vibrations return. My thoughts are hard to grab on to with the multiple strikes to my head and the emotional rollercoaster I've been on since Richard appeared in front of Declan's home. I focus on the faint buzzing sound, and my stomach clenches when I remember my cell phone. My body went numb a while ago, so it's hard to pinpoint, but I know I shoved the phone in the pocket of my pants.

I look back to Richard; his eyes are still closed. My heart begins to race as I shimmy to try and move my arms as quietly as I can. With my eyes locked on Richard, I make attempt after attempt, but it's no use. I can't get my hands to my pocket. I know it's Lachlan calling me because he's the only one I ever gave that number to.

"Richard," I call out to wake him up when I get an idea. "Richard."

"What the hell do you want?" he says on a groggy voice when he opens his eyes.

"I have to go to the bathroom."

"Hold it," he snaps and closes his eyes again.

"I can't, but I have no issues peeing myself if you don't have any issues smelling it," I lash back.

He breathes out in frustration and walks over to me, grabbing my arm and picking me up off the floor. Walking me down one of the corridors, we stop in front of a door.

"Hurry," he demands, and I look at him, reminding, "My wrists."

With a long, distrusting glare, he then says, "Turn around," and I do.

He takes his knife out, and when he slices through the tape, finally releasing my hands, the phone begins to vibrate, and fear crashes inside of me, locking my body up. When I turn to look at Richard, I can tell he hears the phone by the look on his face.

He knowingly cocks his head to the side, and in a moment of fright, I lurch forward and bolt. I'm not even allowed one second of attempted freedom as he immediately catches his arm around my waist, pulling me back.

I fight against him, but the moment his fingers latch around my neck, I freeze. His hand pats my pockets, and he pulls out the cheap disposable phone I've been using since I arrived here in Scotland. He flips it open and holds it out in front of my face while he has me in his chokehold with my back pinned against his chest. He then selects the last number that called and clicks it.

Putting it on speakerphone, he threatens, "Say one word and I'll make you regret feeling like you ever had a chance of one-upping me."

And then the ringing stops when the call is connected. I hold my breath, and Richard remains quiet as we both wait for the contact to reveal themselves.

A few seconds pass, and then my heart pumps hope when I hear the worried voice of the man I never gave this number to.

"Elizabeth?"

His accent wraps around my name, and it feels as if it's wrapping around my body in a soothing hug. I want to speak, to defy Richard and yell out all the details of my surroundings so that Declan can find me, but instead, I hold tightly to my breath.

"Elizabeth, are you there?"

"She's here," Richard answers.

"Who's this?"

"A man that has no conscience or limits," he responds before letting me go and handing me the phone.

In an instant, after taking a couple steps away from Richard, he has his knife to my face as I slowly bring the phone to my ear. Richard then takes my trembling hand as I listen to the gravel in Declan's voice, assuming Richard still has the phone, threatening, "My word is my mark, and if you lay a hand on her, I'll—"

"AHHHHH!" I cry out in white, blistering pain, dropping the phone to the ground, and stumbling back on my feet. Gripping my wrist, I wail and stare in horror at the palm of my hand that Richard just dug his knife into, slicing it wide open. Blood is everywhere, oozing out as I hunch over and cry. Looking up, Richard now has the phone, but my body is in shock so that I can't hear anything he's saying to Declan.

I fall to my knees, forcing myself to calm down by taking in slow, staggering breaths, but all I'm doing is choking in shallow pants. I ball my hand into a tight fist, wincing through the burning sting as I hold my hand against my chest.

"Let that be a lesson," Richard says as he walks over to me, no longer on the phone. "Don't cross me again."

He then reaches down and starts tugging at my clothes and shoving his hands in my pockets.

"You hiding anything else?"

"No."

"Stand up," he orders, and once I'm up on wobbly legs, he grabs the neckline of my top and slashes his knife through the fabric, cutting it right down the center.

Shoving the fabric away, he runs the flat of the blade over the swell of my left breast, and when he reaches my nipple, he flips the knife to its razor edge. I've lost all control of my body as it shakes violently.

My eyes are closed while he taunts, "Defy me now; I dare you."

His words are an echo of Carl's. He would provoke me the same way, daring me to push his limits, as if it was giving him my consent to hurt me even more.

*"What are you doing?"*

Flicking my eyes over Richard's shoulder, I see Pike standing behind him.

*"You're forgetting everything I ever taught you,"* he tells me. *"You're so much stronger than this pussy in front of you. Stop letting him think you're weak."*

Shifting my eyes back to Richard, I take Pike's lingering voice and inhale his words in a steady breath and release it slowly from my nose. I let my walls down with Declan, something I felt was right to do, but I forgot to bring them back up the moment Richard showed up. So with calculated intent, I mend the chink in my armor and steel myself to take whatever comes my way.

The knife continues to roam over my tits as I pull my strength together, and once I feel confident in my shield, I move my eyes to meet his.

"Can I take a piss now?"

*"That's my Elizabeth,"* Pike encourages before Richard gives me a snide nod, and I turn to open the door.

## (DECLAN)

THE CALL DISCONNECTED but not before I heard her blood-curdling screams. Focusing on the threats coming from the unidentified man on the phone was almost impossible when my only concern lay within the girl whose shrieking cries could be heard in the background. I demanded to know what he had done to her, but his priorities were in the instructions he was giving me.

And now, I fly around my hotel suite, shoving my clothes into my suitcase at the same time I wait impatiently for Lachlan to answer my call.

"Where the fuck is Elizabeth?" I bark when he answers.

"I don't know. Why?"

"She's gone. I need a plane. Now!"

"Slow down, McKinnon," he says. "What's going on?"

Blood courses erratically, like a raging stampede inside of me. Zipping up the luggage, I answer, "Someone's taken her."

"Are you sure?" he says in surprise.

"Yes, I'm fucking sure! I need a plane five minutes ago. Make it happen and call me back."

I don't waste time arranging for a driver, instead rushing down to the lobby and grabbing the first cab I see.

"Biggin Hill Airport," I tell the driver.

"You okay, sir?"

"Get me there as fast as you can."

He nods without further question as I wait impatiently for Lachlan's call, but all I can hear are her screams as they play over and over in my head. So many times I've wanted to inflict a pain so brutal to induce that type of reaction, but knowing her torture is outside of my control has my heart racing to protect her. It's a twisted thought, but if anyone is going to hurt her, it's going to be me.

I think of all the people who would choose to use her to get to me, and I'm drawing blanks. Truth is, I don't know the people she surrounds herself with, if any at all. But this person, whoever it is, was targeting her and knew just where to find her.

Logging back into the security cameras from my phone, I click through the rooms looking for any kind of clue I can because I don't know what else to do in this moment. When I check the camera that looks over the drive, I see my car that's missing from the garage. She must have been taken from the house if the car is there, but how? Why would she let anyone in the gate?

The phone rings, and I quickly answer. "Did you get it?"

"Yes. The plane will be ready to go in half an hour."

"Good."

"What can I do?"

"Have you seen her or spoken to her since I left yesterday?" I ask.

"No. I've been home."

"They want money," I tell him.

"Who?"

"I don't know. After you gave me her cell number, I called, but she didn't answer. I dialed the number a few times, and then a man answered. I could hear Elizabeth in the background."

"What did he say?"

"That we each hold something of value to the other. That he will let her go when I wire money into an offshore account."

"How much?"

"Enough to destroy either my foundation or my business."

"What are you gonna do?"

And when he asks, my answer comes easily and without second thought. "I'll do anything to make sure she's safe."

Once the words are spoken, I catch myself in a revelation I wasn't expecting to come to so effortlessly. I hang up with Lachlan and attempt to convince myself that I shouldn't be wanting this. That I should just turn a blind eye to her and let this situation work itself out. She'll be destroyed, and in return, I won't ever have to deal with Elizabeth again. Because if this man owns up to the promise he made on the phone, he'll kill her if he doesn't get his money. And then the book will be closed, and I can move on.

But I can't do that.

I can't turn away.

Taking the laptop from my briefcase, I log into the security cameras again. This time, to backtrack the footage that was recorded. I load the camera that monitors the gate to get a time-stamp on when any cars arrived. It takes a while, but soon, two cars approach, my roadster being one of them. I watch closely and switch cameras when they pull up to the front of the house.

An older man, around the same age as my father, emerges from the one car. They speak and then head inside. I switch cameras again when they walk through the house and down to the library. She grows irritated, and I wish for the life of me there was audio on these cameras.

They sit and talk before the man turns angry, lurching off the couch, moving towards Elizabeth. And what happens next drains all warmth from my bones. I lean in toward the screen while I watch this unknown bastard take a gun out of his suit jacket and aim it right at her face. Her hands are white-knuckled to the chair as he then presses the barrel against her forehead.

Every cell in my body fills with a storm of tumult as I watch my world spin more and more out of control. I watch helplessly when he pistol-whips the side of her head, sending her flying to the floor. They exchange more words, she stands, he slams the gun into the side of her head again, this time, knocking her unconscious. He then goes out to his car and returns to duct tape her lifeless body, binding her ankles and wrists. Anger explodes, erupting in an outburst of seething fire when he hunches over her and spits in her face. Once he's dragged her out of the house and tossed her into the trunk of his car, I slam the computer shut.

My breaths come heavy, loaded with guilt, fury, and an undeniable urge for vengeance.

I want to kill that motherfucker.

"Drive faster, God dammit!" I bark at the driver.

Raking my hands through my hair, I can feel my body shuddering in emotions I need to get in check before I lose all the temperance necessary to keep my shit together. As we continue to drive and the mania begins to dissipate a little, I'm reminded of all the ways this woman has sent my life into an upheaval of disarray—her cunning hypocrisy, her ugly spitefulness hidden underneath her shiny exterior, and the blood that will everlast on my hands because of her malicious and selfish vendetta.

I remind myself of all the reasons why I should let this man kill her, remind myself of all the reasons why I hate her. But no matter how many reasons there are, I can't rid myself of the unyielding need to find her. It tugs on the threads that stitch my heart together, the heart that she ripped from my chest and tore apart. And as much as I want to deny it, as much as the thought repulses me, the fact is, the one that destroys is the one that heals.

I need her.

# thirty-four

MY STOMACH GROWLS as I sit here on the ground with my hands bound with a plastic zip tie around a pipe that runs down the length of the wall. Since restraining me, Richard has retrieved a bag from the car filled with food and water that will never find its way into my stomach that hungers. So, I sit and watch, having no idea how much time has passed, if it's night or day.

We're underground, and I can tell by the looks of his phone that he's also operating on an untraceable disposable, making me worry that no one will be able to find me. Although Declan called and now knows I've been taken against my will, a part of me doubts that he cares enough to even come looking for me. But he's the only hope I have because there's no one else out there that even knows who I am. No friends. No family. Nothing.

Strength wanes.

Hope fades.

The tired fight inside of me vanishes.

Slowly, I open my fisted hand and wince from the sting of

oxygen hitting the gash in my palm. Flesh covered in crusted blood—blood dead—proof that nothing survives forever. Old news to me, but yet I've always chosen to go on.

Why?

What's the point?

Win one battle only to be faced with another, but when will it end?

Will it ever stop?

Cellophane crumpling draws my attention to Richard's hand that holds a wadded chip bag. He stares at me as he throws it my way, but it doesn't reach me as it falls to the ground. I look at the garbage and can't help but compare myself. I sit here, lifeless as well, but marred in swollen bruises, cuts, and scabs. Some are self-inflicted, but others come from my love and this bastard in front of me.

I'm waste.

"What are you waiting for?" my voice cracks.

My words catch Richard's attention, and he looks down at me with question in his expression.

"No one's coming for me," I tell him. "If you think Declan cares about me, you're wrong."

He doesn't respond as we stare at each other, and then I ask what I need clarity on before my time runs out, "How did you know my father?"

His eyes shift to his gun that lies on top of the desk, and when he reaches over and picks it up, he gazes at the steel as if it's his desired beloved.

"You worked together, didn't you?" I ask on a trembled voice that threatens to break. Pieces begin to connect in my theory. "You said you used Bennett's business to wash money from guns."

Keeping his hand around the pistol, he rests it upon his thigh when he leans forward, saying, "You have no clue the tangled web you're caught in. It's almost a privilege to be the one who gets to unwrap this gift for you."

I thought I knew Richard. Thought he was nothing more than an ascot-wearing chauvinist that I didn't have to worry about. But now, I have no idea who this man sitting in front of me really is. I'm wondering if we're more alike in the fact that we mold ourselves in pursuit of self-gratification and manipulation.

"Just tell me," I say, free from revealing the emotions tugging at me.

"Steve worked for me. He worked as the middle man, the eyes and ears on both sides."

"Both sides?"

"Me and the mules."

I can't even attempt to connect the dots that led him to Bennett because all that floods my mind is my dad. Never have I pictured my father other than what he always was to me and still is—my prince with a handful of pink daisies. I can't imagine him working for a man like Richard, a man that dug his knife into my face and hand just to prove a point.

"He was always loyal though," he adds. "Until he took a plea bargain in exchange for names. I guess he thought the Feds would protect him, but Menard is filled with prisoners that are linked to me in one way or another. Although he never gave me up, which I hold great respect for, he did give up names of men who walked the low ladder of the business, and for that, he paid the price."

"You bastard," I breathe in sulfurous hate.

"Me?"

"You knew he gave up names?"

"Yes."

"And out of loyalty to you, he never gave you up?"

"Steve did what the Feds asked of him in exchange for an early release—for *you*," he says, nodding his head to me for emphasis. "But at the same time, he never turned his back on me."

His words are gloats of pride for his assumed stature, and I grow in rage at the price it cost my father. The gravel in my voice thickens along with my animosity when I say, "But you held power. You knew the danger he was in, and you did nothing to protect him from what you knew would be inevitable!"

"It was out of my hands."

Blood boils, fists clench, and I begin to tug my wrists against the zip ties as I seethe, "But you're the boss! You hold all the power, and you did nothing!"

And then it starts clicking. The pieces now begin snapping together. Twisting my hands even more, the edges of plastic dig into the tender flesh of my wrists, cutting the tissue and releasing the blood my wounded heart pumps.

"You wanted him dead," I state in my revelation. "You were scared, weren't you? You knew he gave up names, and you feared it was only a matter of time before he sold you out too, right?"

His head tilts, and his condescending gesture acknowledging my theory as truth sets me off.

"You fucker!" my screaming voice scratching my throat. "It was you! You put the hit out on him, didn't you, you *motherfucker!*"

His only response is a slow upturn to his lips as he sits there.

I've always put all the blame on Bennett, and even though I hate Bennett for being the catalyst for all this shit, it was Richard who had the say in my father's life, and he took it to save himself.

"You're a fucking coward!" I spit out as I feel the bursts and pops of veins and ventricles—heartbreak over and over and over. My daddy risked his life in giving up names just to get to me.

Blood rolls down my arms like teardrops as my skin rips open as I fight against the zip ties. When my frustration snaps, I release a defeated scream and slump over. My bones tremble, and when I hear Richard chuckling, I turn to him in disgust.

"Does this get you off?"

He stands and walks to me. "Seeing the queen of Chicago society fall apart before my eyes? Yes," he responds and then kneels down in front of me, touching his finger to my face and running it along the cut on my cheek and then down my neck.

His touch is vile, rousing my stomach in putrid disgust, and I just can't take it.

"Tell me something," he starts. "When you found out that Bennett cheated on you, did you wish you'd known before he died so you could've gotten even with him?"

He then takes the knife out of his pocket and pops the blade up. My eyes follow his hand as he moves the blade to the zip tie and holds it against the plastic that's now covered in my blood.

"Did you?" he questions again.

"No." I didn't give a shit about Bennett cheating because I never felt anything for him other than pure hate.

Suddenly, with quick movements, Richard cuts through the restraint and frees my hands. He then moves the blade between my breasts. My top hangs open from when he cut the fabric earlier. I hear the lace snap apart when he presses the blade against the fabric, and I know his intentions. Focus is key, and knowing the process all too well, I protect myself and shut down.

He now knows the truth about his wife and son. I could overhear him when he was down the corridor and on the phone right after he bound me to the pipe. I knew he was talking to Jacqueline. He questioned her, and I could tell from the words he spoke, that she admitted the truth to him. He didn't raise his voice or become irate. It was the opposite. He remained collected, but looking into his eyes right now as he cuts through my bra, I see the fire of betrayal burning, and I brace myself for what I know is coming my way—retaliation.

Richard doesn't know how strong I am when it comes to sex. After all, I made it through four years of fucking the enemy, and I did it so well that he was none-the-wiser of my deep-seated hatred for him. My body is used up and polluted. It always was and always will be. Even Declan desecrated it when he raped me. So when Richard pushes the fabric aside to expose my tits, I feel nothing.

The cold, dank air hardens my nipples, and when this happens, he smiles and gloats, "Eager, huh?"

*Fucking idiot.*

When he stands up, I notice his erection pressing against his slacks. He walks over to the desk, exchanging his knife for the gun, and returns to me. My breath catches when he shoves the muzzle underneath my chin.

"Don't get brave on me," he threatens. "One wrong move, I'll put a bullet in you."

Although I now know his true profession, I still want to doubt that he would be a man capable of killing, but his next words disintegrate all doubt.

"But something tells me you won't beg for your life like your little boyfriend's mother did, which is disappointing. I love hearing a woman beg."

My eyes widen is shocked disbelief. "You?" I question, horrified.

"Sometimes in life you have to teach people lessons, and when Callum thought he could screw me over, I made sure he learned I wasn't someone to be fucked with."

He's right—I've gotten myself tangled in the most fucked up cryptogram imaginable.

"What does Cal have to do with any of this?"

He shushes me, running his gun down my belly and shoving it into my pants, the coolness of the metal seeping through the lace of my panties. His grin is scathing when he unzips my pants to earn more room to slip the barrel between my legs. He slides it back and forth along my pussy, all the while smiling. But I'm detached. My mind is in the past with Declan on the afternoon when he opened up to me about his mom being shot in the head.

The pain he hides so well surfaced in his eyes, and just like me, the moment he lost his parent, he was forever maimed with a wound that would never heal. I would do anything for him, and to know that Richard was the one who pulled the trigger that forever fucked up Declan's faith in security and comfort fuels my affinity for revenge.

Richard catches my attention, taking me away from my memories when he begins tugging my bottoms down my legs.

"My wife acted like a cunt," he says. "But she's not here for me to release my anger on, and neither is Bennett. All I have is *you.*"

With my panties gone with my pants, he forces my legs wide open and presses the muzzle of the gun over my clit. My body locks up in horrid fear. I close my eyes, bracing myself for whatever is to come next, and after he makes me wait, I gasp when he forces the barrel of the loaded pistol inside of my pussy. Keeping my eyes pinched shut, I press my lips together and force myself out of this moment while he fucks me with his gun.

I remove my emotions and escape, giving him my body that's proven to be nothing but a piece of garbage. He glides the pistol in and out of me while I dig my fingers into the concrete beneath. Richard lets out a pleasurable groan as he starts fondling my breast in his one hand. I swallow down the puke that burns the back of my throat. My head rings loudly, and when the shield becomes too much for me to keep up, I beg for Pike to come, but he doesn't.

The iron cast cracks, chipping away piece by piece, and behind my closed eyes is Carl. No longer is Richard's gun raping me, but instead, Carl's filthy dick. My body jerks when the numbness wanes, and soon I can feel everything that's being done to me. When my hips buck, my eyes flash open to see the devil above me, and I lose it. With all my strength, I grab his wrist and lurch my hips back, forcing the gun up to my forehead, screaming like a maniac, "PULL THE FUCKING TRIGGER!"

He looks at me bitterly, and with my hands fisted tightly around the barrel of the gun, I shriek, pressing it harder against my head, "Do it, you piece of shit! Pull the trigger!"

He yanks the gun out of my hands and snarls, "What the fuck is wrong with you?"

"What are you waiting for? Declan's not coming, he would've already called by now. So why wait?" I tell him. "Just get it over with. Shoot me."

"Like this?" he questions, cramming the gun into my mouth.

I sit still, tasting the mixture of my pussy and metal. My lips wrap around what I yearn to be my savior. I nod my head and pray for the shot that will end my misery once and for all. But instead, he uses it to degrade me even more. Fisting my hair, he forces my head further down on the gun.

"Suck it," he demands as he bobs me up and down.

I gag, tears springing from my eyes as he makes me deep-throat it. He then pushes me away and stands.

"Put your pants on and shut your fucking mouth."

And as the saliva drips from my chin and I wipe my eyes, the phone rings.

# thirty-five
## (DECLAN)

"THE CELL NUMBER is coming up blank. It must be a burner phone," Lachlan tells me, and it makes sense that she would be using a disposable under the circumstances of her dead husband and all the lies. "Maybe the police would be able to bypass the blocks. I mean, the calls are going through a cell tower, perhaps they can track that."

"No cops," I order. "The call was choppy, cutting in and out, so they have to be somewhere secluded. I'm almost home though, how far are you?"

"Half an hour."

I hang up, and when I arrive at the house, I take my time heading up the drive, looking around for any clues. My black roadster is parked in front of the fountain, and when I get out of my SUV, I walk over to check the door to find it's still unlocked. The car is empty aside from the suitcase I find when I pop open the trunk.

Once inside, I head straight to the library to see the furniture slightly disheveled from the altercation I witnessed on the surveillance. I look around, stomach twisting, heart thudding, questions brewing. Setting the suitcase onto the couch, I start digging through it and realize that she went back to the Water Lily to retrieve the rest of her belongings.

As I'm rummaging through her clothes, my hand hits something hard. Grabbing the object, I pull it out, and the moment I catch sight of it, a chill takes over me. My fingers shake as I hold the picture frame and stare down into my own eyes looking up at me.

*Where did she get this?*

Unlatching the back of the frame, I take the photo out to see if anything is written on the back to find there is:

*Declan*

*6 years old*

I'm sitting by the small pond that was on the land of the home I grew up in. I'm staring up at the camera, smiling. The water is filled with lotus blooms, the blooms my mum loved so much. I remember how much she enjoyed that pond. She would sit along the bank with her legs hanging over the edge, just as I'm doing in the picture. She'd laugh in the sun's edge of spring, skimming her painted toes on the water's surface, calling out to me, her voice delicate and loving, *"Sit with me, sweetie. Dip your toes in."* And I did.

The water was cold that day as we sat together among the fragrant lotus flowers. Her face is still so vivid in my head, flaw-less and milky. She was beautiful, with long brown hair that she would pin up in a bun around the house, but when she was in the gardens or by the pond, she would let it down.

My eyes close to bear the ache in my chest. The memories hurt, and the visions only remind me of what I allowed to be taken from me. I shake the past away, forever weak to let myself think about my mum for too long before I'm reminded of the coward I am.

Reality comes back into play when Lachlan calls from the gate. I let him in and stash the photo back inside Elizabeth's bag, still confused about where she got it and why she has it. But I push the thought aside when Lachlan walks into the room and tosses his jacket over the back of one of the chairs.

"He was in this room with her," I blurt out. "I pulled up the security cameras. He had a gun, smashed it into her head, knocking her out before he taped her up and threw her in the trunk of his car."

"Fuckin' hell," he mutters in disbelief. "Where's the computer? I want to get a look."

Grabbing the laptop, I log in and pull up the footage to show him. He takes the computer and sits at the desk in the corner of the room. I pour two fingers of Scotch and throw it back quickly, not even caring to respect the smoky flavors because I just need it to take the edge off before I completely go ballistic.

"Where's the gate cam?" he asks, and I walk over to show him the particular camera he's wanting.

I watch over his shoulder as he clicks to zoom in on something, which I didn't think to do because I swear to God, I'm losing all sense of focus.

"There it is," he says as he grabs a pen and jots down the license plate number.

"Christ, I'm a fucking idiot."

"Not as much as this fucker," he counters and then grabs his cell. "Try to relax. We'll find her. Let me make a couple calls while I grab a cup of coffee from the kitchen."

I nod and walk over to the couch and take a seat, but the moment I do, I hear a buzzing coming from Lachlan's jacket. Curiosity piques, and I go over to find another cell in one of the pockets. With no name flashing on the screen, I accept the call and stay silent.

"Baby, are you there?" a woman says, and it takes me a few seconds to connect the voice in my head.

"Camilla?"

There's a moment of silence before my father's girlfriend questions in return, "Declan?"

"Why are you calling Lachlan?" I ask, but she quickly pivots, saying, "How have you been? Your father and I haven't heard from you since you—"

"How do you know Lachlan?" I question, cutting her off mid-sentence.

"Umm, well . . ." she stumbles. "Maybe you should . . . you should probably ask Lachlan."

"I'm asking *you*."

There's no immediate response, but it isn't long before she releases a sigh and reveals, "Your father is in a little trouble. I wanted to call you and tell you this sooner, but your father insisted that I refrain. You know how stubborn he is."

"Stop the shit, Camilla. How do you know Lachlan?"

"It's a rental," Lachlan announces when he rushes back into the room, and in the same second, Camilla hangs up, disconnecting the call.

"What the fuck is this?" I question as I hold up the cell.

He's collected and calm, responding, "My personal cell."

"And that is . . . ?" I question, eyeing the cell in his hand.

"My work phone."

"So tell me then, why is my father's girlfriend calling your personal cell? And why, when I asked her how she knows you, did she choke like a cheap whore giving head?"

"Camilla's an old friend. Don't worry; your father knows that. You probably just caught her off guard when you answered the phone."

His composure makes me second-guess whatever suspicions I have, but she called him *baby,* and I can't ignore that, but I also can't waste time right now. I'll have to deal with this shit later as I draw my attention back to what he said about the car.

"McKinnon," Lachlan adds. "Relax, okay? We're going to find her."

"I'll relax when she's back in this house. Tell me, what did you find out?"

"I'm waiting on a call from the rental company. Seems, whoever this guy is, he wasn't aware that the car has a tracking device in it that the company installs on all the vehicles."

"What about the police?"

"The minimum wage kid who took the call was an easy payoff," he tells me.

Grabbing her bag, I say, "I'm going to check her room. I'll be down shortly."

"Sure thing."

Heading upstairs, I walk into the guest room I put Elizabeth in since bringing her home with me earlier this week. I set the bag down and sit on the edge of the bed. When I look over to the nightstand, I see a pair of pearl earrings along with a necklace that catches my attention. I pick up the thin silver chain and stare at the small charm that hangs from it—a lotus.

How could a woman who is so dead inside be so sentimental?

This girl is incredibly damaged. To wrap my mind around her psychotic thoughts and deranged actions would be a wasted effort because there's no way to make sense of it all. The trauma that a person has to endure to get to the state of mental instability that she's in is gut-wrenching to think about. Everything she's told me about her childhood, everything she went through, is morbidly sickening. If I had to walk around holding on to what she does, I'm not sure I could live with myself.

Her past has molded her into a monster. But to look into her eyes as deeply as I find myself doing, there's something innocent inside of her. She's very much like a child in many ways; I see it in small glimpses. It's almost as if she hit pause and stopped living when she lost her dad. Like she's somehow stuck because the life she was thrown into was too heinous that she never let go of the childlike beliefs that the world is a good place filled with good people. You would never know it unless you found yourself in the core of her. She knows how ugly life is, but there's a little girl inside of her that hasn't given up just yet.

I'm helpless sitting here, not knowing where she is or what that fucker is going to do to her or *has* done to her. Never have I wanted to save someone as much as I did when I believed her to be Nina. I would've done anything for her, and I did. My love for her was so strong that I never thought twice about turning myself into a monster too—for her.

As much as I hate her, as much as I want to hurt her, as much as I wish I'd never met her, I can't walk away from someone I love so deeply that she's in my marrow.

The girl is crazy and out of her mind, and for wanting her, I am too. Nothing can deny the force that pulls me to her, even in my most wretched thoughts, I'm still drawn to her.

"McKinnon!" Lachlan shouts. "Get your ass down here. Let's go!"

Flying down the stairs, I ask, "What is it?"

"She's in Edinburgh. The location of the car isn't a pinpoint, but it's close enough."

"One second," I tell him before rushing up to my bedroom to grab my gun.

Energy powers through me like lightning as I move quickly through the house, and when I make it outside and jump into Lachlan's SUV, my heart races out of control.

"Talk to me. Where is she?"

He hands me the phone with the map open, and suddenly, my surge of optimism that we might know where she is morphs into dread.

"There's no way. It's too populated," I say.

"It's all we have to work off of. That's where the car is."

"That may be where the car is, but there is no way that's where he's got her," I tell him as I look at a map of downtown Edinburgh.

"Who're you calling?" he asks when I pull out my phone.

"Her. He's got her phone."

After one ring, the call connects, but there's nothing but silence.

"Tell me where you are."

My demand is met with a sinister laugh from this dick fuck, before he responds, "Now why would I tell you that?"

"I have the money you asked for," I lie.

"Very good, but I don't want to touch it. I'll give you the account information you're to wire the money into. Once I get verification the money has been transferred, I'll text you the location of wherever I decide to drop the bitch off."

"I want to talk to her first."

"I don't know if she's in the mood to talk right now."

"I don't give a fuck!" I shout. "Put her on the phone or the deal is off. I can take or leave the bitch, so it's up to you!" My words, fallacies.

Silence spans before he responds, "I don't think so. You see, I don't give a shit what you feel for the girl. I mean, I'm not gonna lie, I wanted to use her as leverage, but she isn't the only leverage I have on you."

"And what's that?"

His next words drain my veins and then fill them with icy fear.

"Bennett Vanderwal."

*Fuck.*

thirty-six

"WHAT DID HE say?" I ask timidly after hearing Richard tell Declan that if he couldn't use me as leverage that he would use Bennett.

"Looks like you were telling me the truth."

"What do you mean?"

"Seems Declan doesn't give a shit about you."

I knew it. I knew that if forced for an answer that I would never be it. And now I sit here, half-naked, beaten, and raped as the last of my heart incinerates into ash.

*Go ahead and take a breath now because I'm finally ready to be blown into nothingness.*

I now know my lies truly destroyed what I never wanted them to. I knew Declan was conflicted, I felt it in his push and pull, but I hoped there was a piece of him that still wanted me regardless of all my sins.

So I close my eyes, and green meets blue as Declan looks at me the way he did back in Chicago. He will never look at me with adoration as he once did. I ruined it for both of us. Now I'm left with this pain, ripping inside of me. It isn't the pain of heartbreak though, because I've already lost that. My heart no longer exists. And it can't be my soul, because I'm without that too.

But it's real, the pain I feel. It comes from somewhere inside of me, a place I never knew I had, and it hurts deep. Hurts in a way I've never felt before. It's so unbearable my body can't fight it, so it shuts down on me. I'm lifeless, flesh and bone, the weakened muscle inside my chest beating slowly, pumping what I pray is venom into my veins.

I don't want this anymore.

*"What if he's lying to you?"*

Keeping my eyes closed because just hearing his voice is enough to console me, I lie down with my head in Pike's lap, and he places a soothing hand gently over my swollen face.

"He's not," I whisper to him in response. "My destruction went far beyond the capacity of forgiveness."

"What the fuck are you talking about?" I hear Richard's voice bark, but I shut it out and focus entirely on Pike.

Pike is all I want right now. He's the constant that's always been in my life. He never turns away from me, never stops comforting me, never stops caring for and loving me.

My face scrunches in despair as I try so hard to hold myself together. "I can't stop missing you."

*"I can't stop missing you either."*

Battling with my emotions causes my body to tremble, and I know Pike feels it when he says, *"You wanna play a game?"*

I nod. "You can pick this time."

*"How about breakfast foods?"*

"Okay." Pike and I always used to play this word game when

we were kids and I was locked up in the closet. It was his way of distracting me from my awful reality. We'd play this game for hours in the middle of the night while he sat on the opposite side of the door. And in this moment, in his death, he never fails to take care of me. "Pancake," I say, playing my first word.

*"English muffin."*

"NutriGrain bar."

*"Rice Krispies."*

We continue to play our words while he runs his fingers through my hair, careful to not hurt the tender scab that still remains on the back of my head. I never open my eyes, and eventually, before declaring a winner, I drift to sleep.

COLD METAL PRODDING my face wakes me up. My tired eyes come into focus as I jerk my head away from Richard's gun. I look at him, his face pale and his hair messy, as if he's been anxiously running his hands through it. He's jittery, kneeling beside me, and I have no clue if something happened while I was asleep to cause his shift in demeanor.

"Have I given you the impression that I'm one to be toyed with?" he says with a tight jaw, pissed.

I shake my head, and he snaps, "Then where the fuck is he?"

"I don't know."

"I will put a bullet in your head the same way I did the McKinnon woman. I swear to God, I will."

"I won't fight you," I tell him calmly. "You want to kill me? Then kill me."

He grabs my tattered shirt and shakes me, losing control

while he screams in aggravation, "What the fuck is wrong with you?"

"If you wanted me to fight, you picked the wrong girl. There's nothing for me to fight for."

He shakes his head, confounded, and then clues in, saying, "So you don't give a shit what happens to you? I could do whatever I wanted with you, and you'd let me?"

"You can't possibly hurt me; I'm already dead," I tell him, the sound of my own voice creeping me out with its eerie tone. "But first," I add, "Fill in the blanks."

"What do you want to know?"

"Cal. What does he have to do with the guns?"

"He was my washer," he tells me freely, taking a deep breath and sitting next to me with his back against the wall. "Cal used to push the money through a random laundromat he acquired for the sole purpose of covering the money trail. But I later found out he was being greedy and filtering some of the money into an offshore account that was linked to him. That's when I taught him his first lesson in loyalty and killed his precious wife. He never stole from me again."

His words turn the venom of my heart into the blood of life. Just because Declan doesn't give a shit about me doesn't change my love for him, but I hide my shift. I'm like a machine when I continue my quest for clarity. "And Bennett?"

"Bennett was a man who trusted too easily, which made him my perfect asset. His father actually worked with yours."

"What?" I ask in shock.

"I always suspected bad blood between the two, then it became apparent when he put the authorities on Steve. I didn't know this until after Steve was already locked up, but apparently when Bennett came home one day talking some nonsense about how he thought your father was hurting you, that's when he saw his chance to get your dad out of the game."

My hands tingle in fury as I listen to his admissions. I can't even see straight as my desire to kill that piece of shit sparks to life. This man, my fucking father-in-law, was yet another man who had a hand in my father's death and the destruction of my life.

"Later, when Bennett was older and acquired his first production plant, his father convinced him to partner with me. We knew it would serve as a better cover for laundering the money. Bennett trusted me as a longtime family friend, took the advice of his father, and the rest is history, until you came along and fucked everything up with your stupid charade."

I sit in silence, trying with everything I have to control the anger exploding within me as I process what I've just heard, realizing that all of us are linked in one way or another. There was a time I was the one in control and able to manipulate people into my puppets, but I know now I was never in control because I never truly knew the cast of characters I lured my way into.

"But I will admit," he continues, "I'm impressed with your efforts, even though you failed miserably."

"Who says I failed? You're stuck down here with me too. You're not free."

"I will be."

I can't contain my chuckle, and when it grows, Richard fumes, "What's so funny?"

"*You.*"

"Do tell."

"You're so focused on yourself, that you're shadowing the

fact that, in a very twisted way, I won."

He cocks back the hammer of his gun, the snick of the metal sounding when he does, and then points it straight at me, but he doesn't intimidate me.

"Don't you see?" I say in total control. "I *want* you to pull that trigger. So no matter what you do, I win." I take a hard swallow before going on, telling him, "It was *you*. You're right, I did get myself tangled up in something that was much bigger than me, but the root of everything, which I thought was Bennett, is actually *you*. And because of my *stupid scheme*, your family is now tainted in Bennett's blood through your son, your whole cartel is falling apart, and your freedom depends on the money of a man who'd rather see me dead than alive."

His eyes narrow in a murderous glare, but I don't stop, adding, "And if you think you have him fooled by threatening to know about his involvement with Bennett's murder, you're wrong. If anyone is to be pegged for that crime, it's you, the leader of one of the largest international gun trafficking rings, using Bennett as your cover."

Richard pulls the gun away from my face, but doesn't disengage the hammer.

"You've got it all figured out, don't you?" he taunts. "You think you have me played, telling me you want to die to take the pleasure away from me? You say I can't hurt you, but I think you're lying."

"Kill me or don't kill me, I don't care."

"I think you do."

I then wrap my hands around the barrel and place it back on my forehead, stating firmly, "I don't."

Agitation streaks in the lines of his face now that I've taken his bargaining chip away from him. He gains nothing from killing me, not even joy because he knows I won't beg for my life.

Richard drags the gun down my face, along the bridge of my nose, over my lips, and then slips it into my mouth.

*I knew my sanctuary would be in death, and I was ready to be released into the oasis I'd been longing for. But even though I was ready, it didn't mask the fear of having a loaded gun with the hammer cocked inside my mouth. One slip and that chambered bullet would fire. I can still taste the steel of his pistol on my tongue if I think about it hard enough. Can still feel the way my heart ricocheted off my ribs. I had been close to death before, but it was always in my control. Not this time. This time I was on Richard's watch. He would say when. He would be my executioner.*

*I remembered hearing the voices—my ballasts. Daddy, Pike, and even Carnegie, they were there with me while I rested on death's lips, waiting for its kiss. Their words of courage to guide me from evil sang in my head like a melody of deliverance, but it wouldn't be enough, and I was about to find out why.*

Richard uses the gun to guide me down on my back while he pushes it into my mouth. With his free hand, he rips the buttons to my pants open, demanding, "Take them off. You're not going to rob me from feeling gratified."

*Idiot.*

He's stupid to think that he can degrade me for his pleasure by fucking me. I do as he instructs, kicking off my pants while he fumbles with his own. I don't offer any fight when he shoves his pants down just far enough to pull out his dick. Nudging my legs open, he sits on his knees while holding himself in his hand and slapping it against my pussy a few times.

"Hands under your ass," he tells me, and I lift my hips to place them beneath me. "Time to even the score."

This man's pride is fucked up, to be concerned about getting even with his wife in this moment. My body slacks when he slams inside of me. I refuse to give him the satisfaction of tensing up. I keep my eyes focused on the pistol in my mouth as the metal rattles against my teeth while he violently pounds into me. He braces all his weight on his one bent elbow, grunting with each thrust. My tits hang out of my ripped clothes, jiggling while he fucks me with barbaric force.

This is my life.

This is all it's ever been.

Light turns dark as my eyes close, silently begging for him to release me to my paradise.

From across the room, I hear my cell ring, and my heart jolts alive.

*He's calling.*

My eyes pop open when the thought flashes quickly that maybe Richard was lying about Declan. My body jerks the moment the phone goes off, startling Richard in that exact moment, and everything happens in a lightning fast haze when he falters, losing his balance.

The instant the gun slips from my mouth, Pike shouts urgently, *"Elizabeth, FIGHT!"* and without thinking how or why, I automatically react.

Willing my strength, I drive my elbow into his arm, knocking the gun out of his grip. Adrenaline pumps through my system when the gun goes off, firing a bullet into the concrete wall as it skitters across the ground. The blast is deafening, but somehow I'm able to flip onto my stomach, scrambling as fast as I can. I sling my arm out to grab the gun when he locks his hand around my ankle and yanks me back.

My fingertips skim the pistol as I'm being pulled away, and the commotion is a total blur. Ripping out an excruciatingly demented scream, I fight with everything I have in me when I twist around and lurch my shoulders off the ground. With his pants still down, I dig my hands into his thighs, and with all the force in me, bite the ever-living-shit out of his dick, snarling like a wild beast as I do, and his voice erupts in pure acid.

"FUUUUUCK!"

Flesh pops in my mouth as my teeth cut straight through the elasticity of skin and sink into tissue, spurting blood everywhere. I feel the thick heat of it splattering on my face and coating my lips and chin. His screams are deadly as his body falls to the ground, and I jump to my feet, charging for the gun. The moment my hand wraps around the pistol, I turn, aiming it at his head, and scream like a maniac as my body detonates every emotion imaginable, but none of them make sense as they shake me to the bone.

# thirty-seven
## (DECLAN)

LACHLAN AND I located the rental car a while ago with no traces of where they could be. We're wasting delicate time wandering around the usually busy streets of downtown, but it's the middle of the night, and Lachlan and I are the only ones lurking around.

"This is fucking useless," I gripe in frustration. "Every business is closed and locked up. They could be anywhere."

"What do you want to do?"

Huffing out an angry breath, I let my head fall back as I look up into the dark of night. We've been scouring these streets for hours, and nothing. For all I know, this car could've been ditched for another and they could already be in another country.

Lifting my head, I turn to look down the narrow close that's to my right. There are so many of these alleyways in the city, and we've been walking through them all night it seems.

I'm plagued with an unsettling sense of doom that I'll never find her. The thought grabs ahold of me, twisting my gut as I think about not being able to see her face again or hear her say my name in her sweet American accent. I can't stand the thought of her never knowing the truth of my heart. She deserves to have the peace of knowing that I still care about her. After everything she's been through, and even after all the corruption within her, she still deserves to know.

Pulling out my cell, I begin to walk again and decide to call her phone once more. I dial the number, and after the first ring, I startle when I hear a loud crack that splits the night.

"You hear that?" I ask Lachlan, the words flying out of my mouth.

His eyes are wide, alarmed, saying, "That was a gunshot."

Grabbing my gun from its holster, I fly down the steps of the alley, because that sounded like it came from beneath me. My body surges in a rush of power as I go into overdrive.

"McKinnon!"

Darting down the stairs, I don't stop as I shout over my shoulder, "Keep a lookout!"

A man's torturous screaming fuels me, and I follow the echoes into the underground vaults. My heart has never raced so fast when a woman's screams filter in through the man's. With my gun in my hand, I run as fast as my legs will move through the narrow passageways. In an instant, I kick through a door to find a scene so disturbing, my gun immediately finds it target.

Their screams bounce off the cement of the small vault, piercing my ears. I'm horrified as my eyes flick back and forth between the two of them while my mind tries to grasp what's in front of me.

A man I don't recognize is crumpled on the floor, his face utterly pale as he begins choking on his breath. His pants are down, and his lap is covered in blood, and when I look over to see Elizabeth, I turn sick. She stands there naked with only a cut up shirt and bra hanging off her arms. Her mouth is covered in blood, and when I jerk my head back to the guy, I realize that the blood on her is from that bastard's dick.

Cries slice through her screams as her whole body shakes while she steps towards the man with her arm outstretched, holding a pistol.

"Elizabeth, no!" I shout when she rams the muzzle of the gun into his forehead and keeps it there.

She doesn't respond to me in any way as she stares down at the man.

"Don't pull the trigger!" I order, my words coming out fast while I have my own gun aimed at the man.

Her screams are replaced by staggering breaths hissing through her teeth, and I know that any second, she's going to murder him.

"Elizabeth, look at me," I urge. "Don't kill him."

"Why?" she seethes.

"Because you already know it's not going to make you feel better."

"You MOTHERFUCKER!" she screams hysterically at him like a crazed animal.

I take a couple steps closer to her, but she snaps, "Stay away from me!"

"Please," I beg. "No more killing."

"If not for me, then I'll do it for you," she says cryptically. "Consider this a gift."

"What are you talking about?"

She cocks the hammer back before finally looking over at

me, and says, "He's the one that killed your mother."

Looking over to him, I pull back the slide on my gun to chamber a round; the metallic *click* is all I hear in this moment. I can feel the beast inside, digging his claws into the most wounded parts of me. It takes control of me, and without hesitation or question, I squeeze the trigger and put a bullet in his head.

I can't look away from him as blood sprays and chunks of his head fling across the room. His body tips over, still as death takes him instantly, dark blood draining from his mouth.

Elizabeth continues to aim her gun at him, trembling in shock with wide eyes, and I move cautiously over to her. Not taking a moment to process what I just did, my concern goes straight to the distraught girl in front of me.

When I reach out, she snaps, "Don't touch me!" and I immediately recant.

"Let me have the gun."

"No."

"He's dead," I tell her, but she doesn't respond as she keeps her gun pointed at him. "Look at me."

"No."

Her body is battered beyond belief as I scan over her. Added to her self-inflicted bruises is a nasty wound on her cheek covered in crusted blood, swollen contusions on her face, and a black eye. She's not only covered in her own blood, but also the blood from the man who lies dead at her feet.

Her breathing is rigid as I watch her, and eventually, she drops her arms and allows me to take the gun from her hand before falling to her knees. I release the hammer and set the gun down along with my own. As I start unbuttoning my shirt, I kneel down next to her and drape it over her back to cover her up. She keeps her chin tucked down, and I noticed her slashed wrists covered in blood when I take her hand in mine.

"It's going to be okay."

She remains silent as I sit with her. I want to do so much, but all I can manage is to simply observe. Her once-beautiful red hair is dirty, matted in blood. She's a fraction of herself, and I find it painful to look at, but I look anyway. And as sick as it sounds, I've never felt more bonded to her than I do now. Both of us exposed for the evil we are. Killers with mangled souls. No longer can I blame her for my sins because I just murdered of my own free will without her persuasion or seduction. She may have birthed this malignity inside of me, but I'm the one who now embraces it.

"He killed your mom," she says again, and I can barely hear her faint voice when she adds, "He's the reason my dad is dead too."

"Who is he?" I ask in utter confusion to this situation.

"Richard Brooks. He was Bennett's business partner," she answers and then goes on to explain how our fathers worked for him and the hit he put out on her dad. I sit and listen to everything she tells me, the whole time keeping her eyes downcast, almost cowering as if she's afraid of me. But it's when she says, "Cal is in jail," that her eyes finally lift to mine.

"Did Bennett know?"

"No. He thought he was running an honest business. Richard and Cal used him."

Every muscle in my body in tensed up because I know at any minute, I'm liable to break completely. As I ask questions to piece the puzzle together, my heart and mind remain with my mum. The fucker's blood that killed her at point blank pools under my loafers, and I have to swallow down the bile that threatens. I have to get out of here.

"Come on," I say, urging her to stand. "Let's go."

She coils away from me, pulling against my hold on her. "I can't."

"Can't what?"

She looks up at me, tears filling her eyes, blood smeared across her face, and says, "I can't keep pretending that . . . that we . . ."

"Just come home."

"I don't have a home."

Looking past the ugliness, deep into her eyes, into the depths of what's hidden beneath, my heart beats a beat I've never felt before. It comforts all the fears and doubts I have about her and assures me that she's where I belong.

"I know life hasn't been good to you, and I know you've lost a lot, but you haven't lost everything," I tell her. "I still want what I told you back in Chicago; I want to give you a home you can feel safe in. I want us to have a chance to make that happen."

"But . . . you hate me."

"You're right," I confirm. "I do hate you, but I love you and that's not going away."

"Do you forgive me?"

"No," I answer, shaking my head.

"Are you done punishing me?"

"No."

She drops her head, and I immediately cup her cheeks, angling her back to me when I explain, "I don't know if I'm ever going to get over this—if I'm ever going to get to the point where I don't want to punish you for what you've done. But I need you to understand something; I need you to know that even though you may feel pain, I will *never* hurt you. I will do everything to give you what was taken from you. I'm going to make you feel safe, I promise you that. No one will ever lay a hand on you again."

She never allows the tears to fall as I watch her struggle against her emotions, and I know it's a defense mechanism she uses to protect herself from pain, but she needs to feel it.

"Stop fighting yourself," I tell her as I hold her in my hands. "I want to see you cry. Don't hide from me anymore."

"I'm not a person you should love."

"Neither am I, but you do, don't you?"

Nodding her head, she let's go and weeps, "So much."

"And I love you," I say and then gather her in my arms. I hold on to her, listening to her broken breaths before making my selfish request. "Cry, Elizabeth. I want to hear you cry and know that it's for me."

She tucks her head into the crook of my neck, and when I feel the wetness of her warm tears dripping onto my skin, I'm satisfied. She's quiet in her sadness, and her release comforts me. I like knowing that she can hand it over to me and I'm the one getting to soothe her. I know she's right in that fact that she shouldn't be loved. Neither of us deserves it, but I can't help myself when it comes to her. I've never been able to curb my addiction to her, even when I thought she was a married woman. I wanted her regardless, and I want her still.

"McKinnon," Lachlan's voice hollers out.

"In here," I shout as I keep a tight hold on Elizabeth.

When he eventually finds his way to us, his voice is disjointed as he takes in the scene before him, uttering, "Holy fuck."

"Tell me I can trust you," I say to him, and without a second of hesitation, he responds loyally, "You can trust me."

"Call the police."

My arms remains locked around Elizabeth's trembling body while she continues to silently weep, hiding her head against my chest. Without having to even ask, Lachlan hands me her pants before turning around to make the call.

It doesn't take long for the authorities to arrive. Elizabeth plays her part as Nina, explaining her *husband's* murder and the crimes that Richard was conducting through Bennett's company. We twist the story, informing them that Richard murdered Bennett after he'd discovered the money laundering. It takes a while to give our statements that clear me of any involvement in the murder I committed.

The medics offer to take Elizabeth to the hospital, but she refuses, fervent that nobody touches her. Before we go, the detective advises us that we may be called in for additional questioning. He hands us his card with his contact information and we leave.

Arriving at the SUV, we climb into the backseat and I pull her onto my lap, cradling her back in my arms.

"Everything's going to be okay," I try assuring her, confident that we both just got away with our crimes.

She draws back from me, and I can tell she wants to speak, but she doesn't. She simply stares at me, and I'm able to look beyond the blood, dirt, bruises, cuts, and tears to see what I fell in love with when I first saw her in my hotel back in the States. I'll never forget how beautiful she looked at the grand opening of Lotus, standing across the room in a long, midnight-blue gown. She was confident, snarky, and so sure of herself, and in this very moment, I vow to give all those qualities back to her.

Running my hand around the back of her neck and up into

her hair, my fingers graze over the scab that remains from when I pulled her hair out. I stop and she turns her head in shame away from me.

"Look at me."

And when she does, I cup her face once again and swallow against the emotional knot in my throat, saying, "You're safe with me," and then move her head to rest against my chest, banding my arms around her.

# thirty-eight

SHAME AND EMBARRASSMENT only exist in things you value. I feel none of that as Lachlan drives us back to Galashiels. I know Declan assumes I'm feeling that way after finding me naked, raped, and covered in Richard's blood from where I bit his dick, but I don't. My body trembles and quakes in his arms as he holds me, but I tremble from fear. Declan told me everything I've been longing to hear, but who's to say I can trust him? Who's to say this won't fail like everything else?

Life has taught me that heartache is inevitable, proving over and over that dreams are simply that—dreams. Imaginative figments of our subconscious. Why am I to believe this is anything different? I certainly don't deserve it.

So here I sit with two options: die or trust.

Death seems the safest choice, but I'm also not ready to let go of what I'm starting to get back. Declan's like my heroin; I get one small taste, and I'm stuck, feening for more. But I'm terrified of losing it, knowing I can't survive without him—I don't want to survive without him. So if this is undoubtedly doomed, I'd be smart to just end this all now.

Maybe my true home doesn't really exist in the hills of Scotland, but instead, in the presence of all that was and is no more. They say death is the ultimate paradise, and the idea of being back with my father and Pike is beyond tempting. But I can't deny how good Declan's hands feel on me right now. Holding me and stroking my back. He smells like he always has, and I find comfort in the spicy notes of his cologne the same way I used to find comfort in Pike's clove cigarettes.

So as the uncertainty wracks my body in unquestionable fear, I hold on tightly to the one thing I fear the most—Declan. He's the one who holds all the power here. He could easily destroy me or make all my dreams come true, but in order for me to find out which, I have to let go of my control, something I've never done before. It terrifies me to hand all the parts of me over to him and trust that he'll take care of them.

For now, I selfishly take the affection he's offering me and nuzzle my head more deeply against his chest so that I can hear every sound his heart is making. Allowing its rapid beats to sing to me, I cling more tightly to him. The closer I get, the more senses I open up to him, the more I let the fear consume me. All I want is comfort, but I'm too scared of the pain I'll have to endure when it's gone—and it *will,* one day, be gone.

When we arrive at Brunswickhill, Declan helps me out of the SUV as I wince in pain. The long drive back gave my body time to dissipate the adrenaline, and now my muscles and bones scream angrily at me, causing me to hunch over. Bracing my hand on Declan's arm to steady myself, he moves to pick me up and carries me inside.

Neither of us speaks as he takes me up the stairs, but instead of going into the guest room, he carries me into his. He sets me down on the edge of his bathtub, and I watch him as he wets a washcloth. When he kneels in front of me, he begins wiping my face, and my eyes focus on the terrycloth as it turns from white to pink to red, collecting Richard's blood.

I'm a tomb, sitting in the palace, observing. I couldn't move if I wanted to.

So I sit.

Maybe my body's in shock.

Or maybe it's just numbing itself for departure.

There's no feeling, only sounds as Declan moves about, tending to me. He holds out a toothbrush, but my hand won't move to take it.

"Open," he gently requests, and I do.

Mint touches my tongue as he brushes my teeth, but it doesn't taste right. And when I look up at Declan, he doesn't look right. Sounds don't sound right, as everything begins to vacuum itself into a tunnel of fog. And now, my chest doesn't feel right. Pins prick along my body at the same time my eyes swim out of focus.

"Are you okay?" Declan's lips ask, but his voice is muted and a million miles away as I sway.

My brain tells my mouth to speak, but the wires don't connect the message as Declan's face morphs into a concoction of colored specks.

And then he's gone.

Strong hands press through the pins; one on my chest, and the other on my back, lowering my body down.

"Drop your head," he instructs.

I reach out for him when I let my head fall, and his hands quickly move to mine, and I latch on to him. Everything's disconnected, floating in an abyss, causing my pulse to pick up in a panic.

"I'm here. I've got you. Just close your eyes and take deep breaths."

My tongue is completely numb as I attempt to finally speak, but my words only slur when I say, "I feel sick."

"It's okay. Just focus on breathing."

Soon, I feel the heat of my blood flow, warming my insides, and when my vision comes into focus, I move slowly to sit up.

"Better?"

I nod.

"Let me get you some water," he says before going to fill a glass from the faucet. "Here."

I take a few sips, and Declan turns the water on in the shower. He undresses, and I can't peel my eyes away from him as I watch. Every part of him is smooth and cut in deep, muscular lines. Walking over, he takes the glass from me, and helps me stand up.

With my hands gripped to his shoulders to steady myself, he begins unbuttoning the shirt he put on me. I let go of him, letting the shirt fall to the floor along with my other top and bra that Richard cut with his knife. My body is sore as I help him remove my pants, and he then leads me to the shower.

Hot water rains down on me, washing away exterior grime. If only I could turn myself inside out, I'd do anything to cleanse the grime from inside of me, but I can't. And I wonder if that rot will always remain.

Declan's fingers run along the open wound on my cheek

where Richard dug his knife in, and I hiss against the sting.

"Sorry," he whispers, and as I look up into his harrowed eyes, I'm overtaken with guilt, and it becomes too much to hold on to.

Heated tears slip out, merging with the heated water as I let my emotions roll down my cheeks. Declan sees it coming out of me, takes my head in his strong hands, and presses the side of my face tightly against his chest. I curl my arms between our bodies and cuddle into him.

As we stand here under the water, naked and boundless, exposed and vulnerable, I feel the faint line-fracture begin to split. It's a sharp razor, slicing a jagged line through the scar tissue of my deepest pain. A part of me is terrified, but another part of me is ready to end the war inside. But I'm not even given a choice when I feel it taking a life of its own, shredding the fibers of the walls I've spent my whole life erecting.

*"It's okay,"* I hear Pike whisper. *"If you shatter, he'll put you back together."*

His voice, his words, they allow the severing to happen, and I rip open.

Tremors quake through me and Declan feels it, banding his arms around me. And when he speaks his next words, "I've got you, darling. If you shatter, I'll put you back together," I bleed it all out.

Dropping to the floor of the shower with me, he tucks me in his arms, and for the first time ever, I cry for everything I've suffered through—I *really* cry. It's ugly and messy, screaming and sobbing, bawling harder in an attempt to drain all the misery out of me. Salt burns, sadness scathes, memories devastate, but somehow, his hands alleviate.

I'm tired of being steely and callous. I'm tired of pretending and always fighting against my own skeletons. I'm tired of the uncertainty and hatred that drives the tenebrific evil in me. My wish is that his arms hold the magic to intenerate my heart—to make me good—to make me worthy—to make me lovable. But I doubt any man's arms are that powerful, and that doubt adds more fuel to my fear of Declan.

So I cry for fear as well.

Because I'm scared.

I'm *so* scared.

It's always been there though—the unease, the worriment. It's lain dormant inside of me since I was five years old, coming to life every now and then, but Pike taught me how to quickly silence it in order to survive. The dormancy is gone now. It's a live wire of unfiltered anguish that pours out of me and into the arms of my prince on earth while my other prince exists only in the nirvana I've yet to become a part of.

Warm breath feathers over my ear with a tender, "I'm so sorry."

"It's me," I blurt out through the unwavering tears, lifting my head to look into his eyes that own responsibility for things he was never responsible for. "I'm the cause of everything, not you. It was all me."

"You were just a kid. You didn't deserve what happened to you."

With his words, I reach out to his chest and run my fingers along the two bullet wounds that mark my deceit and give him *my* words, "And you didn't deserve *this*."

His hand covers mine, pressing my palm against his scars, saying, "I did. Because without it, I would've never found the truth in you."

"But my truth is so ugly."

"Like I said before, the truest part of a person is always the ugliest. But I'm ugly too, so you're not alone."

As the water cascades over us, I feel weighted down in guilt for what I've put this man through. Because none of it mattered when all I truly cared about was simply him.

"Tell me how to make you forgive me. I know I'm not worthy of your forgiveness, but I want it."

"I wish I knew, but I don't," he tells me. "We're broken people, Elizabeth. You can't expect me to not have my issues, because I have thousands of them. But just because I hold a hate for you doesn't take away from the love I have for you."

His words might not make sense to most people, but for me they do. I just have to choose whether or not to risk handing myself over to him.

"Come here," he says as he stands to help me up.

I take a seat on the built-in slate bench, and allow him to wash me as I sit here, drained to depletion. Closing my eyes, I relax into his touch while he washes my hair and cleans my body. But it's when he opens my legs and curses under his breath that I open my eyes and tense up.

"What?" I ask, looking down at him as he stares in horror between my thighs.

Shifting his eyes up to mine, his jaw grinds before demanding, "Tell me exactly what happened."

I look down to see the nasty collection of bruises.

"He raped you?"

I nod.

"What else?"

His hands remain on my thighs, spreading me open, when I admit, "He used his gun."

"What do you mean *he used his gun?*" he seethes through his teeth.

"To fuck me with. He used his loaded gun and then forced it in my mouth to suck."

His fingers sink into my skin as he drops his head, and I can see the muscles in his shoulders and back flex in anger as he tightens his grip on me. His words strain when he goes on to ask, "And all the blood on your mouth?"

"He was raping me with his gun in my mouth, but I managed to get away and I bit him."

"His dick?"

"Yes," I whimper, and when he looks up at me, I reveal, "I wanted to die. I begged him to shoot me."

"Don't you dare think about leaving me," he scolds.

"He told me you didn't care what happened to me, that you weren't coming."

"I *did* come for you," he affirms. "All I could think about was finding you. I was going crazy not knowing how to get to you."

Grabbing a washcloth, he runs it between my legs and begins to gently clean me. Once he has me washed, he keeps me naked as he helps me up into his bed. Nestled in his sheets with his scent all around me, I want to smile, but I can't. Regret consumes, hating the darkness I've brought to us, wishing I could erase it and go back in time to do it all over again.

"I need you to know something," he murmurs, wrapping me up in his arms. "I'm not the same as I was."

But I already know that. It's evident in his eyes. From the

moment he stepped out of his SUV and I knew he was alive, I saw the corruption inside of him.

"I keep trying to process what I did to Bennett, find reason for allowing myself to lose control, but I can't."

Reaching my hand to his face, I press my palm against his stubble, and all I can manage to get out is a breathless, "I'll love you no matter how dark you turn."

And with that, he finally kisses me, pressing his lips to mine in a fever of emotion that tells me everything that is buried deep within him. His body, heated in bands of roped muscle, rolls on top of me. We're flesh on flesh, transparent, bare. Scars opened wide for each other to see.

His lips move with mine, opening me up to reunite, claim, and control in carnal ustulation. He growls, rolling his tongue with mine, as I tangle my hands in his hair, savoring his taste.

His cock is thick and hard against me, but the moment he grinds himself over my pussy, I wince in pain, crying out as I flinch away from him. He tenses above me, and I try pushing him off of me, but he doesn't budge.

"Are you okay?"

"I'm sorry," I blurt out as he allows me to sit up.

"It's okay," he soothes.

"I just—"

"You don't need to say a word."

Coming in, he takes my breast into his mouth, sucking my nipple, all the while keeping his eyes pinned to mine as I look down at him. He feasts in primal need and I don't deny him of his need for closeness in this limited capacity. With my legs bent and spread, he lowers himself on me, dropping his lips to my pussy.

"Don't let me hurt you," he tells me as I run my hands in his hair, fisting it the moment his tongue dips through the seam of my core.

He keeps his touches soft in a very un-Declan-like way that I'm not used to. Dragging his tongue over my clit and then pressing the flat of it against me in slow circles, sending a chill up my spine. Gently, he sucks the bundle of nerves into his mouth. His deep groans vibrate against me, and I know he's restraining himself, so I grant him permission, saying, "It's okay. You won't hurt me."

As soon as my words are out, he bares his teeth, sinking them into my most tender flesh as I pull his hair. I hiss in a pleasurable pain that only Declan is able to give, and I'm satisfied in knowing he's content to inflict it upon me. I sink down into the bed when his hot tongue begins fucking my pussy, dragging in and out of me in torturous delight.

Grabbing on to my hips, he begins to move me over his tongue, up and down, push and pull, forcing me to now fuck his face. Sparks flicker when I close my eyes, and I give in, grinding down on his face, and his approving growls to selfishly take this pleasure he's offering spurs me on more.

Thighs quiver, hips buck, heart thuds, and I don't deserve this.

"Stop."

I push him away and scoot back.

"No," he barks at me, pulling me back down, wrapping his lips around my clit as he grips his cock and starts jerking himself off.

"Declan, please," I whimper as he draws me closer to my orgasm, but he ignores me.

His tongue laps over me, teasing, sucking, biting, licking. He's fervent in his movements with only one goal in mind, and when he rolls my hips against his mouth, I explode.

Shattering waves of electricity burn and spark through nerves and veins, heating me in a frisson of passion. I come sinfully hard, feeling every pulsing contraction of my pussy gripping Declan's tongue as he moans out his own orgasm. Our sweat-covered bodies writhe together as internal wounds open in vulnerability. Tears spill from the corners of my eyes when he kisses his way up my battered body, over my breasts, along my neck, and up to my lips where he says, "Taste how perfect you are for me," before dipping his tongue in my mouth so I can taste myself on him.

And we kiss.

We kiss like no two humans have ever kissed before.

We're tear-stained savages, sharing a single breath of life, death, and love. Giving, taking, bruising, and reuniting what I thought was forever destroyed.

And for the first time in a very long time, when I tire out and close my eyes, I spend my slumber with Carnegie.

WAKING UP, DECLAN is sitting up in bed next to me, drinking a cup of coffee and watching the world news on the flat screen above the fireplace that's across the bedroom. As the rain falls outside, pelting against the windows, I lie still, allowing my body to wake up slowly as I watch a breaking news segment.

When I stretch out, Declan notices I'm awake, saying, "Morning, darling," and opens his arms up for me to curl into.

"What time is it?" I ask in a groggy voice.

"After one. We slept all day."

Turning my attention back to the television, I listen to the report on an American aircraft that crashed after there was a malfunction with the landing gear. I melt into Declan's hold as I watch the reporter give an update as the passengers are deplaning in the background. He announces everyone's survival and that only a few were injured and are being taken to the hospital. But it's when the camera pans over the passengers that my heart stalls and I immediate sit up.

"What is it?" Declan asks, but I can't speak, and then the segment is over.

"Can you rewind this?"

"What's going on?"

"Just rewind it," I say on a trembled voice and my body goes into high alert.

Declan rewinds the segment, and as soon as the camera zooms in on the passengers, I tell him, "Pause it."

My eyes widen in shocked disbelief as my pulse races out of control.

*It can't be.*

Crawling to the edge of the bed, Declan's worried voice calls to me in question, "Elizabeth?"

*Oh my God.*

"He's alive."

# from the author

Thank you for reading *Echo* book #2 in the Black Lotus series.
If you enjoyed this book, please consider leaving a spoiler-free
review.

Need to talk to someone about the Black Lotus series?
There is a discussion group on Facebook for those who have
finished reading.

Discuss the Black Lotus series
*https://www.facebook.com/groups/bangdiscussion/*

# acknowledgements

SOMETIMES IT TAKES a village to make things possible, so let's get straight to it.

My fans, *thank you* will never be enough for all you do for me. You have waited so patiently for me to write this book. You stood by me, supported me, encouraged me, and everything in between. This book would not have been possible if it weren't for each and every one of you. I've said it before, and I'll say it again: E.K. Blair fans are the best fans!

My husband and children, I know the sacrifices you all make to allow me to pour my soul out onto paper for the world to see, and I love you for that. The three of you are the blood my heart pumps, the air I breathe, the fibers of my soul, the salt of my tears, and the icing on the sweet life I've been blessed with.

My editor, therapist, and dear friend, Lisa, what would I do without you? Through tears and laughter and more tears, you've proven to be a steady rock for me. When life gives me lemons, you have a way about you that turns those lemons into a lemon drop martini. Thank you for loving me both professionally and personally.

To my fellow writers who helped me out of the burning flames, Aleatha Romig, K. Bromberg, Corinne Michaels, Adriane Leigh, Pepper Winters, and Kathryn Andrews, your uplifting words and supportive messages, no matter how big or small, provided me with the threads needed to create the rope that helped pull me above the under.

Sally, Bethany, and Teri, the time you girls sacrifice for me is simply unreal! I couldn't ask for a better team to assist me. The three of you make it possible for me to spend more time with my family, and that time is so precious to me. Thank you!

My brave beta readers, Jen, Kiki, Ashley, Jennifer, you girls are amazing! Thank you for giving up months to go with me on this wild ride and for embracing the darkness in my head.

Tarryn Fisher, for supporting me and sharing me with your fans. And also for being my Twilight-Bestie and for loving the series as much as I do! We crazy psychos must stick together.

Thank you, Denise Tung, for always being there to organize all my promotional marketing from cover reveals to reviews. You have been with me from the very beginning, and without you I'd be lost.

Erik Schottstaedt for another beautiful cover photo.

And last but certainly not least, to every blogger and book reviewer who has read my words, reviewed my books, and promoted me, THANK YOU! No, seriously, THANK YOU!!!! Everything you do for me and the lengths some of you go to for me is valued immensely.

**Ways To Connect**

www.ekblair.com

Facebook: https://www.facebook.com/EKBlairAuthor

Twitter: @EK_Blair_Author

Instagram: https://instagram.com/authorekblair/

**Coming Soon**

**in**

**The Black Lotus Series**

*Hush*

(book 3)

https://www.goodreads.com/book/show/21860945-hush

**Other Titles by E.K. Blair**

**Fading** (book 1)
**Freeing** (book 2)
**Falling** (book 3)

**Bang**
(Black Lotus, book 1)

# marrow

## by tarryn fisher

THE PEARL STARTS ITS LIFE AS A SPLINTER—something unwanted like a piece of shell or shard of dirt that accidentally lodges itself in an oyster's body. To ease the splinter, the oyster takes defensive action, secreting a smooth, hard, lucid substance around the irritant to protect itself. That substance is called "nacre." So long as the splinter remains within its body, the oyster will continue to coat it in nacre, layer upon beautiful layer. I always thought it was remarkable that the oyster coats its enemy not only in something beautiful, but a part of itself. And while diamonds are embraced with warm excitement, regarded to be of highest, deepest value, the pearl is somewhat overlooked. Its humble beginnings are that of a parasite, growing in something that is alive, draining its host of beauty. It's clever—the plight of the splinter. A sort of rags to riches story.

# chapter 1
## age 13

THERE IS A HOUSE IN THE BONe, with a broken window. A sheet of newspaper covers the hole, secured around the edges with thick pieces of duct tape. The siding on the house sags like old flesh, holding up a roof that looks as if it's bearing the world's burdens.

I live in this house with my mother. Under the rain, under the oppression, in the room with the broken window. I call it the eating house. Because, if you let it, this house will devour you, like it did my mother. Like it tries to devour me.

"Margo, bring me the washcloth."

My name followed by a command.

I do. You can barely call it a washcloth. It's just an old rag, smoothed over by too many uses and discolored by the dirty things it has scrubbed. She takes it from my hand without looking at me. Her fingers are elegant, nails painted black and chipped along the edges. She moves the washcloth between her legs and cleans herself roughly. I flinch and look away, offering her minuscule privacy. That's all the privacy you get in this house—the aversion of eyes. There are always people—men mostly—lurking around the doors and hallways. They leer, and, if you give them the chance, they reach for you. *If* you give them the chance. I don't.

My mother steps out of the bath and takes the towel from my hand. The house smells like mold and rot, but for an hour after she takes a bath, it smells of her bath salts.

"Margo, hand me my robe."

My name followed by a command.

She hates taking baths alone. She told me her mother tried to drown her in the bathtub when she was a child. It still scares her. Sometimes, at night, I hear her whimpering in her sleep, *No mama, no.* I didn't know her mother. After the drowning incident, my mother was put into foster care. *A nightmare,* she calls it. By the time she'd matriculated from the system, my grandmother had died of a massive heart attack and left her only daughter the house—the eating house.

She looks at herself in the mirror as I unfold her robe—a red thing, filmy to the touch. It is my job to launder it twice a week. I do so with care, as it is her most prized possession. My mother is beautiful in the same way that a storm is beautiful. She is wild and destructive, and in the middle of her fury you feel her God given right to destroy. We both admire her reflection for a few more minutes as she runs the pads of her fingers over her face, checking for flaws. This is her mid-afternoon ritual before things get going. She takes out the little tubs of creams that I bring her from the pharmacy, and lines them along the chipped sink. One at a time, she dabs them around her eyes and mouth.

"Margo," she says. I wait for the command, breath bated.

This time she is looking at my reflection, slightly behind hers. "You're not a pretty girl. You could at least lose the weight. What you don't have in the face, you can have in the body."

*So I can sell it like you do?*

"I'll try, Mama."

Submission. That's my job.

"Margo, you can go now," she says. "Stay in your room."

My name followed by a double command. *What a special treat!*

I walk backwards out of the bathroom. It's what I've learned to do to avoid being struck in the head with something. My mother is dangerous when she doesn't take her pills. And you never know when she's off. Sometimes I sneak in her room to count them, so I know how many safe days I have left.

"Margo," she calls when I am almost to my door.

"Yes, Mama?" I say. My voice is almost a whisper.

"You can skip dinner tonight."

She offers it like it's something good, but what she's really saying is, "I won't be allowing you to eat tonight."

That's all right. I have my own stash, and there's nothing in the cupboards anyway.

I go to my room, and she locks the door behind me, pocketing the key. The lock on my door is the only working lock in the house, besides the one on the front door. My mother had it installed a few years ago. I though it was to keep me safe, until I figured out that my mother was stashing her money under a loose floorboard in my room. Her money is all there under my feet. She doesn't spend it on clothes, or cars, or food. She hoards it. I skim money off the top to buy food. She probably knows, since I'm still alive and also fat.

I sit on my floor and slide a box out from under my bed. I

choose wisely in case she's listening at the door: a banana and two slices of bread. No noise, no crunching, no wrappers. The banana is black and sticky, and the bread is stale, but it still tastes good. I pull off pieces of the bread and squash it between my fingers before putting it in my mouth. I like to pretend I'm taking Holy Communion. My friend, Destiny, took her first communion. She said the priest put a flat piece of bread on your tongue, and while it was sitting on your tongue it turned into the body of the Lord Jesus. You had to wait for the Lord Jesus's body to melt before you swallowed it, because you couldn't very well bite the Lord Jesus's body, and then you had to drink his blood. I don't know anything about the Lord Jesus or why you have to eat his body or drink his blood to be Catholic, but I'd rather pretend to eat God's body than stale, old bread.

When I'm done with my dinner I can hear muffled thuds and the floorboards groaning under the weight of feet. Whose feet? The tall man? The man with the gray, curly chest hair? Or perhaps it's the man who coughs so hard he makes my mother's bed rattle.

"The croup," I say to my limp banana skin. I read about the croup in one of my books. A library book I keep checking out because I don't want to give it back. I slide it out from my school bag as I eat a Honey Bun, and look at the pictures while licking the sticky off my fingers. When I hear Mama's headboard creaking against the wall I eat another. I'm going to be fat for as long as I live in the eating house. For as long as the house eats me.

*New York Times Bestseller*

# THE
# FADING
## SERIES

"Heart-wrenching, jaw-dropping, and absolutely
beautiful."
-Aleatha Romig, *New York Times* bestselling author

"One of the most incredible, breathtaking stories I have
ever read."
-Word

"Beautifully written and emotionally charged."
-Vilma Gonzalez, *USA Today* HEA blog

Made in the USA
San Bernardino, CA
02 March 2017